The Returned

The Returned

Dr Laurence B. Brown

2011

Other Books

by
Dr. Laurence B. Brown

Fiction
* *The Eighth Scroll*—Amazon.com's #1 bestselling Kindle book in the category of Religious Fiction, described by one reviewer as, "*Indiana Jones* meets *The Da Vinci Code. The Eighth Scroll* is a breath-holding, white-knuckled, can't-put-down thriller that challenges Western views of humanity, history and religion. Bar none, the best book in its class!"

Nonfiction:
* *The First and Final Commandment*
* *MisGod'ed*
* *God'ed?*
* *Bearing True Witness*

To this day, there are areas of the Amazon rainforest
from which few explorers have ever returned.
Those who survive have rare stories to tell.

Prologue

"You have to understand. We didn't mean to kill him. We just didn't know any better...back then."

Nathan Jones felt himself tense up in the cozy microfiber embrace of his favorite recliner and pinched the sting out of his eyes. Was he talking to himself? He dabbed his budding tears away with a tissue, then looked up, a little startled, as the doorway facing him filled with a familiar form.

"Hey, Pops. You ready?"

At forty-two, his son Martin's tight afro was as dark as ever—unlike his own still-thick hair, which was grey on the sides and speckled on top. With a melancholy pang, Nathan remembered that Martin's soft, kind eyes were a tribute to his mother. *May she rest in peace.*

Martin leaned down smoothly and made an adjustment on the tripod that supported the camera pointed at his dad.

His athletic build, Nathan thought proudly—*that's all mine.*

"You sure you're up for this, Pops?" Martin asked, gently.

"Ready as I'll ever be," Nathan said. It took an effort to hide his welling emotion.

"It's recording to hard drive, Pops. I'll edit it later. You can talk all day if you want."

Nathan nodded, and then collapsed the recliner's footrest as he swung himself forward and leaned toward the camera.

"You want me to stay while you tell it?" Martin asked.

"That would be nice, thanks."

"Okay, Pops. Don't worry. I think you need to get this out once and for all. It'll be good for you."

Nathan sighed heavily and rubbed the side of his face. "Okay, then...once more, from the beginning..."

1

The Amazon, 1965

"Hey, Nate. Remind me why I volunteered for this trip."

"I dunno. 'Cause you're dumb?"

"That must be it." Mark Jones slapped his hand to the back of his neck. Sweat splashed from between his fingers and a well-fed mosquito flew off to a safe distance. "Why aren't they biting *you?*" He inspected his empty hand for casualties, and then wiped the sheen of sweat onto his pant leg.

Despite being fraternal twins, Nate and Mark were about as different as two young men could be. Nate glanced at Mark's auburn-grey skin, and held up the back of one of his own hands by way of comparison. Nate was tall, thin—and as their Aunt Clara always said—"nearly as black as a Negro could be." Mark was short and husky with auburn-tinted hair, a "red Negro" on Auntie's color scale.

"Maybe they don't bite me because they like lighter meat," Nate said. "Maybe I'm too spicy for them."

Nate's strong, angular features contrasted sharply with Mark's round, less defined face. Mark's dull, faraway eyes and slow words hinted at dimwittedness. But Mark wasn't dumb. Mostly, Nathan mused, he was just a big goof-off.

"Oh yeah?" Mark thumbed at the expedition leader, who stood to one side, directing the packing of the group's equipment onto the backs of their five mules. "Then why don't they bite *him*?"

Nate smiled at Professor Gwyn Wogan's unusually pale complexion and wavy red hair—a source of quiet jokes among their native Indian guides. They had taken to calling him "the ghost" behind his back.

"Skeeters like it *less* spicy, not *totally* bland. Ask 'em if you don't believe me." Nate winked at his brother and got a smirk and lowered headshake in reply. "You using the bug spray?"

"Naw. Makes me itch."

"And those mosquito bites don't?"

"Naw, those itch, too."

Nate looked at his brother and shook his head. He scanned the remnants of their camp. Clingy tan soil was exposed beneath the cleared undergrowth. Well-spaced tree trunks disappeared into the misty ceiling of the tropical rainforest. A muddy path led down to one of the myriad tributaries that coursed through the Amazon.

Mostly, Nate eyed the seven Americans and three Indians that completed their motley group of twelve. Except for the professor, his long-haired assistant Scott Campbell, and Charles Hawley, who represented the company that sponsored the expedition, the Americans were all student volunteers. Nathan and Mark were the only blacks and the only undergrads—two social stigmas that ranked them only slightly above their native Indian helpers in the team pecking order.

Four of the Americans—Arthur, Duke, Frankie and Hugh—were grad students hoping this trip would pad their resumes and improve their career prospects. Hawley was tagging along in case they discovered anything of value. If they did, ADR Chemical wanted immediate closure, meaning containment and perpetual mining rights.

Nate watched Professor Wogan work. At 5'8", the professor was trim, energetic, and corded with muscles. Nathan squeezed one of his own rock-hard biceps and wondered if he would be in as good shape when he reached his mid-fifties.

His gaze swung skyward, but his mind drifted back to Wogan's sophomore class in Geochemistry at Cornell. They quickly found the professor's generous grading scale to be only one of the course's attractions. Not only did he create interest in the subject, but he also shared alluring tales of previous students who had achieved wealth and success through modern-day prospecting, or by selling their skills to the petroleum industry.

If Nate had known then what he was just beginning to understand—that the vast majority of prospectors returned home frustrated and penniless—he would have prospected a summer job at the university library. Instead, he was serving as an unpaid pack-bearer for a professor whose only real, measurable success was in the classroom. *How had Wogan persuaded an industrial giant to sponsor a grant for him to prospect in the Amazon, anyway?*

Raised voices and another neck-slap from his brother jerked Nathan out of his reverie. He stood up from the stump he sat upon, grabbed his pack from the ground by one shoulder-strap, and motioned his brother to follow him to the source of the noise.

It was nothing new. For the last two weeks, the guides had argued for better wages on a daily basis. The farther they led the group from civilization, the more their demands increased.

The Indians, dressed in ragged shorts—their only concession to civilization—gesticulated threateningly in Wogan's direction as the professor shouted back at them, red-faced with anger and frustration. The native translator stood between the two factions with outspread arms as if to part the waters of the Red Sea, his head jerking back and forth as he struggled to keep up with both sides of the verbal battle. Other team members ringed the foursome in a loose circle. Everybody was aware that the guides were bargaining with the lives of the expedition. Paying them too early or promising too little could threaten their willingness to lead the group home. For the guides, the forest *was* their home; they could slip off into it at any time. Only the promise of payment kept them from doing so.

As the two brothers drew closer, the translator threw up his arms, turned his back and stomped off to the edge of the clearing. He sat on the tree stump Nathan just vacated, concern etched in the furrow between his wide-set brown eyes. With their translator gone, both sides launched a few more shouts and gestures but then recognized the futility of any further effort. The two guides turned and stormed off, casting malignant glances over their shoulders, hissing warnings like snakes.

Another step would have taken Nathan into the loose circle of observers, but Charles Hawley glanced over his shoulder and saw him coming. He sidestepped directly into his path, blocking him from the group. Nathan almost stumbled into the man's back, and briefly considered slamming into him, as if by accident.

Instead, he brought himself up short and turned to roll his eyes at his brother, who now stood behind him. Scott Campbell glanced in their direction. He flung a beaded, blond hair-braid over one shoulder with a flick of his head and said to Hawley, "Be cool, man." Then he stepped aside to make space, reached out to take Nathan by his elbow, drew him alongside and collegially draped one arm over his shoulders. Mark stepped to Campbell's other side.

Hawley just shrugged and edged away from him without so much as a glance in his direction.

The quiet ones are always the most danger-ous, Nathan thought to himself. *Not like that big-*

oted graduate student in their group, Duke, who can't stop talking about Malcolm X's murder, and how some "righteous Son of the South" is going to "do the same for Martin Luther King, Jr. someday."

"You know, Campbell, you're all right," Nathan said, "For a white guy, that is. When we wean your Scottish ass off of that shortbread and butterscotch, who knows? You might even darken up a bit."

"When we get back home, swing by for supper," Campbell said, smiling. He dropped his arm from Nathan's shoulders. "When you taste my fried chicken, you'll know we're members of the same club."

Campbell got both the inflection and timing just right. If he had flubbed either, his taunt wouldn't have come off as a joke. It might even have backfired. As it was, they just glanced at one another and laughed.

"I hired two guides in hopes of avoiding this," Wogan said, his eyes never leaving the guides, who now sat huddled together at the base of a tree.

"Think they'll desert us?" one of the graduate students asked.

"Not a chance. I'm paying them six months' salary for two months' work."

"It's still peanuts," Nathan said.

The professor tore his eyes from the pair and turned to face him. "Maybe to you. To them, a hundred dollars a month is a fortune. I really can't understand their problem. Twenty years ago, at the end of the war, they'd have made fifty cents a day." Turning to the group, he said, "Just in case, we'll post a guard at night. To keep an eye on our gear, and to make sure nobody tries to sneak away."

A couple team members groaned, but most nodded soberly with understanding.

"Okay," Wogan said, turning a circle among them, "one more week and three more sites, then we're all going home. Sort out your packs, load the animals and let's get going."

2

Picking their way single-file along a narrow animal path, Nathan paused to wipe sweat from his eyes and glance back.

They're still keeping us at the back of the line, he reflected. *Now, is that because we're young, undergraduate, or black?*

He shrugged his shoulders and scanned the forest. Many times over the past six weeks, he had been struck by the numbing sameness of the rainforest. Although parts looked different, he could never tell where he was.

Trees grew tall and straight, buttressed by wide, powerful root systems. Their lush green crowns bunched together in the forest canopy, over a hundred feet above. Emergent trees such as the Kapok, or Ceiba tree, penetrated the canopy to create a towering overstory layer favored by eagles and bats. Most of the forest's wildlife lived at the level of the understory—the branch layer—and above, completing their entire life cycle without ever descending to the ground. In the spots where the thick canopy blocked the sun's rays, the starved undergrowth remained sparse, permitting easy passage.

Where the canopy thinned, the undergrowth responded to the sun's nurturing rays by exploding with growth. Shrubs and saplings knotted together in a competition to suffocate one another—to survive. Vines and liana wove the dense mess into jungle, rendering areas virtually impassable. Those brave enough to venture into those areas found that certain vines struck and bit, only to recognize them as vipers too late.

Where forest gave way to jungle, the composting groundcover perpetually stewed in its own fermented juices. Mud sucked at the feet and clung to the boots until they were caked. Insects and snakes, many of them poisonous, teemed in this fertile environment. The groundcover squished underfoot and rebounded with each step. If it moved on its own, you ran.

Despite the beauty, the atmosphere was stifling. Temperatures bordered on intolerable, humidity tickling one hundred percent. Nathan felt as if his lungs could barely squeeze enough oxygen from the hot, humid air, thick with the ripe odor of an ecosystem recycling itself. The treetops and groundcover misted for hours in the mornings. Rain fell virtually every afternoon, filling scoop-shaped epiphytes overhead and then emptying like tipped buckets upon whatever lay below.

The calls of the rainforest only stopped for a reason. When the birdsongs and monkey chatter stilled, a person quickly discovered the reason. At that point, they hid, ran, or died. Equally disconcerting was the fact that when the rainforest transformed to jungle, visibility decreased to a matter of a few yards.

Progress was slow. Nathan stopped for a moment and pondered his surroundings. The native translator bringing up the rear stepped up beside him. Mark, directly in front of him, had advanced only a few steps. All the same, Nathan knew he had to keep up or he would lose him in the thick vegetation. Keeping an eye on his brother's dun-colored backpack, he nodded in greeting. "How's it going, Tonto?"

The Indian was a member of the Mandahua-ca tribe. His given name was such a convoluted mix of H's, X's and Y's that Nathan had given up on mastering it. To the rest of the team, the interpreter was Bud. To Nathan, he was Tonto. Unlike the guides, who were nearly naked, Tonto wore a t-shirt and shorts, although he moved through the forest barefoot. He'd been educated by American missionaries, and had made a bit of a career for himself translating for tourists and explorers.

Early in their acquaintance, some mystery had bridged their cultures and persons, and they had formed a bond. Neither had saved the other's life or honor, nor had they stood side-by-side battling a common adversity. Theirs had simply been a meeting of souls.

"Copacetic," the Indian replied. It took a sharp mind to be a translator, and he'd been doing the job long enough to have picked up some decent American slang. "How you doing, Jane?"

"No, no," Nathan chuckled. "It's Kemosabe. Ke-mo Sa-be. Work on it."

"You call me Tarzan, I call you Kemosabe, Jane."

Nathan laughed. Tonto's sense of humor was one of the things that had drawn the two young men together. "Man. It's so hard to get good help these days."

"Not that easy to find good bosses, either."

Mark was as far ahead as Nathan dared let him get, and Nathan started to move forward with Tonto at his side. His face grew serious.

"What's the situation with the guides, Tonto? Is it really that bad? You think they might ditch us?"

Tonto shook his head. "Where Dr. Wogan wants to go—is very dangerous. Nobody wants to go there. But they need money. I think they'll stay. But they're not happy. They want more pay. I understand why."

"You're not thinking of taking off on us, too, are you?"

"Not my style, Jane. I signed up, I stay on."

"If they run off, can you guide us back?"

"I translate for a reason. I've spent more time with books than in the jungle. Amazon's larger than America. Easy to get lost."

Tonto pondered for a moment, as if struggling to explain a complex formula. "Look. We walked in a circle for six weeks." He drew a big "C" in the air in front of them. Then he closed the mouth of the C with a straight line. "But we walk home straight.

Two weeks, maybe. How, though? What rivers and zigzags? The guides know—but I don't. Do you?"

Nathan digested this. He was glad Mark was not close enough ahead to overhear their conversation. "Can we retrace our steps?"

This time Tonto's headshake was accompanied by a shrug of his shoulders. "After rain, I'd have a hard time even finding yesterday's camp.

"It rains every day," Nathan said.

"You got it, Jane."

Tonto fell back to his place at the end of the line.

Nathan reflected on the danger. Their beans, rice, flour and dried fruit would easily last another three weeks. The mules could go from pack animals to pot roast if protein took priority over the soil samples they carried. For five weeks, they'd supplemented their rations through fishing, hunting, and trade with natives they had encountered. Food shouldn't be a problem if they stayed on schedule...*If.*

If they lost their guides, their rations could easily run out before they chanced upon civilization on their own. Furthermore, it was the guides' job to steer them to receptive villages. Without guides, they could stumble upon hostile natives as easily as they could upon friendly ones.

There were other uncomfortable signs besides the guides' restiveness. They'd lost one mule to snakebite early on. About a week in, a grad student had come down with a life-threatening fever. He'd recovered, but they'd had to leave him behind in a small village that, fortunately, had a radio.

Now, almost a third of the group was slowed down by mild dysentery—and the threat of malaria was ever-present.

I guess things could be worse, Nathan thought.

Just then, a gun blasted up ahead, followed by a burst of short, shrill screams.

The gun exploded again, severing the screams, and the forest fell silent.

3

Nathan stood frozen for a moment in the sinister silence. Finally, a lone insect chirped off to one side. Its neighbor joined in, and together they jump-started the familiar chorus of animal sounds.

Tonto slid to Nathan's side.

"I've never heard an animal scream like that before," Nathan said as he peered ahead. "What was it? A wild pig?"

"Pigs squeal, Jane. You're a city girl for sure. Woolly monkeys—they scream."

Nathan forced himself to smile. "Woolly monkey for dinner, then. Um…what do they taste like?"

Tonto grinned mischievously up at him. "Woolly monkey? Tastes like human."

"Oooo-kay. I know I'll regret asking this…but what does human taste like?"

"Pig. So I hear."

Nathan nodded slowly, then turned back to the animal trail. "I was right," he said. "I'm sorry I asked."

A couple of minutes later, Nathan stepped through a thick curtain of shrubs and found the group scattered and resting around a small clearing. Professor Wogan sat on his pack, leaning his back against a tree, his M2 carbine propped against one knee. The guides dexterously skinned and gutted the monkey, chatting cheerfully among themselves.

"A favorite of theirs," Tonto said, after listening to their chatter. "They say we need one more. Then everybody have enough."

"They can have my share," Nathan said as he swung his pack to the ground at his feet. "After what you told me, I'm sticking to beans and rice tonight."

Nathan nodded to his brother, who settled onto the ground, one arm draped across the upright pack beside him. Mark raised an eyebrow in his direction, then leaned back against a tree trunk and closed his eyes.

Nathan eyed Wogan's carbine enviously. "Three M2 selective fire carbines in the group, two 12-gauge shotguns and one M1 Garand. Not to mention Hawley's fancy lever-action Winchester. That's a lot of firepower."

"Amazon's dangerous." Tonto motioned to the light survival rifles lashed to Nathan's and his brother's packs. "You forget those?"

Nathan snorted, and then almost immediately regretted his derision. Most natives couldn't afford even the poorest quality rifle. Here in the interior, firearms were virtually unknown. "Combination 440 shotgun and 22-caliber rifle," he said. "Good for small game. Almost useless against anything big." He shrugged.

Nathan knew the pecking order. The adults carried the big guns. He and his brother toted the survival rifles, to be used only in emergencies. The Indians were allowed nothing other than machetes.

Nathan's mind drifted, and he found himself back in the college classroom. The overhead lights illuminated his final exam paper, laid out on a pitted wooden desk. He sat hunched over his essay, pencil hovering at the end of his final paragraph. Glancing up, he saw only seconds left on the clock. A whispered *"Psst!"* drew his attention. Looking over his shoulder, he found Mark bridging his pencil between fingers and thumbs of both hands, grinning at him. He grinned back, the bell rang, and Mark snapped his pencil in two with a spray of graphite and splinters.

"Hand 'em in," Wogan shouted from the front of the room as he snatched a test paper from the nearest student's desk. "Grades will be posted on the bulletin board outside the department office next week. Excepting the two of you scheduled to join me on my Amazon trip, I'll see the rest of you next school year. Have a good summer vacation."

Ten days later he and Mark were packed, ready to go, and sharing their last dinner with family. He had expected their last meal together to be a jovial affair, but instead their father recounted the many dangers of the Amazon. He concluded by reminding Mark of the many serious blunders he had made in his nineteen years—and that similar mistakes could be fatal in the wild.

Mother rose from the table, patted Mark's head and pinched their kid sister's cheek as she turned to the kitchen, plates in hand.

"You take care of yourself down there, Nathan, you hear?" she said.

Mark forced down a mouthful of meatloaf with a bob of his head and said, "I'll take care, too, Ma."

She stopped by the kitchen door and turned halfway. "I meant both of you, honey. *Both* of you take care down there." Plates balanced in both hands, she pushed through the swinging door.

Mark turned hurt eyes across the table. Nathan couldn't meet his brother's gaze. Their father cleared his throat and stared across the room, out the window.

Nathan grit his teeth and dropped his eyes to his plate.

Nathan snapped back into the present suddenly, the flattened brown features of his Indian friend only inches away from his own face.

"You want to live?" Tonto asked with a shrewd smile. He held the rough, rusted blade of his ancient belt knife between them, pointed directly at his chest. "Turn around."

Nathan held both arms out to his sides, as if to be frisked, and obediently about-faced. He felt a gentle pressure from the native's blade on his back and asked, "What is it *this* time?"

Tonto held his knife out for inspection. Draped over the edge slithered a ten-inch-long grey centipede, waves of movement rippling down both rows of legs. Behind its evil-looking black head were two modified legs for delivering its poisonous venom, and two fleshy, wicked-looking appendages he presumed to be stingers protruded from its tail. "*That* would kill me?"

"You want I put it back?" He leaned closer and Nathan reflexively took a step back. "No, no, that's okay. Give it to our redneck buddies," he said, nodding in the direction of Duke and Hawley.

"Take a rest," the native said as he flicked the centipede into the brush. "Drink water."

Good advice. The temperature and humidity had sweated him dry, and his urine was darkening. He hoped his kidneys were still healthy. It was amazing how many ways a man could die down here.

4

At midday they entered a broad clearing beside an even broader river.

In the center of the clearing stood a dozen thatched huts on stilts. Some sort of domesticated bird, whose exotic plumage looked more typical of pheasants than chickens, dodged and clawed between the naked Indian children as they played in the dirt.

Seven dugout canoes lined the muddy riverbank, their long, thin bodies jutting into the murky green water and bending to the weak current like fingers of a palm frond.

As soon as they stepped into the clearing, a woman shouted an alarm. Villagers poured from their huts and ran straight at them, weapons raised. In a moment Nathan found himself surrounded by tattooed and scarified men with wild, unkempt hair, wearing only chest bands and waist strings for supporting their genitalia—but brandishing spears and bone-knives as they shouted threats. Beyond them stood a reserve army of half-naked women adorned with beaded jewelry, hefting a variety of camp utensils that could double as clubs. The children jostled at their feet, their expressions alternating between menace, in imitation of their parents, and open curiosity.

The guides and translator shouted a few words above the din, and Nathan watched as the men lowered their weapons slightly and stilled. After a few more words the tribal leader, identifiable by his extravagant body paint, shouted a command to his people. Instantly the natives lowered their weapons to their sides, gave their best yellow-toothed smiles, and the crowd opened a channel to guide the newcomers into their village.

"I never get used to this," Mark said, as he stuck close to Nathan's side.

"What, the half-naked women, the threat of being killed, or the mood swing from menace to welcome?"

"Yeah. All of those. And by the way, I noticed which one you mentioned first."

Nathan grimaced. "Well-played, bro. Displace the focus from your wimpiness to my—"

"Hey, do you think they're going to feed us?" Mark asked in mock excitement.

"God, I hope not," Nathan said with a groan. He recalled the last village meal—how he had thrown up everything he had ingested less than a half-hour later. He felt his stomach turn queasy at the memory. "At least when we cook for ourselves, we know what we're eating." He turned to a native who poked and prodded him out of curiosity, and exchanged well-meaning smiles with him without breaking stride.

"Probably never saw a black man before," Mark said. "Remember that roast capybara and jungle root? *That* was pretty good."

Nathan nodded. Glancing ahead, he saw the huts drawing near. "And I know you dug those frog legs. The snake wasn't half bad, either."

"Uh, bro," he said, "Don't even mention—"

"The live beetle grubs and insect larvae?"

Too late—Nathan's stomach flipped at the memory. The problem with village meals was that they couldn't refuse. As visitors, they were the guests of honor. And a mood that had swung from malice to welcome could reverse just as quickly, if provoked by a refusal of native hospitality. These were simple people, with simple emotions, simple codes of conduct—and simple but deadly weapons.

"Oh, sorry," Mark said. "I guess you don't want to talk about those—"

"No, I really don't."

"Those fat, pasty-white beetle grubs and slimy, squirmy insect larvae. Sort of like eating living spit."

Nathan halted in his tracks and faced his brother. "Mark, quit it. You've got a garbage disposal for a stomach. You can eat anything. I can't, and you're going to make me sick just thinking about it. Now, *stop*."

As he stood there, a young native woman reached through the throng of men and patted Nathan's cheek with the backs of her bent fingers.

Then she ran her open hand down his shoulder and chest, unabashedly squeezing, as if to see if he was real. Nathan shrugged her hand off and turned back toward the village.

"You know, you should probably do the same thing to her," Mark said.

Nathan shot his brother a sidelong glance, but then shook his head, unable to suppress a smile.

"No, seriously, she'll probably like it," Mark persisted. "Expect it, even. It's probably their local custom. Oh, don't worry about her husband or father decapitating and disemboweling you—that's probably just part of their custom as well. On the bright side, it might just save you from having to eat dinner with them."

5

"Good news and bad news," Professor Wogan said. He had just returned to the group, where they sat waiting in an abandoned village hut.

Nathan gazed out the open doorway, out past other huts to where Mark tended the hobbled mules as they grazed at the edge of the clearing. *What's the problem this time?*

Wogan leaned back against the wall of vertical wooden poles lashed together with dried vines. "They'll allow us safe passage. But only if we pay."

"What's new about that?" Hawley sat cross-legged to one side, stroking the polished wood stock of the Winchester repeating rifle laid across his knees. One of the expedition rules was that in a village, your rifle never left your hands and your pack never left your sight.

Nathan reflexively dropped his hand to the survival rifle he had laid on the reed-matted floor beside him. *Safety on,* he reflected. *Bore clear.* That, to him, was the weirdest, but perhaps the most sensible of Wogan's rules.

"What's new about it?" Wogan asked. He picked his teeth with a black thorn the size and shape of a two-inch finishing nail, then stuck it in his mouth and spoke through clenched teeth, "What's new is they want money."

"Money?" one of the graduate students said, jumping to his feet. "*Money*? What for?"

Some of the expedition members thought Wogan paranoid. Others felt his rules made perfect sense. Nathan shared Wogan's fears that the natives, especially those who hadn't had much contact with the outside world, could steal their guns and turn their weapons against them. Most natives had never seen a gun before. But once they witnessed their awesome power, they might literally kill to own one.

Wogan dealt with this concern in two ways.

First, he did not allow the natives to see how the guns were stripped, cleaned and oiled, reassembled and loaded. This daily ritual kept the weapons in working order under the wet and humid rainforest conditions—and was always performed at night, in the privacy of the team's tents. The result was that an Indian would never learn how to load a gun, take the safety off, or even what a safety was. He might not even know the thing needed bullets.

Second, the only maneuver they showed the natives was how to stuff a plug of paper or leaves down the barrel, like tamping wadding down the bore of a muzzleloader. Without doing this, they lied, the guns wouldn't work. What they didn't tell them was that they would later push the plug through the barrel and remove it from the breach.

A gun with a plugged barrel would explode when shot, destroying the weapon and maiming or killing the shooter.

Fair punishment, in Wogan's judgment. Stealing a man's gun in the Amazon was tantamount to robbing him of his livelihood, like stealing a cowboy's horse in America's frontier days—a hanging offense.

"That's like, far out," Campbell said as he toyed with one of his beaded hair braids. "These dudes have nothing from the outside. Have you checked out this village? They're like, totally in touch with the earth. Everything they've got is from the forest. Even this hut doesn't have a nail in it. What do they need bread for?"

"Don't know. Doesn't make sense." Wogan turned his back on the room and leaned into the open doorway. "Where's the fifth mule?"

"What?"

Wogan turned back to the room. "I said, where's the fifth mule?"

"Oh, crud!" Hawley jumped to his feet with his beloved Winchester in hand and stared challengingly at Nathan. "Is that muck-up of a brother of yours trying to kill us again?"

In an instant he was out the door, followed by the rest of the team, each man bearing his rifle. Nathan felt Wogan hook his arm as he tried to pass.

"You stay here and guard the gear," he said, and nodded to the packs strewn about the floor.

And then he turned and was gone, following the ragged line of men as they raced across the clearing to the forest's edge.

Not again, Nathan groaned to himself. He hefted the light survival rifle in his hand, leaned into the doorway Wogan had just deserted, and squinted at the forest edge. He could see his brother sitting cross-legged in the grass and weeds, back bowed and head bent to his chest, both arms outstretched to where he held the barrel of the rifle like sagging guy wires supporting a post, the gun's butt braced against the ground.

The short, spindly grad student who had bolted from the hut halted beside Mark and shook his shoulder. Mark jerked his head up and straightened, reflexively clutching his gun into his arms. He gazed around in confusion before stumbling to stand up. The others fanned out and ran past the four remaining mules to the forest's edge. After walking the tree-line, sweeping away branches and vines with their hands, Campbell called out. Two men disappeared with him into the foliage, and three minutes later they emerged, struggling to haul the reluctant mule into the clearing by its halter rope.

"Thank God." Nathan sank down to sit on the floor, leaned against a stack of mule packs and dropped his head into his hands.

6

The group filed wearily back into the hut, after tethering the mules nearby in their direct line of sight.

Mark threw himself down on the floor opposite Nathan. "Sorry," he muttered, his eyes on the floor. He flicked his gaze up to meet Nathan's frosty stare, and then instantly lowered it once more. "There was that long walk this morning. And then, sitting out there, baking in the sun..."

"Y'all fall asleep watching our animals agin'..." Duke drawled as he stormed past, leaving the sentence unfinished. He propped the group's heavy M1 Garand against a wall, then turned and squatted in the corner. He pointed an index finger at Mark. "Y'all screw up *anything* agin', *boy*, me an' Hawley here, we're gonna...make it right."

Duke noticed Wogan looking in his direction and stopped himself from saying more. But the Southerner's implication was clear.

Nathan noticed that Hawley swayed on his feet, his Winchester cradled in his crossed arms, but kept silent. *The dangerous one*, he thought. *And those eyes? The hatred in them speaks more than words.*

Even Campbell kept quiet this time. Nathan wasn't surprised. His brother had made too many careless mistakes on this trip. Nobody came to his defense anymore.

Hawley let his gaze drift away from Mark. He scratched his head and glanced over his shoulder toward the corner. "Let it go, Duke. Nobody's going to take the law into their own hands here. He was just passed out from the heat. It's our fault. We asked too much of him."

Mark looked up in amazement, as if questioning his ears. He followed Hawley with his eyes as he strode past to lean on the sill of the cut-out that served as a window. Glancing over his shoulder again, Hawley lowered the butt of his rifle to the floor with a thump. "Try not to do it again. Alright?"

Mark nodded, still looking as though he was in shock.

He wasn't the only one. Hawley turned to stare out the window.

Uh-oh. Nathan felt a tingle at the base of his spine. He suddenly realized he and his brother might be in more danger from these two than they were from anything in the forest.

Wogan broke the uncomfortable silence. "The chief isn't asking for a lot. I just don't understand why he wants money to begin with. There's no trade here. These people never leave their village, never go anywhere money would hold value. All the other natives have accepted our trinkets as if they were gold. Heck, they even fight over our garbage!"

This last point was not an exaggeration, Nathan reflected. The natives of the interior snatched plastic wrappers and empty steel cans from the team's refuse as though they were treasure. Most of them still used bone or stone knives, so even the razor-sharp lid from a soup can was a useful novelty to them. Certainly the machetes and belt knives they traded to the Indians were a vast improvement over the crude, rusted pot-metal implements a few of them toted.

Hawley turned from gazing out the window. "What are you going to do?"

The professor shrugged, and turned to leave. "Pay them, I guess. Let's pack the animals and get ready to go. I shouldn't be long."

"Fresh mangoes?" one of the graduate students asked, hopefully.

Wogan turned back and nodded. "Bananas and plantains, too," he said, and then patted his hands together in their direction. "Now, packs, mules—let's get moving, okay? And leave room on one of the mules for the fruit."

Nathan grabbed a mule pack from the stack he leaned against and got up. "Come on, bro, give me a hand." Mark pulled himself up, grateful that the attention was moving away from his mistake. Together they lugged a pair of mule packs outside and settled them onto the back of one of the animals. As he had expected, none of the others followed right away.

"Wow," Mark said, his eyes bright as he glanced back at the hut. He spoke across the back of the mule as he lashed the pack in place. "Did you see how Hawley—"

"Yeah. We're in danger, bro. You, especially."

"Huh? What're you talking about?"

Nathan checked over his shoulder. He leaned over the animal's back. "What do you think? Hawley's had a sudden change of heart after thirty years of chronic racism? Not likely. He's setting us up, I'm sure of it. Those words? He's just acting nice to take the suspicion off of him—when whatever he's planning happens to us. Or maybe just to you."

Mark's smile faded. "Wait a minute. What Duke said was out of line. Any *decent* person would've spoken out—even Hawley. My own twin *brother* didn't come to my aid, but Hawley did."

Nathan felt a rush of heat in his face, a burn of anger in his eyes, and his voice came out harsher than he intended. "Nobody spoke up for you because we're all sick of your screw-ups, me included!"

Mark's face was tense. "I've been doing the best I can. Okay, maybe I messed up a few times..."

Nathan held his first impulse to yell *"A few times?"* at Mark. He had to admit his brother had a point. The two of them were family. Brothers. Twins. Not to mention being the only two blacks on the expedition. And what Mark lacked in capability and intelligence, he usually made up for in loyalty and sincerity. The problem was, those qualities weren't enough here. Maybe not even enough to stay alive. Still, he had a right to expect loyalty back from Nathan. Nathan felt a pang of guilt. *Mark could be back home, basking in the sun while snoozing in a lawn-chair on their front lawn. But he chose to stay with me.*

Nathan started to form an apology. Mark glanced up at the hut, saw others coming near, and waved him silent. Wordlessly, Nathan finished lashing his side of the pack as the others joined them and started loading packs onto the other mules.

"Finished?" Nathan said. "Then come on." He motioned his brother toward the hut. "There's one pack left."

As he stepped away, Nathan noticed an odd bulge in the pack. Passing around to Mark's side, he found one strap so loose he could put his two fists under it. With a deep sigh, he took out the slack, retied the knot, and then followed Mark back to the hut.

Halfway across the clearing, he glanced over his shoulder and saw Duke and Hawley, working on opposite sides of the same mule. They were staring right at him. The moment he caught their gaze, they turned their eyes back to their work.

Mark popped his head out the doorway. "Everything okay?" he asked.

With another glance backward, Nathan caught a surreptitious flick of Hawley's gaze. "Somehow..." he muttered to himself, "somehow, no, I don't think so."

7

Nathan stayed watchful for the next three days. He noticed nothing untoward, other than Hawley becoming uncomfortably chummy with him and his brother. But every time the bigot tried to ingratiate himself to them, Nathan felt his insincerity meter implode.

On the evening of the third day, Nathan sat by himself on a split log watching the campfire burn down to cinders. An occasional flame jumped and flared, only to dwindle and die into its glowing grave. Nathan raised his gaze to where the tethered mules stood huddled together at the edge of the fire's weakening ring of light. Each mule balanced on three legs, the forth leg cocked at the knee, the tip of the hoof resting nonchalantly on the ground. Periodically one animal would shift his weight, bumping his neighbors and setting off a wave of rebalancing.

With a deep sigh, Nathan scraped the last mouthful of stew from his aluminum dish and spooned it into his mouth. Still chewing, he got to his feet and walked over to the animals, tied and hobbled beside Wogan's tent, which glowed in the darkness from a camp light within.

"You don't hate the others for being colored, do you, big guy?" he whispered to the only pale roan in the bunch. "Didn't think so. Animals don't kill each another over color."

Nathan toyed with the animal's thin forelock for a moment. He ran his hand over the arched neck, down its coarse-haired mane, and patted his rump. Then he sauntered over to the improvised serving table, a short board balanced between two cut logs.

Nathan had opted for an early rest and a late dinner due to having pulled watch duty for the first half of the night. By the time he had risen, the sun had set and the others were already heading for their tents in anticipation of an early morning.

Nathan sloshed water from a pan into his dish. He swished it around with the stained dishrag they boiled daily, and then flung it to the side. The ribbon of water hit the ground with a running splat. Nathan stacked his dish upside down on the pile in the center of the board to dry.

A twig snapped behind him and he spun around, ready for anything.

Tonto squatted on the other side of the fire, his brown face dancing with shadows from the dying flames. His friend held up two ends of a twig he had deliberately broken, and then tossed them into the fire. "How," he said, raising the open palm of his right hand. "Can't say 'paleface,' though."

Nathan steadied himself and returned the salute. *A sign of peace, to show the warrior's strongest hand empty of weapons.* "How, Chief."

Tonto rose and hefted the M2 carbine Nathan had been assigned for guard duty—but which he had negligently left propped against his split-log seat. With an inscrutable wink, the native handed him the weapon, gathered an armful of firewood from the pile at their feet, and set it down beside the nest of glowing embers.

Habit, Nathan thought. Slinging the semi-automatic rifle over his shoulder, he walked over and sat beside his friend. The resinous wood sizzled and popped as Tonto laid it on the coals, and almost immediately burst into flames.

The light in Wogan's dome tent blinked out, leaving all five of the two-man tents in the dark. The Americans paired up, but Charles Hawley slept alone. The natives, as always, occupied a lean-to.

"Quiet out there," Nathan said.

"Too quiet," Tonto said. "Insects start talking in an hour. Should be."

The brief silence was broken by a tropical bird, crooning a haunting goodnight song far overhead. A nearby bush shook with the rustle of a rodent drawn by the smell of food, and a chorus of snores drifted out from the tents to blend with the sizzles and pops from the fire.

"You're worried," Tonto said.

"You're not?"

The native nodded slowly. "Not the same worry."

"What, then?"

Tonto jerked his chin past the tents to the black shadow where the guides slept under the lean-to, indistinguishable in the dark. "Three days, no fights for more money. Not normal."

Not normal. Huh. Nathan realized he had been so wrapped up in his own concerns he hadn't noticed. But Tonto was right. Had they given up on trying to squeeze Wogan for higher wages, or was there another reason? Suddenly he felt wide awake.

"Do you know something?"

"No, Jane. Not normal is all."

"Can you talk with them? See what they're thinking?"

The native tossed another log onto the fire, now fully ablaze, sending a shower of sparks dancing up the swirl of vapors. "You're worried about Hawley."

"And Duke."

"I'll sit with you—sleep outside your tent later." Tonto fixed his gaze on the fire.

Talk about not normal. Nobody would ever do that for me back home. With a start, Nathan realized he was unlikely to ever find a more loyal friend than Tonto—here or anywhere—perhaps for the rest of his life.

After turning over the guard at midnight, he went to sleep beside his brother with the same peaceful thought, having watched Tonto bed down outside the tent flaps.

He awoke to shouts, followed by a gun blast that shook the very core of his being.

The camp exploded with cries. Grabbing his survival rifle, he rolled over, only to find the sheet Mark slept in empty. In one fluid movement he pushed to his knees and launched himself through the tent flaps. He expected the ties to tear, but the flaps flew open without resistance and he caught a half-naked body with one shoulder. Instinctively wrapping his arms around the man, together they tumbled to the ground. A melee of shouts at the camp's center were punctuated by another explosion of gunshots. Nathan felt a rush of adrenaline, and struggled in the darkness to get the better of his opponent. Pitching to one side, he quickly reversed, caught the native off balance, rolled on top and pinned both the man's arms to the ground beneath his knees. Raising his rifle butt in both hands to bash in the man's skull, only then did Tonto's cries of "Kemosabe! Kemosabe! It's me, Kemosabe!" penetrate the haze of his panic-fogged mind. For a moment he froze, and then he leapt off as if electrified.

Tonto nimbly jumped to his feet and grabbed him by the arm in the dark. Together they turned and ran toward the din of voices in the center of the camp. They found the expedition members milling around in confusion, the scene dimly illuminated by the campfire.

Nathan grabbed one of the grad students as he raced by, carrying an unlit lamp. "What happened?"

"Murder," he said. Pulling away, he stepped back. "Got a match?"

"Here. I've got a lighter." With a shiver of fear, Nathan realized the calm, controlled voice of the man who stepped forward was Hawley's. A metallic snap in the dark was followed by the rasp of a lighter's striker on flint, and a long daisy-petal of flame leapt from his silver lighter. The pale hand that held the lighter was smeared with blood.

Nathan felt his world close in upon him. "Where's my brother?" he asked, unable to keep the chill from his voice.

"Don't know."

"Wait until we get this lamp lit," the grad student said.

The mantles of the Coleman lantern sputtered to life, just as Scott Campbell stepped from a tent holding another lantern high. Together they bleached the scene white, and for a moment nobody moved. Spread-eagled on the ground was a body, arms wide as if to embrace the earth. He was dressed in the same safari khakis they all wore, even to bed. One hand was stuffed under the split log seat Nathan had sat upon earlier that night, the other lay draped into the fire where it sizzled and sputtered with an unholy stench, engulfed by flames.

A huge puddle of blood spread out from where the body's head should have been.

"Mark," he said, his heart and hopes sinking.

"Yeah? What happened?"

He snapped his head around as his brother stepped into the circle of light, only three feet away.

8

Nathan jerked his disbelieving eyes back to the corpse. One of the grad students knelt beside the body and said, "Oh, God, no! It's Hugh."

The second shift watch.

Nathan watched as the student pulled Hugh's arm from the fire and tossed dirt onto the curled, burning hand to put out the flames that licked the fat from the flesh. Only when he pulled the other hand from beneath the split log could Nathan see that the victim was white.

"His hea...hea...his *head*." He motioned toward Duke. "It's...it's at your feet."

Duke looked down. His eyes widened and he jumped to one side. "Jesus Christ! Get that thing away from me!"

Hawley stepped forward and picked up the head, cradling it in both hands like a bowling ball, and placed it beside the body. "I've already got his blood on my hands," he said. "I found him."

Or killed him, Nathan thought, wondering how Hawley kept so cool, when the rest of them were in shock.

"What's wrong with *you*?" Frankie said, staring at Campbell.

Everybody turned in his direction, and for the first time Nathan saw the blood that streamed down one side of his face. The hair braid on that side was soaked.

"Wogan's dead," Campbell said, his voice quavering. "It was the guides. They tried to kill me, too, but I got a shot off. We struggled. One grabbed my gun and ran."

"Wogan's dead?" someone asked.

Campbell nodded, then half-fell to sitting. "They killed him with a machete. I think. Turned it on me, but missed in the dark. Well, not completely..."

Nathan noted that in his shock Campbell had completely dropped his hippie act and reverted to his native Manhattan accent.

After they cleaned and bandaged his head wound, the group moved the bodies to the edge of the clearing. Then they gathered around the fire. Every light in the camp blazed, pushing the blackness of night into the recesses of the forest.

"Let's review what we know," Campbell said, clenching and unclenching his fists by his sides. Nobody seemed to question his assumption of Wogan's command. "The guides must have snuck up on Hugh. They killed him and took his gun, an M2 with a thirty-round clip."

For a brief moment, Nathan recalled how easily Tonto had snuck up on him, just a few hours earlier. He shook a chill away, and tried to follow Campbell's words.

"He must have died instantly, so we have to assume he left the safety on. Was the gun loaded?"

Nathan scanned the faces and realized all eyes were fixed on him. "Uh, yeah. First bullet chambered and ready to go."

"But safety on?" Campbell asked.

"Safety on."

"Okay, then. If they figure out how to work the safety, they've got some serious firepower in their hands. They've also got my 12-gauge shotgun, less one cartridge. It's a semi-automatic and I took the safety off when I fired, so let's hope they plug the barrel before pulling the trigger, the way we showed them. If they don't, they'll get four more shots out of it."

"You're sure you didn't hit one?" Hawley asked.

Campbell shook his head, then grimaced and laid the palm of one hand on the bandage over his temple. "Too dark. I'm not sure of anything."

"Did *anybody* hit them? As they ran away?" Nathan's question was met with silence.

"One of the guide dudes snuck into our tent," Campbell continued. "He split his...I mean, he killed Wogan with a single blow of his machete. I woke to find him searching the body. I jumped him. He started to get the better of me and I grabbed my gun. We wrestled over it, I got a shot off. He connected with his machete and stunned me. Then he grabbed the gun from my hands and ran. Into the forest."

"Damn savages got two of our guns, and left us to rot." Nathan knew Duke's words expressed everybody's concerns. Without guides, their chances of survival were slim.

Frankie, the short, spindly graduate student who woke Mark from his nap when tending the mules in the village, gazed over the fire at him. "It's not all about us, Duke. Wogan and Hugh are dead."

"Which means their problems are solved," Duke said.

Frankie turned to Campbell. "Why didn't you wake when he came into the tent?"

Campbell shook his head. "Wogan's snores could shake fruit from a tree. Heck, after the first week of sleeping beside him, I could have slept with a cement mixer going full-bore without waking. It's not a surprise I *didn't* wake. It's a miracle I *did* wake."

"All right, then," Hawley said, his arms folded over the Winchester in his lap. "Why didn't they kill you first?"

"Don't know. Maybe..."

"They like him," Tonto said.

Duke jumped to his feet. "Nobody asked *you* about your damned buddies! They're your *people*. You're probably in league with 'em on this. How do we know you're not hangin' back to signal 'em when to finish the job?"

"I don't think so." All eyes turned to Nathan, who went on to relate how Tonto had tried to protect him that night.

"Oh, yeah?" Duke said. "Well that proves he knew the guides had something planned." He turned on Tonto. "How come you didn't warn us all?"

"He wasn't protecting me from the guides," Nathan said.

"Well what, then?" Duke said.

'He was guarding me—and Mark—from you. You and Hawley."

"Us? You thought *Charles and me* were plotting against you?" Duke gestured in Hawley's direction, his face flushed. "Can you *believe* this?"

Hawley blew out a "pfft," then said, "Ridiculous!"

Nathan was about to argue his case when he scanned the circle of faces—and realized he didn't need to. Everybody could see that Mark and Nathan weren't unreasonable to be concerned about Hawley and Duke. Duke saw it, too. He sniffed nervously and rubbed his nose. "Anyway," he said, suddenly eager to change the subject, "they can still come back and try an' finish us off."

"Two against seven? I don't think so."

"*Three* agin' seven." Duke said, and pointed at Tonto.

"Tonto's innocent," Nathan said. "Unfortunately, while he was trying to protect me, it gave the guides a chance to slip out of their lean-to unnoticed. Normally, he would have slept beside them. He would have known if either of them had left. That may be why they didn't attack before. If he hadn't been protecting me...they probably would have killed Tonto first!" Nathan nodded to the Indian. "Finish what you were saying," he said.

Tonto scanned the circle of faces. "They hated Wogan. He was always fighting with them. Worked them too hard. Treated them bad. Flower-child," he said, with a gesture in Campbell's direction, "—he treated them good. Shared food with them. Candy sometimes. They liked him."

"So what were they after, Mr. Ein-jungle-stein?" Duke shot him an upward glance from where he sat hunched in front of the fire.

"Same thing you're after. Money. Guns, maybe."

"Well," Hawley said, "They got the guns, that's for sure."

"Wait a minute," Campbell said. "This is beginning to make sense. As soon as we left that village three days ago, they stopped demanding higher wages. Wogan was happy about it at first, but he was worried. He talked to me about it before we went to sleep last night. Maybe..."

"Maybe..." Hawley said, poking the fire with a stick, "Maybe they set us up. They convinced that village chief to ask for money instead of goods—to see if we had it with us. When they saw Wogan dip into his money belt, they realized they could have it all."

"And leave us t' die in the forest," Duke said. "Dead men tale...I mean, dead men don't tell a lot. They don't talk, know what I mean?"

Dead men tell no tales. And you're a graduate student? Nathan swallowed the words and glanced around the circle. Campbell held Wogan's M2, and the others had the guns they started out with. "So what do we do now?"

Campbell shrugged. "They've got Wogan's money belt and a couple guns they never dreamed to own. They'll probably run home to celebrate. Come to think of it, maybe we can track them back to civilization."

Duke ran a hand down the barrel of his M1. "And then we'll be home, and they—they'll be dead."

9

They broke up into two groups. Using flashlights, they searched the area where the guides had disappeared into the forest.

"Duke says our lights will make blood stand out as black blotches on the leaves," Campbell said.

"Guess he should know." Mark peered fearfully into the forest. "He's been bagging Bambis since he was a kid."

Campbell flicked a blond braid over his shoulder and turned to Nathan. "How old are you?"

"Nineteen."

"You talk like a man." Beside him, Frankie grunted agreement.

"I *am* a man."

"You know what I mean. You talk more like an adult than a nineteen-year-old. Years beyond your age."

Nathan replied, but kept his focus on the forest. "Funny, I was going to say *you* talk like a teenager. I'm glad you dropped that hippie lingo. It dumbed you down."

"See there you go again, sounding like my old man."

"Sorry."

"No, it's good. Really. You speak what you feel. I like that. You also know when to keep quiet. I like that more."

The silence that followed seemed to ask for an explanation, so Nathan said, "Whenever my mom saw us trying to talk 'cool,' she'd slap the jive out of us." After a pause he said, "Do you think Hawley and Duke are still a threat to us?"

"Not after what you said back there. They're exposed." He turned from inspecting a broad-leafed plant. "Tell you what, I'll talk to them anyway, just to be sure."

Nathan nodded and turned to his other side. "Mark, what happened back there? Where were you?"

"What? Oh, yeah." He straightened from ruffling the undergrowth with one hand and stood. Obviously embarrassed, he scratched behind one ear, his face scrunched up. "I went to do my business. In the woods. Bud didn't tell you?"

Bud. Tonto's other name. Nathan shook his head.

"When the first shot went off, my pants were around my ankles." He shook his head and shrugged. "I couldn't tell what was happening, so I hung back. When I heard everybody gathering in the center of camp, that's when I came back."

"Why didn't you use the slit trench we dug at the edge of camp? That's what it's for. I told you not to go into the woods by yourself. Not to go *anywhere* by yourself." Mark scuffed the ground with his feet, his face downcast. "Bro," Nathan said, "you're going to get yourself killed some day, and I'm going to have to be the one to tell Mom and Dad. And you know what they're going to say?"

Mark shrugged, still staring at his feet.

Heaving a sigh, Nathan reached out and lifted his brother's chin with a crooked forefinger, so he could look him in the eyes. "They're going to say they're not surprised."

Mark blinked, his eyes dull. "Look, how can I do my business where people can see me? I'm doing the best I—"

"You have to do better, Mark. Right now, your best could get you—or all of us—killed. Some feel it'll be safer if you were dead, or left behind. Now, I'm not saying I agree—"

"Over here," Tonto yelled from twenty yards away. His shout carried clearly in the still, early morning air, and everybody turned in the direction of his voice. "Blood here."

10

Nathan had to strain his eyes to see the single drop of blood on the tall grass stem, at knee level. "How on earth did you see this, Tonto?"

"I have an idea," Duke said, leaning nearby on the barrel of his rifle. "Maybe he knew where to look."

Nathan shot him an annoyed glance. "You'd better learn to trust him," he said. "At this point, he's our best hope."

"Here, too. Look here."

They walked over to where Tonto now stood pointing, ten feet away. This time the quarter-sized blood smear on a vine leaf jumped out at them.

"Okay," Duke said. "This here gives us our starting point. When they stop to bandage the wound, we'll lose this blood trail. We gotta get moving at first light."

"You heard him," Campbell said, turning a circle. "Let's bury the bodies, then get packed up and ready to go. And nobody steps into the woods until we can see what's out there. Understand?"

"Got that, Mark?" Nathan looked at his brother sternly. "I mean, do you really, *really* understand that?"

"I got it." Mark gave Nathan a pitiful gaze. "No problem."

"Okay, then. You help bury the bodies, I'll come back and spell you after I load the animals."

The moment Nathan saw the mules, he knew something was wrong. They weren't standing together in a bunch outside Wogan's tent anymore. The mule closest to the tent stood apart from the others, swaying on all four feet. The rest seemed to avoid him as if he had a disease. When Nathan got close to him, his flashlight clearly illuminated the dark patch of ground at the animal's feet. "Oh, no," he said. "No, not this, too."

He heard a rapid dripping sound, and walked around to the tent side of the animal. There, he saw the apricot-sized hole in the tent's canvas. Squatting down, his flashlight lit up a wet mess in the mule's belly, dripping blood to a pool that soaked into the ground. The splatter had speckled all four of the animal's white stockings red. He reached to prod the animal's side, and his fingers sank into the soft hole. He recoiled at the feel of slimy viscera mixed with rough fecal matter, released by ruptured intestines, and snatched his hand back. A gush of blood followed, but stopped almost as quickly as it had started. *Intestines plugging the hole.* He stood and took a step back, just as Campbell arrived to stand beside him.

"The shot you got off," Nathan said. He waved his blood-smeared hand between the hole in the tent and the swaying mule's belly. As they watched, two of the animal's legs buckled at the knees, but he recovered and stood upright. Then all four of his legs gave out, and he fell to the ground with a meaty thump, letting out a throaty huff of air as he hit. As he flailed his legs in his death throes, the other animals pulled at their tethers and shied to one side as a group, blowing out the peculiar mule call that starts with a whinny and ends with a grunted "*aw-ah-aw*"—the wind-down of a donkey bray inherited from their fathers.

"Ugh," Campbell said. "There go the soil samples."

"Tents." They turned to find Hawley standing behind them, staring at the dead mule as its chest heaved in its last agonal breaths. Looking up, he said, "Don't you mean, there go the tents? The soil samples are what we came for."

"We might have *come* for the samples, but we're going to try to *leave* with our lives," Campbell said.

Hawley's face contorted as his survival instinct waged battle with his corporate responsibilities. "We're down two men, not counting the Indian guides. We'll ditch their gear and any unessential goods."

"We're going home," Campbell said. "And we need to travel fast. No more prospecting. Can ADR Chemical live without their prospecting tools?"

Hawley nodded. "Hold onto the basics, just in case we come across something interesting and have to do some digging. Toss the rest." He slung his rifle over his shoulder, turned and strode away in the direction of his tent.

Campbell shook his head, then laid a hand on his bandaged head. "Somehow," he said, "I have a hard time imagining Hawley digging anything more on this trip—except maybe a grave."

"Yeah," Nathan said. "Let's hope it's not one of ours."

11

Morning brought a mist layer in and above the canopy, as well as along the forest floor. As soon as the day warmed up enough to burn the fog from the ground-cover, Duke led the group into the woods, Tonto close at his heels.

A hundred yards into the forest, Duke stopped beside a blood-smeared leaf and leaned on his rifle. "This here's the scoop," he said, as the group gathered around him. "The blood trail is thickening, which means two things. First, he's hurt bad. Second, he's slowing down. Close to camp, there was little blood in one place, 'cause he was running. Here, he's leaving larger trace evidence, which means he's slowed down to a walk. Y'all can also see that from his tracks. Back at the beginning, his footprints were toes and balls of his feet—parts that strike the ground when sprinting. Here, y'all can see the imprint of his whole foot. Lastly, all blood trace is at this here level or below," he said, marking a point slightly above his knee. "Now, sure as the South will rise again, I'm taller than both of them—so whoever shot this one connected with his thigh."

"Why's there so much blood in this one spot?" Frankie asked, pointing to the ground.

Duke pointed to a line of broken stems and trampled vegetation. "This here's where he stopped and waited for the other one. See, their paths converge."

"So, is he going to bleed out?"

Duke shrugged. "Don't know. But we have to proceed with caution. If he gets too weak, he might hole up and wait for us—like a cornered animal."

"So what do we do?"

Duke hefted his M1 and flicked the safety off dramatically. "I'll take point, you all follow—well back to keep out of danger."

After a mile, the injured man's track became irregular. Even to the untrained eyes of most of the group, it was clear the guide favored one leg over the other, leaving a deeper imprint in the earth with his right foot. He also seemed to be having a progressively harder time walking in a straight line.

Duke crouched, half-turned in their direction, the rifle in his hands aimed straight ahead. "He's getting weak." Despite being only five yards ahead of them, Nathan could barely make him out in the dense foliage.

As Duke turned to face forward, Tonto lifted his nose in the air and sniffed. "Wait," he said.

Duke looked back, gave him an annoyed look, took a step forward, and the bush beside him exploded.

Duke fell and Nathan reflexively jumped back. Tonto threw himself forward, scrambling into the thick foliage on all fours. A moment later he re-emerged, dragging the shorter of the Indian guides by one arm. The others all ran forward to hold him captive, except for Arthur, the fastidious graduate student charged to lead the string of mules. *Wouldn't want to muss his khakis,* Nathan thought.

Tonto ducked back into the bush and emerged with Campbell's shotgun. The breach and magazine were blown out, the metal twisted and blackened.

"Duke!" Hawley threw himself to the ground beside the man's motionless body. Sitting up and cradling his friend's head in his lap, he stroked Duke's forehead, careful to avoid the oozing shrapnel wounds in his head and neck. "Aw, hell, Duke, what did you go and do that for?"

Duke's body seized up suddenly, then he said in a gasping breath, "Tell my wife..." His eyes turned dull and his lids slid closed, his last breath came out with a rattle, and his body seemed to collapse in on itself.

Hawley bent over his dead friend, tears silently streaking down his cheeks.

Nathan turned to the stricken Indian guide, lying on the ground with the remaining members of the party looking down at him. The guide moaned painfully. Tonto was trying to talk to him, and he was answering, weakly.

"Dying," Tonto said, from where he sat, hunched over him. "Lost too much blood."

At a glance, Nathan understood why Tonto had pulled the man from the bush by only one arm. The guide's right hand was blown completely off. He must have pressed his face against the stock of the gun before pulling the trigger, as he had seen the Americans do when shooting game, because the right half of his face was an unrecognizable, bloody pulp. "What's he saying?"

"He said the other guide left him. Says he went for water, never came back. Two, three hours ago." Tonto bent close to the man's ear and whispered something, then put his ear by the guide's mouth. He glanced up at Nathan. "He says he's sorry. He followed a bad man. He wants forgiveness. He says we can survive if we follow the other guide. He went the way of the red macaws." Tonto paused to listen as the dying Indian spoke. "He says we should kill the other guide. He's a bad man."

"Yeah, well he's not exactly an angel, himself," Nathan said. "What does he mean about the macaws? What is the way of the red macaws?"

Tonto relayed the question to the dying man, but there was no answer. He spoke again, louder and more urgently this time, and still no answer. He pressed his hand on the man's chest to detect a beating heart. After a few moments he sat back and looked up at Nathan. "He's not going to speak more."

12

Nathan scanned the circle of men who stood around Duke's corpse, laid out on his back in the undergrowth, as the remaining four mules grazed behind them.

Hawley, his face drawn with grief, struggled to hold back his tears. Campbell, cold and analytical, looked like he was thinking hard about what to do next. He'd had a lot of responsibility thrust upon him suddenly, and he was a completely different guy than he'd been just a couple days earlier. Arthur and Frankie stood awkwardly, heads bowed and feet shuffling, as if in nervous prayer—though Arthur in his always-neat clothes looked less rattled by the experience than Frankie, Nathan thought, imagining him attending services at a High Anglican church. Tonto, looking grim, and Mark, his face lined with worry, completed the circle.

"We should bury him," Frankie said. "It's the Christian thing to do."

"Unfortunately, there's not time," Campbell said. "When the rain comes, we'll lose the other Indian's trail. If that happens, we're all dead. We have to keep moving."

Hawley got to his knees. He wrestled Duke's pack off and straightened the dead man out on the ground, crossing his hands over his chest. He carefully removed Duke's wedding ring, then pushed himself to his feet and wiped his face roughly with his forearm.

"He was my friend," Hawley said. "He lies where he died. Let's get going before we join him."

Campbell bent over and picked up Duke's M1. He flicked the safety back to the "on" position, then glanced at Mark and Nathan inquiringly.

"I can take that," Mark said, and held out his hand.

Campbell eyed him calmly for a moment. "That's alright, Mark," he said.

He pushed the gun into Nathan's chest. "That's a lot of gun," Campbell said. "Don't forget to take the extra ammunition from his backpack."

Nathan weighed the heavy rifle, the mainstay of the American infantry in World War II, in his hands. As the others started to gather their things, he stooped to rummage through Duke's backpack. He found the stripper clips of ammunition underneath the change of clothes and personal articles they all carried, quickly transferred them to his own pack, and then fell into line behind Tonto as the Indian led them deeper into the forest.

"Tonto?"

"Yes, Jane."

"You tried to warn Duke. How did you know the Indian was nearby?"

"I smelled him."

"So why is the other guide only a few hours ahead of us? He didn't walk through the night?"

"Too dangerous. He left in morning, like us, but before the mist died. He doesn't know we're tracking him. You've seen plenty of red macaw before, right?"

"Sure. We call it scarlet. Scarlet macaw. But I don't know what the 'way of red macaw' means."

Tonto shook his head grimly. "Me neither."

Nathan's mind wandered to thoughts of his grandparents and parents, kid sister and brother, friends at college. *What are my chances of making it back?* His memories coasted back to his father's lecture on the dangers of the Amazon—and the thought of it almost made him laugh. *Dad, you don't know the half of it.*

"Tonto?"

"Yeah?"

"Just in case something else happens—it's been nice knowing you."

"Likewise, Jane. You have a wife at home?"

Wife? I don't even have a girlfriend. "No, Tonto. You have someone in mind for me? A sister, maybe?"

On any other day, Tonto would have laughed. Today, he squatted and carefully inspected some cut vines. "I'm not an expert at this, but it seems like he doesn't know we're tracking him. He's hacking his way with a machete, see? He's cutting. That slows him down. We follow in the path he makes, which speeds us up. We're going to catch him for sure."

"Any idea how close we are?"

Tonto held up one of the vines and inspected it. He cut a deep notch a foot above the severed end with his rusty belt knife. After a minute, he said, "Not dripping. Cut hours ago. When water drips from these, we'll be close."

Three hours later the sun had passed its zenith. The rainforest chatter never seemed to ease. The heat and humidity was squeezing them again like a hot, wet blanket.

Tonto stopped to hold up a vine end. Nathan could see it was dripping. Slowly, but still dripping. Tonto swung his machete and cut another vine with a metallic chinking sound. He held the two together, and water flowed from the freshly cut vine in a fine stream. "Not close yet," he said. "But closer."

Three hours later, when he held up a vine the runaway guide had cut, it dripped more quickly.

"We're getting closer," Tonto said in a low voice. "We need to keep quiet now."

Nathan passed the message down the line.

13

"Look," Campbell said, "I'm just pointing out the obvious problem with our plan."

Nathan sat on the ground next to his brother and rested along with the others. He, like everyone else, had to admit Campbell had a point. Campbell swung a hair braid behind one shoulder with a flick of his head. Even though his speech and manner had changed dramatically in just a couple of days, this old gesture remained.

"If we catch him, he's going to fight," he said. "He might die. That's the last thing we want to happen. Because then we're lost. Even if we catch him unharmed he might not cooperate. He'll know we'll throw him in jail as soon as we reach civilization. But if we hang back—he'll continue to lead us home."

"Tonto," Hawley said, "You feel like you can keep tracking this guy, even if the rain washes away his footprints?"

Nathan smiled thinly. Ever since the native had taken charge of tracking, everyone had started calling him Tonto.

The Indian nodded thoughtfully. "I'm not a tracker, but I've spent a lot of time in the forest. Right now the undergrowth is thick. As long as he's cutting, and we don't get too far behind, we should be able to follow him even in the rain. If the forest thins out, things could get tricky. But for now, it's about as easy as tracking gets."

"Well," Frankie said, plucking a grass stem from between his teeth as he leaned heavily against his pack, "if we're going to hang back, we need to hang *waaay* back. If he hears one of the mules cut loose and bray, he's going to know we're on his tail. Who else has mules around here?"

"You're right," Campbell said. "We hang back as far as we can, but we keep following him until we hit some kind of civilization. Mules bring up the rear. We're all agreed? No dissenters? All right, then. We'll take a long break and let him trot on ahead for a while."

With that, he plunked down among the tired, somber men and started rooting through his pack for something to eat.

They roused themselves a couple of hours later and walked until sunset. When they stopped to make camp that night, the vines the guide had cut were definitely drier than the ones they'd seen earlier in the day.

They tracked the guide for the next two days, always staying in the "slow drip" zone. On their fourth day out, however, Nathan woke to find Tonto restlessly pacing their small camp.

"What's wrong?" he asked.

Tonto sat down and shook his head. "Bad dream, bad feeling. Couldn't sleep."

Nathan wouldn't say he had known Tonto long enough to trust his feelings—but he wasn't about to dismiss them, either. "Any idea what might be wrong?"

"Just…something's not right."

"What, the sounds? The forest doesn't sound right?"

"The forest doesn't *smell* right."

Tonto's foreboding made Nathan feel even worse—if that was possible. For the past week Nathan's relations with his brother had progressively worsened. After Campbell had given Nathan the M1, Mark had barely spoken to him. In fact, Mark hadn't really spoken to anyone. He'd kept to himself in the middle of the line, head down, lips pressed tightly together, clearly terrified at the thought of screwing up one more thing. Nathan realized he missed his brother's gentle humor and faithful companionship, even though he was relieved to see him making an effort to stay out of trouble.

Now Tonto felt the forest didn't smell right. *What on earth could that mean?*

As they did every morning, they put their gear together and fell silently in line, with Tonto in the lead, and Nathan behind with the M1. Forty-five minutes into their hike, Tonto stopped abruptly.

"What is it?" Nathan asked. Campbell drew alongside, holding his carbine at the ready. Tonto pointed, and for a minute neither of the Americans saw anything out of order. Then, taking a tentative step forward, Nathan saw cut vines off to the side. Advancing a few more steps, he saw a crisscrossing of naked footprints converging onto the guide's trail.

Tonto bent down to examine them. "Three," he said, and then, touching a smaller print, "No, four."

"They joined him?"

"Maybe," Tonto said, his voice sounding unsure.

"Who could it be?" Nathan asked.

"Don't know," Tonto said.

"We'd better tell the others," Campbell said. "If we're up against four or five...that's going to make a difference. Let's stay alert."

Nathan fell back next to Mark. "Hey, bro," he said. "How you holding up?"

"Fine," Mark said, without looking at him. "What did I do wrong, now?"

"Nothing. You're doing fine. It just looks like the guide might have reinforcements. So keep your eyes open for trouble. You should probably take that rifle off your shoulder and keep it ready."

"In case of what?" Mark said, glancing at the small-bore weapon. "In case I get attacked by a rabbit?"

"It may not be the best firepower we've got, but it can still stop a man," Nathan said. *And he already knows that.* "Just stay alert, bro."

Nathan returned to the head of the line and took up his position behind Tonto. They advanced for another ten minutes. That's when Nathan smelled it.

"What is that, Tonto?" he asked in a whisper. "Is that pork roasting?"

"Don't think so, Jane."

"Tonto, that's pork. If that isn't pork, what else could it..." He glanced at Tonto's taut, concerned face. A chill shot up his spine. "Not woolly monkey?"

Tonto shook his head again, never taking his eyes off of the path that lay ahead. "So...cannibals?"

Tonto nodded.

"Oh. My. God. What do we do now?"

14

Campbell gathered them into a huddle on the trail. "Okay, what can we expect?" he asked in a whisper.

"Four," Tonto said, and held up his fingers. "Very dangerous. Now they're cooking. When they finish eating, they come this way."

"Can't we just go back the way we came?" Arthur asked.

"These men are the terror of the rainforest," Tonto said. "If they want to, sooner or later they'll kill us. When they finish eating, they'll come back down this path to return to their village. It's easier for them to retrace their steps than to cut a new trail. They'll find our tracks, and come after us. Or maybe they'll go to their village and bring the whole tribe to run us down. We've left too many tracks for them not to notice."

"Okay then," Campbell said. "We stand and fight."

Nathan scanned the faces of the group. He read grim resignation on Campbell's, fear on Arthur and Frankie's, and absolute terror on Mark's. Hawley's poker face gave nothing away.

"Any military experience?" Campbell asked. When nobody raised his hand, he fixed his gaze on Hawley. "Korea?"

"I'm younger than I look."

"In that case, we'll have to wing it." He bent down and with one hand swept a patch of ground clean of leaves. "Okay, here's the trail," he said, and drew a line in the soil with a stick. "Somewhere ahead of us, they're gathered around their fire." Drawing a circle, he mapped out how two of them would assault the camp from the trail. The remaining four would divide into two pairs. Each pair would fan out to one side of the camp to intercept any cannibal who took to the woods, aiming to swing back around to the trail. "We can't have any survivors. If even one of them gets away, he'll bring the rest of his village back. Maybe their village is close, maybe far. Either way, they'll get us sooner or later and kill all of us. Does anybody not understand that?"

"How are we going to divide up?" Hawley asked. "The two who rush the camp from the trail...I mean, it's going to be four of them against two of us. We've got guns, sure, but the odds will still be against those two."

Campbell plucked a tuft of grass stems and stood up. "I don't see any way around it. Do you?"

No one answered.

"Okay," Campbell continued. "We don't have much time." He turned from arranging the stems in his fist. "Who's first?"

Everybody stared for a minute, the sounds of the rainforest chirping and chattering along.

Clearly, the cycle of life couldn't care less who would live and who would die.

"Come on, Arthur," Frankie said, nudging him with an elbow to his side. "Let's get this over with." In unison, they reached—and each plucked a long stem from Campbell's fist. Mark watched with wide eyes. He shook his head when he saw their good luck, sweat breaking out on his forehead. The victorious two dropped their grass stems to the ground, not wanting to rub their good fortune in the worried faces of the rest of the group.

Hawley hesitated, then teased a stem from Campbell's fist, his furrowed brow betraying the otherwise impassive expression on his face. When he saw the short end lift clear, he cursed softly and turned from the group.

Mark swayed on his feet. His nostrils flared and his lips quivered, and Nathan wondered if his brother might faint.

"You want me to do it?" Nathan asked, and reached forward tentatively.

Mark shook his head, trying to look brave. "Naw, bro. I'll take my own fate." He reached in, snatched his choice, and then stared at the short stem as he held it in front of his face.

Hawley cursed again quietly. Campbell dropped his hand to his side and let the remaining grass stems flutter to the ground. Nathan reached across the circle. He took the short stem from his brother's pinched fingers and held it up. "It's okay, bro," he said. "I might only have a minute on you, but I'm the oldest and I'm pulling rank. Mr. Hawley and me, we'll do this together."

Hawley lowered his rifle and stared at Nathan in disbelief.

Mark looked defiant for a moment. "I drew it. I can go."

"It's okay, bro," Nathan said, holding up the big M1. "Like you said, that's not much gun you've got."

"Nobody's going to hold it against you, Mark," Campbell said. "And there's plenty of danger for everybody. But we've got no time to waste. Leave the mules here with Tonto. We'll stay together till we're close to their camp. On my signal, Arthur and Frankie, you'll go left. Sneak off slow and quiet, and don't get too close. We don't want to spook them. Remember, you're not there to charge the camp, only to intercept if one of them tries to escape into the woods. Mark, you're with me. We'll fan out to the right. You two—" he said, turning to Hawley and Nathan, "You two give us a couple of minutes to get into position. After that, we're going to hunker down and wait till we hear shots. Everybody make sure you've got a bullet in the chamber. Keep your safeties on till we're in position. Even then, keep your fingers outside the trigger guard. We don't want a premature shot blowing our surprise. Last thing. Don't shoot each other. Any questions? No? Then good luck—and may God bless."

Nathan watched Campbell switch his M2 carbine to fully automatic fire, suddenly remembering that the man standing in front of him was a hippie—not a field sergeant leading his soldiers into battle.

15

"I'm not sure I can do this," Hawley whispered hoarsely as they snuck forward on the trail.

"You've got to be kidding."

"I've never killed anything in my life—nothing. Not even a rabbit."

Nathan turned and stared into his partner's narrowly set steel-grey eyes. Augmented by his white hair and thin, bloodless lips, he appeared to be the picture of an ex-Green Beret—slightly gone to seed.

"You were ready to kill my brother and me."

Hawley grimaced. "C'mon. Did anybody do anything worse to your brother than badmouth him? Everybody was frustrated. Duke was a bigot, I admit it. But it was just talk. We were just letting off steam. If it'd actually come down to doing something, I would've gotten cold feet—like now."

Voices speaking a strange, guttural language cut through the dense foliage, as did a sweet, choking smoke. Nathan peered ahead to where the trail opened into a clearing, only a few yards ahead of them. He watched as the others slipped off into the woods on both sides, then faced forward again.

"Safety off," he whispered, and slowly teased his own safety into the "off" position, so as not to make a clicking sound. The heavy rifle felt like doom in his hands.

He watched Hawley do the same, and then remembered how Campbell had broken the ice in their friendship. Using sarcasm, he had boldly transgressed the boundaries of racial sensitivity. "Look," he whispered. "If it makes it any easier, just pretend you're back home shooting darkies, okay?" He forced a smile he didn't feel.

"I never..."

"Well, here's your chance," Nathan whispered, bouncing his head from side to side, as if to a raucous rhythm only he could hear, "you red-necked, pea-brained cracker. Now...you ready?"

Together they rose from their crouching position and faced each other on the narrow trail. "Three," Nathan whispered. "Two," they whispered in unison, as they raised their rifles to the ready. "One...and go!"

Together, they charged forward, guns level.

16

They burst into the clearing and spun to the right, toward where they had heard the cannibals' voices. Nathan hoped to catch them sitting or at rest, but in a forest where rustling bushes could bring friend or foe, predator or prey, the savages had sprung to their feet as quickly as any jungle animal, their own weapons in hand. Four stood encircling the cooking fire—two facing them from the far side, the closer two in the act of turning. A fifth squatted at the edge of the clearing, holding his grass skirt open at the back with one hand.

Nathan's mind snapped a mental picture as he pulled the trigger. All five natives wore grass skirts and were naked from the waist up. Their brown chests were covered with tattoos. In fact, every inch of skin was tattooed or scarred. Their pierced noses, earlobes and lips bristled with bones, thorns and sculpted pieces of snail shell. Their hair protruded in wild tufts, streaked grey with the ashes they had rubbed into it.

The clearing erupted with the explosions of their guns and the battle cries of the natives. At such close range Nathan felt he couldn't miss, but the recoil punched his shoulder with the rifle butt like a fist. His first bullet caught the nearest man in the act of turning, and spun him around even further. The cannibal behind him took two rounds directly in the chest, sending him flying backward as if tossed, landing on his back, legs splayed over his head in a half-completed somersault. Beside him, Hawley shot from the hip, firing as fast as he could lever bullets into the gun's chamber. The nearest savage's leg flew backward, as if kicked from beneath him, as puffs of dirt blew from the ground around him with each shot the Winchester fired. He fell, jostling the older native behind him who was just releasing an arrow from his bow with a *zing*. It missed its mark, streaking between Nathan and Hawley with a *whoosh*, while bullets from first Nathan's, and then Hawley's guns blew blood mist from the man's chest and abdomen. As he tumbled to the ground, Nathan saw motion to his left. The native he had spun around with his first shot had recovered and raised a short spear, pointed directly at him.

Nathan watched in slow motion as the savage drew back his arm to throw, heard a dry click from Hawley's gun beside him, and saw the lamed cannibal in his peripheral vision push himself up from the ground and draw his one good leg beneath him. He felt the M1 Garand explode in his hands, saw the shot blow a hole in the spear-thrower's chest, and his gun gave off a loud *twang* as it spat out the empty stripper clip.

Eight shots, gone so fast?

The savage, standing straddle-legged with one arm cocked, toppled backward into the fire with a spray of sparks, just as the nearest man launched himself at Hawley. Hawley fell backward with a shout, holding his empty rifle straight-armed between them in both hands, as the cannibal bore him to the ground. The savage raised himself up to sit on Hawley's hips, pinning him to the ground. Grabbing Hawley's rifle in one hand, he snatched at the sheathed knife that hung by a leather thong around his neck. Nathan reversed his hold on his M1 Garand and, just as the native raised his knife for a killing blow, swung the ten-pound weapon like a baseball bat. He felt the gun shiver in his hands as the butt smacked the native's head with a wet thud. The savage dropped his knife and fell to the side, rolling off Hawley.

Nathan's hands screamed from the burn of the hot rifle barrel, and he dropped the weapon to the ground.

Hawley jumped to his feet just as the native who squatted at the far edge of the clearing turned and dived into the foliage, empty-handed. Nathan yelled, "Mark! Campbell! One's coming at you!" He pulled a loaded stripper clip from his pocket, snatched his rifle from the ground and slammed the stacked ammunition into the empty magazine. He released the slide with a *ching* and a click, chambering the first round, and ran to where the savage had disappeared. He felt, more than saw or heard, Hawley close at his heels. A womanly scream was followed by mad rustling sounds, and then the bush in front of them erupted with gunfire. Bullets whizzed past like hot wasps, showering them with shredded plant fragments, and they dived to the ground together.

"He's down," Campbell shouted. A deep, guttural yell ended with a single gunshot. "He's finished! Are you all right in there?"

Hawley raised himself up on one knee, then stumbled to his feet. "You okay?"

Nathan sat up and glanced around the clearing. The dead bodies lay in spreading pools of blood. One cannibal had suffocated the fire with his body. Thick clouds of oxygen-starved smoke billowed about his chest and spiraled upward. He spotted their runaway guide's corpse at one edge of the clearing, partially covered with broad leaves, but minus one leg. He felt himself retch when he realized the missing leg lay skewered, roasted and half-eaten beside the fire, overturned on its spit by the dead cannibal's fall. The savages' weapons lay scattered where they had died.

Nathan forced himself to swallow and nodded. "Yeah. I'm fine," he said, with a voice that croaked.

"We're safe!" Hawley shouted.

Arthur and Frankie burst into the clearing, their guns leveled.

"Three dead," Hawley said authoritatively, and pointed. "Nate clubbed that one senseless." The way he said it, Nathan reflected, made it sound as though Hawley had shot all of the savages himself, while Nathan had done nothing more than bonk one over the head with his rifle butt.

The two grad students rolled the savage over onto his stomach. Yanking the leather thong from his neck, they tied his hands with it.

Nathan looked up at Hawley, who stood over him as he sat, propped on one arm, his right leg bent at the knee. *Would it be too much to expect an extended arm and an open hand? Typical. We're all good when he trusts me to save his life, but after the smoke clears...*With no small effort, Nathan pushed himself up to his feet as Hawley stumbled over to a clear spot of ground and sat down. Hawley glanced at him furtively, then deliberately avoided his eyes.

Huh, Nathan thought. *This is a new lesson. If a black man saves a white man's life, the white guy gets all embarrassed. Acts almost as though I'd insulted him. Man, if it had been a brother I'd saved, he'd have been all over me with hugs and kisses and...*

As if to confirm his thoughts, Mark bolted into the clearing from the trail. He swept the scene with his eyes, ran over, wrapped Nathan in his arms and lifted him off of his feet. Tonto followed behind him, machete in hand, and checked him for damage while Mark praised him to the heavens. Nathan watched as Hawley scratched one arm. One of his fingers slipped through a hole in his shirt sleeve and he recoiled immediately, as if in pain.

Is that blood? A dark patch extended down from the hole to his elbow. As he watched, Hawley gazed up at him with eyes clouded with fear and confusion. He opened his mouth to speak, but before any sound came out all expression slipped from his face, as if all his muscles shut down at the same time. His head drooped, his shoulders slumped, and he collapsed to the ground in a heap.

17

Nathan was helping the others stretch Hawley out on the ground just as Campbell entered the clearing.

"Scott," Nathan called. "Over here!

"Sorry," Campbell said, casting a quick look around before kneeling down beside them. "I was checking our back trail. All clear. What's going on? Hawley said you're both fine. Did he faint?"

"Don't know. He just went limp and collapsed."

"Fainted," Campbell said, his eyes settling uneasily on the surviving cannibal, who lay bound but unconscious. "Is that one alive?"

"We just finished tying him up," Arthur said. He stood over them, the shotgun in his hands dangling beside Campbell's face. Campbell pushed the barrel away with one hand.

"Arthur," he said, looking up and once again taking command, "Secure the mules and then watch the back trail. Frankie—stand guard over the prisoner. Tell me the minute he wakes. Everybody else got your safeties on?"

"Oops," Mark said, and fumbled with the safely on his survival rifle before clicking it into place. Mark looked at Nathan for a sign of disapproval, but Nathan kept his expression neutral.

"Find Wogan's money belt and the rifle the guide stole," Campbell said.

Mark spun around and started searching the clearing. Nathan turned his attention back to Hawley.

"He didn't faint," Tonto said. They had stripped Hawley of his shirt, and Tonto now leaned close, examining the man's puncture wound. Then he sat back and held up two arrows he had lifted from the dead archer. "These arrows are poison. If they stick in the body, the man dies."

"The arrow passed straight through," Nathan said.

"Then maybe he dies, maybe lives."

Campbell leaned close and lowered his voice. "This is a problem. We need to keep moving. If the cannibals' village is nearby, they might have heard the shots. If they come looking for these guys," he swept his hand in the direction of the corpses, "we'll be at war. We got lucky this time. Next time, it could be *them* surprising *us*."

"They might be coming after us?" Mark stood facing them in the center of the clearing, his face once again the picture of terror.

Campbell swore softly, then turned and faced him. "The money-belt and the gun, Mark. Okay?" He turned back and jerked a thumb at their captive. "Tonto, see if you can rouse that dude. Find out what you can get out of him."

Nathan sloshed water from a canteen into his hand, letting it dribble through his fingers onto

Hawley's forehead. "He's breathing, but barely." He raised one of Hawley's eyelids with a finger, realized he didn't know what to look for, and let it close again. "I'm not leaving him." After a moment he said, "Who screamed? When the cannibal came at you?"

Campbell unslung his backpack and dropped it on the ground beside him. Then he checked his carbine and slung it over his shoulder. He glanced to where Mark crouched on the other side of the clearing, beside the corpse that used to be their guide. "It was Mark."

"I was afraid of that."

Campbell nodded. "He freaked. If we face danger again, we have to remember we can't count on him."

Just then Mark walked up to them triumphantly, holding the stolen money belt and M2.

"Finally," Mark said as he raised the carbine and held it in front of him. "Finally I've got a *real* gun. I'll stand up and fight, long as I'm holding this."

Nathan and Campbell locked eyes for a moment. *Maybe*, Nathan thought. *It's easier to feel brave when you're holding some real firepower.*

"Bring it here." Campbell rocked back from kneeling to sitting, his eyes fixed on the shallow excursions of Hawley's chest.

"He's awake," Freddie said. Nathan glanced over his shoulder to where Tonto was trying to communicate with the cannibal. The savage sat under

Freddie's watchful eyes, hands and legs tied. He appeared groggy, but mumbled something in response to Tonto's questions.

Campbell accepted the money belt Mark offered him, rolled it and stuffed it into his backpack. Then he took the gun. He flicked the safety off and tried to work the slide, but it refused to budge. When he turned the weapon over both he and Nathan could see it was crippled beyond repair. With a sigh, he released the clip of ammunition and stowed it in his pack. Then he returned the safety to the "on" position and passed the gun up to where Mark stood hovering over him.

"You're going to have to toss it into the woods, Mark. They forced the trigger trying to make it shoot, and broke it. And the mechanism is frozen with rust. Daily rains, but no care."

Nathan nodded, recalling their daily ritual of drying and oiling the weapons, a critical step in the rainforest, where a gun's mechanism could freeze in a day if not properly serviced.

Mark stared at the useless weapon in his hand, refusing to let it go. His face downcast, he looked like a child who couldn't believe his favorite toy was ruined. Campbell stood and shrugged his own carbine off his shoulders and into his hands with one fluid movement. He swept past Mark and stepped over to where Tonto kneeled, interrogating their prisoner.

"Anything?"

Tonto shook his head. "Don't know his language. I don't think he'd tell me anything anyway." He shrugged, his brown face strangely serene. He stood and walked to stand over Nathan and Hawley.

"Bummer," Campbell said, and then turned to address all of them. "People, we've got to get moving. Ditch the soil samples and strap Hawley over the back of a mule."

"What about this one?" Freddie said, and gestured to their prisoner with a jerk of his rifle.

Campbell turned, swinging a beaded hairbraid over his shoulder with a flick of his head. He raised his gun and fired. A foot of flame blew out the barrel, the savage's nightmare face puffed outward and then drew in upon itself, and a pink mist flew from the back of his head. He toppled to one side as Campbell grimly shouldered his rifle.

"Let's move," he said.

18

Ten minutes later, a pile of precious soil samples lay discarded to one side of the mule train, and the last animal in the line stood bareback, a jungle ambulance awaiting his human load. Campbell extended an open hand down to where Nathan sat beside Hawley's bare-chested body, his fingers on the wounded man's pulse. "Come on, Nate, Tonto—let's load him up and go."

"He's barely alive," Nathan said. "How do you expect him to keep breathing when you fold him over the back of a mule?"

"I don't. But we can't stay here, Nate. If you don't want to come with us, we'll be forced to leave you behind."

Nathan looked up in wonder at the erstwhile hippie and realized he really didn't know Campbell at all. Scanning the camp, he realized he really didn't really know any of them. Tonto and Mark were the only ones he knew well enough to trust, and even then, Mark was often unreliable, at least here in the jungle, even when he had the best of intentions.

Mark walked over and squatted next to Hawley and Nate. He eyed Hawley's rifle, then put his hand on the gun. "Well, I guess he won't be needing this...."

Nathan slapped his hand onto the gun and Mark recoiled in surprise. "C'mon, it's no good to him anymore, and I need a real—"

"Look," Nathan said, swinging his eyes between Mark and Campbell, "Y'all can run scared if you want and leave us behind—but you're not taking our firepower or our rights."

"Bro, what are you *talking* about?" Mark's eyes narrowed in consternation as his voice rose. "This junkyard dog was acting like he wanted to kill *us*—and now you're putting your life on the line for *him*? When have I ever, ever deserted you? Why can't you stand up for me?"

Nathan laid his hand on Hawley's chest, felt its shallow rise. "I know what Hawley is," he said, "but I'm not going to abandon him here to die. If it were you or Campbell or anyone, I'd take the same stand. That's all there is to it."

"You'll die with him," Campbell said.

"If I believed that, I wouldn't be doing this. Each of us is going to have to live with what he does here today. I know I'll never sleep anything but nightmares for the rest of my life if I run, so I'm staying."

"Have it your way." Campbell turned, an arm raised as if to signal a caravan. "All right, guys, let's move out!"

Nathan raised his rifle, slapped the safety off with a loud click, and Campbell froze. "I said nobody is going to take our firepower *or* our rights." Campbell turned slowly, and looked down the barrel aimed straight at his chest. Nathan nodded at him. "Leave our share of the mules and food."

Campbell half-turned and spoke over his shoulder. "Arthur, Frankie, leave a mule and food for one."

"Food for two," Nathan said. "Hawley's going to live."

Beside him, Tonto cleared his throat. When Nathan glanced at him, the Indian said, "I'm staying with Kemosabe."

"Now wait a minute. You just wait one God-da—"

Nathan held his rifle steady as Tonto stepped to one side, slipping his machete from its hardened leather sheath with the whisper of death.

Campbell raised both arms, as if in defeat. "Okay, okay. Food for—"

"I'm staying, too."

Campbell glanced at Mark, and seemed to do some mental calculations. Nathan was sure he was not nearly as concerned about losing Mark as he was about losing rations. He looked past him to where Frankie and Arthur stood whispering together by the mules.

"You're free to stay with us," Nathan called in their direction, "if you want."

Arthur rested his shotgun butt on the ground and leaned on the barrel. "Sorry, Nate. We think Scott's doing the right thing. We respect what you're doing, but we're sticking with him."

"In that case," Nathan said, "the sooner you divide the mules and food, the sooner you can cut trail."

"You can put away the gun," Campbell said.

"Can I?" In a few short days Campbell had gone from flower child to General Patton, to stone-cold killer. "Take a couple steps back, if you don't mind, Scott. And keep your rifle slung behind you until you're out of sight, okay? We're in survival mode here, and I'm just not sure what wild ideas might be going through your head right now."

Campbell stepped back and dropped his hands to his sides. "Look, Nate, these last few days have brought out the best and the worst in us. But we'll stand a better chance of surviving if we stick together. You know that. Now you're asking us to leave our translator behind."

"And you're asking me to leave a living member of our team behind. That's where we part company. You'll be moving slowly, cutting trail. If Hawley revives, we'll catch up with you. But let's agree on one thing: If either group makes it out of this forest, they bring back a search party for the others. Deal?"

After a few minutes, Frankie turned back in their direction. "We reloaded the soil samples, since we don't need an empty mule for Hawley." He waved a hand between the animals. "Half of the samples are with you, half with us. Same with the food, equipment and trade items."

Nathan watched him tie two loaded mules to the brush. He thought to mention that their four men deserved more rations than the other three, but decided not to push his luck. Machete in hand, Frankie led two mules into the woods in the direction they had been traveling for the last four days. A few rustling branches and machete-slicing sounds, and he was gone.

Arthur took a step forward. "There's something called mouth-to-mouth resuscitation. Have you heard of it?" Nathan shook his head. "It's something new. Two doctors at Johns Hopkins invented it a couple of years ago. From what I read about it in the newspaper, it's saving lives."

"How's it work?"

He explained, as best he could, but then added, "Hawley's still breathing, so you'd only use it if he stops."

"For how long?"

Arthur shrugged. "Sorry, that's all I know. Good luck, guys." He shook hands with Nathan and Mark, and nodded to Tonto. Then he turned and disappeared down Frankie's trail.

For a moment the clearing lay silent. Campbell was the last to leave. "It doesn't have to end like this," he said.

"You're right. It doesn't. You can stay."

Campbell squeezed his lips thin and tight, then shook his head. "I hope you're right. I hope he lives. I hope you catch up with us. Stay cool, Nate." He nodded at the others. "Mark, Tonto."

Nathan followed him as far as the entrance to the new trail. "Scott."

Campbell stopped and turned, and Nathan jerked his chin at him. "We'll probably be a little trigger-happy, sitting here by ourselves. Anything that rustles in the bushes is likely to get shot. If for any reason you think about coming back, you'd best announce yourself before you walk into camp—dig?"

"Nate," Campbell said with a sad shake of his head, "if you're thinking I'd come back to do anything other than team up again...you're trippin'." Then he turned.

After walking five yards, Campbell's safari khakis melded with the green shadows of the forest, and Nathan could only distinguish his form by its movement. Another three yards and the matrix of the forest, both substance and shadows, swallowed him whole.

19

Why? Nathan wondered, as he sat over Hawley's supine form once again. *What made me turn on Scott like that?* He looked up to where his brother stood, strapping the cannibals' weapons and personal effects into one of the mule packs. Tonto had dragged the natives' bodies to one side, and busied himself with rebuilding the fire. *I killed three of them. Campbell killed two. Doesn't that make me worse than him?*

No, he realized, *that's not the point. Both of the men Campbell killed were defenseless, and he killed them so coldly. The three I killed were armed and ready to kill Hawley and me. The one who ran into the woods was empty-handed. The other was tied up. A guy who can do that, no matter how nice he seems, is dangerous.*

Nathan had watched Campbell with growing surprise during his shocking transformation from peace activist to executioner—and he was deeply concerned at how easily he fell into that role. He'd started to change only moments after Wogan was dead, and from there to...*what? Budding psychopath?* At first, Campbell's calculated practicality seemed to be exactly what the group needed in a leader. But when Campbell shot the prisoner in cold blood his ruthlessness was exposed. Still, Nathan wasn't at all sure what other options they'd had with the prisoner. The problem was that Scott had decided for everyone—and that worried Nathan.

"Hey, Tonto."

"Yes, Jane?" He looked up from stirring the coals of the fire.

"The first time you called me Kemosabe, I practically had to beat it out of you, remember?"

The Indian smiled a mouthful of yellowed teeth.

"A few minutes ago, you called me Kemosabe again." The native shrugged and stared down into the coals. "So, my question is—am I going to have to threaten your life or kill somebody every time I want you to call me by my rightful title?"

"I didn't call you Kemosabe because you killed the bad guys. I called you Kemosabe because you did the right thing. You're a real cowboy—just like Lone Ranger." Tonto looked up from the fire and motioned to Hawley. "It's a hard way, but it's the right thing. You're no—how you say?—you're no dusuf."

"Dufus."

"You're no dufus. You earn Kemosabe—I'll call you Kemosabe."

Nathan nodded and smiled—the first smile he'd allowed himself in a long time. He checked Hawley's pulse again. *Still here.*

Nathan cast a glance at the light as it filtered through the tree cover, more than a hundred feet overhead, and realized they were entering the second half of the day. "You know," he said, "there weren't four of them. There were five."

Tonto flashed another smile. "I'm a translator, Jane, not a tracker."

Mark came over and sat on the other side of Hawley's naked chest. Leaning across, he handed Nathan a tuft of straight black hair attached to a palm-sized curl of leather. "Bro, I stayed with you because we're family—but these cannibals are seriously scary." Motioning toward the scalp, he said, "I got that off one of their belts. They all had one or more of those. I still think we should get the heck out of here, before one of these cannibals' relatives adds our scalps to his collection. It's too late for this guy," he nodded his head toward Hawley, "But we could still catch up with the rest of the group."

"Hey, Mark," Nathan said, looking at his brother with genuine affection. "I don't want you to die on my account. If you want to follow Campbell, then go. I won't hold it against you. If our luck, or God's grace, or whatever's been keeping us alive holds out, Tonto and I will catch up with you later. Hopefully with Hawley in tow."

Nathan read the mystified expression on his brother's face and wondered for the umpteenth time, *why am I doing this?* As always, the answer was the same: *I don't know. But I'd do it for any one of them. And I sure as hell hope one of them would do it for me if I were in Hawley's spot.*

Whatever Hawley's shortcomings, the two of them had faced death together and survived—just like everyone in the group. For the first time in his life, Nathan began to understand his father's silence whenever the subject of World War II came up in their family. Granted, Nathan had been on his own "front line" for only the briefest of moments, but like his father, he felt changed—an ineffable transformation that, since the dawn of warfare, had reset warriors' perspectives on life and reordered their priorities. With that transformation came an unwritten code, irrational and inexplicable, that bound a warrior to values he may never have held before. And part of that code for Nathan was to never abandon a fellow warrior—even if you didn't give a damn for them under normal circumstances.

Nathan watched the stricken man's chest rise feebly, fall shallowly. A worm of muscle squirmed in one bicep and started to jerk. The worm turned into a snake that bunched and writhed, and Hawley's chest suddenly heaved in a wet cough. Tonto scrambled to Hawley's side, and together they raised him to a sitting position. His back spasmed into an arch, and threw him to the ground again. They turned him on one side as his coughs started to throw sputum, but his arms and legs jerked uncontrollably, as if he were in a seizure.

As quickly as the fit started, his body fell slack again. Slowly, his entire arm shaking as if with palsy, he raised one hand to his brow, and rested a compress of fingers on his forehead.

"Thanks, guys," he said, his voice thin and wavering as though a gremlin were strumming his vocal cords. "I'll never forget you for this."

20

"Come on, you loafers!" Hawley called over his shoulder, as he surged ahead of them on the trail.

"Slow down," Mark said, pulling on the lead mule's halter rope. "Even if I wanted to keep up with you, the mules don't."

Hawley turned and exultantly threw out both arms, a jungle warrior rattling his Winchester. "Man, I feel like every muscle in my body just got a two-hour massage. Now," he said, dramatically levering a round into his rifle's chamber, "I'm going to track down that coward Campbell, and see how he wriggles outa this one. So move it, you slackers!"

"Maybe I should have left him to die after all," Nathan muttered. Tonto raised an eyebrow in his direction. He expected a snicker from his brother, but Mark just lowered his head and struggled to coax the mules along.

"I heard that!"

"That reminds me," Nathan said as he ducked a vine. "You were saying you heard everything? Explain that to me."

"Uh, guys?" Mark muttered, his head down.

"Curare," Hawley called back to them. "The natives use it for hunting and war. It paralyzes the muscles but doesn't have any effect on the senses. A fatal dose stops the breathing, but thank God I didn't get that much. I could breathe—just barely sometimes—but the rest of my muscles were completely shut down. I heard everything you said and felt everything you did, but I had no way of letting you know. Let me tell you, those damn mosquitoes buzzing in my ears practically drove me crazy."

"If it happens again, we'll tickle you and sing your favorite songs off-key," Nathan said.

"Uh, guys?" Mark stumbled on a tree root, but regained his feet.

"Not funny. Anesthesiologists use a curare derivative for muscle relaxation. But every now and then they forget to give the pain reliever. The patient hears everything the doctors say, feels every cut and stitch of the surgery. Being paralyzed, they can't signal or speak, can't tell anyone the anesthesiologist forgot to knock 'em out. They go practically insane from the pain."

They swung the mules around the wide, buttress roots of an ancient Kapok tree, and Nathan stopped at the base to wipe sweat from his brow. As he spoke, he realized Mark was swaying on his feet. "All of which boils down to...?"

"It boils down to you being A-okay, and Campbell being a skunk. So kick it into high gear, all right? I want to find him before sundown and wipe this forest floor with his butt."

Mark turned in the direction of the trail and slung the mules' halter rope over his shoulder. He leaned into it, but the stubborn animal planted its feet, leveled its head and pulled in the opposite direction, huffing and snorting. Mark fell to his knees, dropped one arm to the ground and lowered himself onto his back. "Sorry, Nate," he gasped, one hand flat on his chest. "Can't...can't go on."

Nathan glanced at the empty trail behind them, which at any moment could fill with warriors and battle-cries, then at Hawley's back as he charged his way through the undergrowth. He knelt down beside his brother and felt Tonto, at his back, do the same. "What's wrong?"

"Just...I'm just done. Burning up."

Nathan laid a hand on his brother's head, and instantly realized this was no joke. "Hey, Hawley, come back here! We've got a problem."

He looked up and saw nothing but dense forest. "Oh, heck. Hawley! Hey, Hawley!" Nothing but aggravating silence. Glancing over his shoulder, he said, "Tonto, go get Hawley and bring him back here. And hurry."

A few moments later, Hawley came back running, Tonto at his heels. Like Nathan, his eyes were on their back-trail as he knelt down beside Mark. "What's wrong?"

"Feel for yourself."

"Whoa. The sun could warm its hands on his forehead." Hawley glanced nervously at the back-trail as he withdrew his hand, and then hugged his rifle. "Look, I may not be the best guy to say this... but we can't stay here. Can you ride, Mark?"

Mark rolled his eyes and then closed them with a flutter of lids. His breaths came haltingly in puffs through cracked lips. "Dunno," he managed. "Can try."

"It's Golden Rule time, Hawley," Nathan said. "We didn't do that to you, but you'd do that to him?"

"Look, I told you I heard *everything*. Your brother wanted to leave me behind. What's he done to earn my loyalty?"

"What's he done to earn *your* loyalty? What the heck did *you* do to earn *mine*? Ugh, I can't believe this. White gratitude."

"What'd you say?" Hawley squinted one eye as he cocked his head at him.

Nathan avoided his gaze. "Tonto, you're watching the trail?" When he got a nod in return, he stood and motioned Hawley to one side. Once they were out of earshot, he said, "I said, 'White gratitude.' Like we owe you our service just because you're white—but you owe us nothing in return. We're still sitting in the back of your mental bus, aren't we, Hawley?"

"What!" Hawley dropped the butt of his Winchester to the ground between them and leaned his fists onto the barrel. "Come on, you know it's not like that." He looked down and cocked his head at his feet. "If that were you over there, I'd... well, I'd..." He looked up, and Nathan realized he couldn't tell if Hawley met his gaze to try to give weight to his words, or to try to convince himself that what he was saying was true. "I wouldn't leave you, okay?" He dropped his gaze back down to the ground and, head shaking, muttered, "I just wouldn't leave you. Not after what you did for me."

"Wow, that was hard for you, wasn't it?"

He raised his steel-grey eyes, bloodless lips clenched, and said, "You'd better believe it. If anyone had ever asked me before if I would ever say those words..."

"To a nigger?"

Hawley's chest seemed to collapse as he blew a sigh of disgust and then spoke to his feet. "Yeah." He looked up quickly, his eyes both pleading and apologetic, "But look, I'm not proud of my old attitude. And I'm never using that word again. I swear. I owe you that much, at a minimum."

Nathan watched Hawley scuff the ground with his boots and huff a bit to fill the uncomfortable silence. Finally he bobbed his head in understanding. "Yeah, man, I know what you mean. I just don't know if I believe you." He shifted his feet and poked a finger at Hawley's chest. "But that's not the issue. The issue is what kind of a man *you* are. You wouldn't leave me to die after what I did for you?"

"I wouldn't."

Nathan watched as the man shuffled his feet, head bowed to the ground, digesting this thought.

"Look, Hawley, I didn't put my life on the line for you because I *like* you. You and Duke were plotting against me, remember? Me *and* my brother. Now, I don't know if you were serious or just blowing smoke. But you were damn sure never a friend of mine. Of either of ours, for that matter." Nathan waved a finger between his chest and his brother, where he lay on the path under Tonto's watchful eyes. "So I didn't do it because I like you or because I owe you anything. And I *certainly* didn't do it because you saved my life. You blew one cannibal's leg out from under him before you dragged your shots out of the dirt. Then you only raised your rifle high enough to shoot the stomach out of another, after I'd already turned his chest into a Whiffle ball. Do I need to mention the one who was about to carve his initials into your heart?"

Nathan read Hawley's headshake, but had to get in one more dig. "If there had been two of you in that clearing, Hawley, you both would have died. And then? Then I wouldn't be having this talk with *either* of you."

Hawley raised mournful eyes, and shrugged. "So why did you do it? Why *did* you stay behind for me?"

Nathan stared at him and, as quickly as his anger had come, felt his face go soft. He exhaled a deep breath and felt himself deflate. "I don't know, man. Something in my gut. I just couldn't leave you to die and rot. I wouldn't do that to anybody on this expedition."

"And now you wish you had?"

Nathan didn't even need to stop and think. "Naw, I don't regret a thing. That's not just because I saved *your* life, but because I learned something important about my *own*."

21

"Jeez, Mark, why didn't you tell me sooner?" Nathan asked. They had circled back around and made camp ten yards off their trail. Anybody tracking them would have to pass by their position, so any rustling in the brush or animals screaming alerts would give them advance warning of their pursuers. To avoid detection and afford cover, they had bedded down in the wedge of a tall pair of buttressed roots. Nathan daubed his brother's forehead with a wet compress, which he knew would do little good. The still, humid air prevented any effective evaporation, leaving the compress little cooler than their surroundings.

"I knew we had to move. I messed up so many times on this trip...I tried to stick it out. It just got to the point..." His face screwed up, his chest heaved with sobs, and tears began to stream down his cheeks. "I just couldn't...couldn't take it any longer."

Nathan cradled his brother's head in his hands and wiped away his tears with the compress. "It's okay, Mark. You did well. This isn't your fault. You just need some rest, okay?" He patted him on the shoulder and then, feeling totally helpless, wandered over to where Hawley sat on a tree root, oiling his disassembled rifle. "The aspirin doesn't seem to be working. He's still burning up."

Hawley grunted.

Nathan looked back at his brother, and realized he was asleep. "Tonto's been away for hours now."

"Takes time to hunt with that cannibal's bow and arrows."

"Water?"

"Said he'd bring that back, too."

Nathan chuckled. "Let's hope he keeps his promises better than our guide did. How's your wound?"

Hawley flexed his arm with a grimace. "It hurts if I move it, but not too badly. For some reason, I didn't even feel it at first. It stopped bleeding, though, and the bandage is holding." He gazed thoughtfully at their trail. "If anyone comes along that path, their noise should give us about five minutes warning before they loop around to where we are."

"We could teach Tonto how to use a survival rifle. Since I've got the M1, I won't need it."

"Good idea. We'll use the buttress roots for protection. After we leave here, if we have to we can shoot the mules and use their bodies as cover. We'll fight back to back, if we have to."

Sounds good in theory, Nathan thought, knowing full well they would never survive the onslaught of a whole tribe of cannibals. *And he knows it too.* To voice that realization, however, could be fatally disheartening. Somewhere he had heard the first step toward death was lost hope. He decided to change the topic. "So...who's cooking tonight?

"I'm thinking I'll boil up some beans, thicken it with flour, stir in the herbs Tonto picked today, and add whatever bush meat he brings back."

"You don't want to roast it?"

Hawley nodded back. "The smell of roasting meat carries. Having learned that lesson, we don't want it to come back and bite us, do we? Anyway, your brother will need the broth." Hawley stilled his hands from reassembling the rifle in his lap. "Look, this isn't our last meal, okay? We're gonna survive. Put that in your head and seal it with wax."

Nathan glanced over to where his brother lay, murmuring incoherently in a fitful sleep. Speaking in a voice too low to carry, he said, "You think he'll make it?"

Hawley finished the assembly and started feeding bullets into the rifle's magazine. "Nope. Then again, I didn't think *I* was gonna make it. Nobody did. And I feel great, considering. We just never know, do we?"

"Moments like this could make a man religious."

Hawley grinned as he jacked a round into the chamber and then flicked the safety on. "Hell, boy...I mean, Nate. Nathan. Sorry, old habits die hard." When Nathan shrugged, he went on, "Like I was saying, if you want to get religion, try lying half-naked and paralyzed in a rainforest, a few thousand miles from home, listening helplessly as your teammates argue over abandoning you. Then one measly teenager you've been raised to hate for his color starts arguing for your life, and you realize he's your only chance. Since then...I'm a believer."

He swung his rifle to one side and leaned it against one of the few saplings that had found a spot of sunshine to grow in. Reclining against his backpack, he stared at Nathan long enough to make him nervous.

"What's on your mind, Hawley?"

"Call me Chuck. Nobody but my dad ever called me Chuck. I figure you've earned it."

"That's all you're thinking about?"

He laughed and slapped his thigh with one hand. "Nate, you get me to thinking too much. What's on my mind is this: You said you couldn't leave anybody behind to die and rot. As for me, I know I could if I had to—and I'd do it without a backward glance."

"Not me, I'd sleep nightmares for the rest of my—"

"Yeah, you said that before. Me, I'd sleep the slumber of the righteous, a full eight hours without even turning. That's what I'm saying. You've got something special inside. Back there, when you decided to stand by me, you didn't sit down and figure the pros and cons of what you were doing. You just did it. That's the person you are. From that standpoint, you might be better than the rest of us."

"Might be?" Nathan asked with a cocked eyebrow.

"Don't let it go to your head, Nate," Hawley said with a broad smile. "But you've gotta find a path in life that'll nurture that...sensitivity—not suppress it."

Nurture my sensitivity? This is the last guy I'd expect that kind of talk from. Nathan was about to formulate a snide comment to that effect when, from the direction of their old trail, a horn-billed toucan let off a cry of alarm. Hawley snatched his rifle from where it stood propped against the sapling and rolled to the ground, clicking the safety off. Nathan crab-walked sideways to where his M1 lay on his bedroll. Kneeling, he leveled it across the edge of a buttress root, in the direction of the toucan's call. Careful to keep his finger outside of the trigger guard, he silently eased the safety into the off position. Glancing down at his sleeping brother, he briefly considered waking him. No, he decided, he might wake with a shout and give away their position. *He wouldn't have much fight in him, anyway. Not in his condition.*

Hawley half-rose from the ground and crept past where the mules stood tethered at the entrance to their buttressed root hideout. Silently, he slipped in beside Nathan.

"Tonto?" Nathan whispered.

"Don't think so. We agreed he'd return to camp from the other side, right?"

A rustling of bushes sounded from somewhere off to their left, then passed to the right, from the direction of their old trail. Together, they repositioned themselves to aim their weapons at where the trail looped around to enter their camp.

"Doesn't sound like many," Hawley whispered. "Maybe only one or two. We might have a fighting chance."

"Then again, it might be a scout," Nathan whispered back, "with the main party somewhere behind him."

Nathan closed his eyes, said a silent prayer, and took a moment to interpret the sounds of the jungle. Then he snapped his eyes open and sighted down the barrel of his weapon, prepared to fight for all of their lives.

22

"This is taking too long," Hawley whispered. "It's been ten minutes now."

"There's no way they lost our trail." Nathan glanced at their pack animals doing their shifting three-footed dance only a few feet away from them. "Not with those deep mule prints."

"Maybe they're wondering why our trail changed direction."

"Or they could be waiting for dark." He glanced up at the canopy and saw a few snatches of reddened sky. "The sun's set already. In another hour it'll be easier to sneak up on us."

"Kemosabe...Kemosabe..." Tonto's call came from the opposite side, but Nathan's nerves were wound so taut that he swung his rifle in the direction of his voice.

"Shh!" he called back in a harsh whisper. Catching his breath and shaking his head as if to throw off his fears, he whispered, "Come here, quickly." Then he swung back to face forward, his rifle leveled.

With a rustle of branches Tonto slipped from the bushes behind them. He unslung a load of canteens and quietly lowered them to the ground. Nathan noticed that one of the arrows he dropped to the ground, alongside the cannibal's bow, was streaked with fresh blood. After duck- ing to palm-test Mark's forehead for fever, the na- tive squeezed in between them. Together, they kneeled and stared, only their heads and weap- ons showing above the tall buttress root.

"What is it?" Tonto whispered.

"They passed on the trail," Hawley whispered. "That was ten minutes ago. We don't know if they're waiting for dark, or for the rest of their tribe to join them before attacking."

"How many?"

"One, maybe two."

"Ten minutes ago," Tonto repeated.

Hawley nodded.

"If it sounds like one to you, it might be two or three. Indians are quiet." He puffed out his chest and slid his machete from its sheath. "You stay here." Holding up an open hand, he turned from one to the other. "Don't move. You move, I die."

"Tonto, what are you talking about?" Nathan hissed, staring at him in bewilderment. Mark let out a moan at their feet.

All three of them glanced down at where he lay, his face beaded with sweat, his shirt soaked dark. He rolled his eyes in delirium and shut his lids again.

"Whatever you hear, don't move. And keep quiet. Understand?" Tonto said, hitching the belt of his ragged trousers higher, "Wish me luck."

Almost silently, Tonto vaulted over the buttress root and rushed to one side of the trail entrance.

Halting in a crouch, he looked back at them and put a finger to his lips. Then he spun into the trail entrance and disappeared. Nathan counted a silent minute and a half of "one Mississippi, two Mississippi" before the jungle ahead of them rang with rattling brush and Tonto's war cry. A scream was cut short, followed by another scream that faded into silence. A wet gurgle ended in a gasp, and the jungle fell silent once again.

"What the..."

"Sshh," Nathan whispered, his knuckles white against his rifle's dark wooden stock. "Just listen."

Nathan measured the next four minutes of silence as the longest of his life. Then they heard the brush rustle in front of them.

"Kemosabe," Tonto called.

Tonto slipped out of the trail entrance, machete dangling in one hand by his side. He slid to sitting position on the ground, evidently exhausted. Nathan and Hawley jumped the buttress root and rushed to meet him.

As they drew near, he held up his other hand. They both stopped short when they saw the bundle of black hair clenched in his fist.

23

Nathan knelt down beside Tonto, his eyes scanning the Indian's bronze body for injuries. "What happened? Are you hurt?"

"No. Just tired. Feel a little sick."

"What happened?" He checked Tonto's back, ran his hands over his arms and legs. "Did any of them get away? Are there any survivors?"

"There were *three* of them?" Hawley asked incredulously, gingerly holding up the scalps Tonto had handed him, now divided between two hands.

"Looks like it, doesn't it," Tonto said.

Nathan eyed Tonto with a whole new level of respect—and a little horror. His friend was taking scalps, now? "Three? You've got to be...Tell you what," he said, clasping him by the shoulder, "You're Tarzan from now on, buddy."

"Wait a minute," Hawley said. "What little blood I see on these is dry."

"Dry?" Tonto said, his expression changing. "So...I don't get to be Tarzan?"

Nathan looked from the scalps in Hawley's hands back to Tonto. Tonto's face split with a mischievous grin and bugged with laughing eyes.

Nathan glanced down at Tonto's machete and realized there was no blood on it. "Wait a minute...what's going on?"

Tonto jumped up, sheathed his machete, threw his head back and spread his arms wide, as if to address the heavens. "I, Tonto, from powerful tribe Mandahuaca. I great warrior." He thumped his chest with a fist, then laughed and looked down at them. "I'm also a big joke."

"Big joker," Hawley said, a sour expression on his face.

"Big joker. Yes." He pulled two more scalps from his belt-pouch, and dropped them beside where Hawley had placed the other three.

24

"So," Nathan said as he watched the pot Hawley stirred simmer over their fire. "You went back to the clearing to see if we were being followed. No wonder you took so long."

"Right," Tonto said. "Then I got a big idea. I scalped the dead man-eaters. Not exactly my style. But I thought, if their friends come, what they see is going to make an impression. Five dead men, big holes in their bodies, scalps gone...and eyeballs ripped out? They're going to be afraid. Not gonna come after us."

"Eyeballs?" Hawley said, voice rising in disgust.

Tonto smiled and shrugged. "I'm kidding."

"Jesus, Tonto," Hawley said.

"Maybe," Tonto said.

"Whatever," Nathan said hastily, patting the air with his hands. "Eyeballs or not, it was a smart move, in my opinion. And then you came back by the same trail, so it was you we heard passing by us in the woods."

"Sorry about that. I didn't know where the trail ended, so I passed you. When the trail bent back, I cut through the forest to return the way we agreed." He finished butchering the animal he had shot with the cannibal's bow and arrow.

Standing, he scraped the chunks of meat into a pile and handed the board to Hawley, who tipped the meat into the pot.

"What's that taste like, Tonto?"

"Not Tarzan?"

"When you actually kill a couple man-eaters, not just fake it."

"Okay, Jane." He pointed to the pot. "It tastes like yapok."

"It *is* yapok."

He shrugged. "Nothing else tastes like yapok. Only water opossum in the world. How do I tell you how it tastes?"

"Okay, never mind. I'll find out soon enough." Nathan bowed his head to the survival rifle in his lap. "It's time to give you a little more firepower." He held the rifle up so Tonto could see. "You press here, and it opens, like this." He cracked the chamber open, and showed how the gun ejected spent rounds. Then he ran through the care and use of the weapon. "Think you can handle that?"

"Hmm," Tonto looked thoughtful. "Not sure, boss. When do you put the paper down the barrel?"

Hawley spluttered the sip of stew he was tasting. "No, no. No, Tonto," he said hurriedly. "That's why the guide's gun blew up. Don't ever put anything down the barrel. If the barrel is not clear, it will explode when you shoot it."

There were a few seconds of silence. Then Tonto's face broke into a mischievous grin.

"Yeah. I know, Mr. Hawley. Just can't seem to stop joking today."

"Jesus, Tonto. Knock it off," Hawley said.

"Look—both of you—I've known all along you don't really trust me," Tonto said. "I'm basically just another native, right? Maybe give me a machete to show I'm a little better than those cannibals back there?"

"We're teaching you how to use that gun, aren't we?" said Hawley.

He turned to face Nathan. "You trust me now?"

"I trusted you...from before," Nathan said. "But I get your point. Believe me. Tomorrow you'll take some practice shots. After that, you're on your own. Is the safety on?"

Turning the weapon over in his hands, Tonto checked. "You know, this isn't the first time I've held a gun. Couple of expeditions actually thought it was a good idea to have their translator armed."

After a few minutes of uncomfortable silence, Hawley lifted his stir-stick from the stew, draped with limp leaves like wet laundry on a line. "How long do I boil these herbs you picked, Tonto?"

"They're ready," Tonto said. "Those herbs make strong medicine. Good for Mark. Good for all of us."

Nathan scooped a cup of broth from the pot as Hawley fished the spent herbs out with his stick and flung them into the woods.

With Tonto's help, Nathan raised Mark to a sitting position. He spooned half of the broth for him, but then Mark slid back down and curled up in the fetal position on his sweat-soaked bedroll. Nathan raised his eyes to meet Tonto's gaze. The Indian just shrugged and pointed to the heavens.

That night, Mark flung himself about in his sleep as if he were being tortured. At one point he babbled incoherently. Later that night he screamed for a full ten minutes, as if to wake the stars.

Nathan sat over his brother, alternately applying compresses he knew did little or no good—and praying. Tonto laid poultices of herbs on his neck and chest.

By morning all three of them felt certain that Mark would die.

Two hours later, his fever broke.

An hour after that he sat up and drank the herbal brew Tonto steeped over the fire. By mid-afternoon he could stumble along on his feet, but they decided to wait until the next day before resuming their trek.

Tonto disappeared into the jungle to gather herbs and hunt, leaving the others behind to prepare for the next day's journey.

As he lay down to sleep that night, Nathan wondered if their small run of good fortune would last. As if to mock this hope, a distant monkey call drifted down to him like the demented cackle of a malevolent spirit.

25

They had hiked a mile from their camp when, in one of the wicked tricks the rainforest plays on its invaders, the canopy inexplicably thickened again. With the reduced sunlight sifting through, the undergrowth practically disappeared. It took with it all trace of Campbell's trail, except for the occasional mule print the daily rains failed to wash away. As the jungle reverted to rainforest, cut vines and trampled foliage vanished.

Hawley took a compass reading and led the group on a straight line, occasionally readjusting whenever they discovered the pocket of a mule print in the mud. After another mile, Tonto spied a deep gouge in a tree trunk at eye level.

"Finally," Hawley said. "They got this far before remembering to mark their trail for us. Maybe now they'll keep us in their rear-view mirror."

They followed the hatchet marks to a wide tributary, where they found an arrow of rocks on the riverbank pointing downstream.

By midday Nathan felt they had covered good ground. He was just thinking of suggesting a break for lunch when Tonto called from a small clearing up ahead. They tramped through the clingy vines that lined the riverbank and rushed to his side. Standing in a semicircle, the four of them stared down at the latest riverside marker. Beside the arrow of rocks, still pointing downstream, lay an oblong rock pile that could only be a fresh grave. Hawley pointed to a rock that pinned down a ragged scrap of paper. When he lifted it a large black beetle crawled out from underneath. He held the scrap of paper aloft, so all could see the neatly clipped sawtooth edge. Whatever message had been written there almost certainly was lining the bottom of a bird's nest by now.

"I wonder what happened here," Mark said. He'd been subdued since his illness, and hadn't said much all day.

Hawley stood and stared, his Winchester cradled in the crook of one arm.

Nathan wondered if Mark was considering how close he had come to filling his own grave, just two days ago.

Tonto scouted the brush and riverbank for signs in an ever-widening circle.

Mark sat and cradled his head in his hands.

"How are you feeling?" Nathan asked.

"Better than whoever's in that grave. Headache, sore throat, aching muscles. Nothing I can't handle."

Nathan reached down and patted him on the back. "You're doing a good job, bro. You're keeping up with the rest of us, even though you're still sick. Before the fever broke, I didn't think you were going to pull through."

Mark motioned to the grave. "Somebody didn't. I wish I knew who's in there."

"When we find the others, they'll tell us."

Mark turned his weary eyes up to where Nathan stood over him. "And if we don't find them?"

Nathan glanced at Hawley, staring at the rock pile, lost in thought. Squatting down beside his brother he whispered, "If we don't find them, they might already be dead."

"That could be me in there, too," Hawley said, still staring at the grave.

Mark splashed water from his canteen onto a black bandana, wiped his forehead with it. "Man. That could be *any* of us in there."

Hawley coughed into his fist and then shook his head, as if to clear his thoughts. "Anyway," he said with a wry smile, "it's not over yet, is it?"

Nathan wanted to remind Hawley of his own words, his commitment to survival. *Put that conviction into your mind and seal it with wax.* But faced with their helplessness, the fragility of their lives in the face of the daunting power of the Amazon, he simply couldn't bring himself to speak with such impotent bravado.

Hawley sighted over their heads and beyond them. "What do you have there, Tonto?"

All of them stepped over to where Tonto was crouched down, studying the ground beneath him. The Indian swept a hand across the contoured mud, thrown up into concentric waves like a giant fingerprint. Even to Nathan's untrained eye, it was obvious something big and powerful had thrashed around in the torn-up weeds and grasses. Then it dragged itself to the river, clearing a muddy swath through the vegetation.

"Some kind of battle here," Tonto said.

"What was it?" Hawley asked.

"Something big."

Nathan shifted impatiently. He was in no mood for another of Tonto's jokes, if that was what he was working up to. He was about to say as much when Tonto said, "Not a black caiman. They're afraid of men. They'll only attack if they're guarding their eggs. No caiman nest here, anyway. Also, no..." He clawed at the air with a crooked hand.

"No claw marks," Hawley said.

"Right," Tonto nodded. "Black caiman leave a lot of claw marks."

"So..."

Tonto rubbed his smooth chin. "I think this was a snake. A big snake."

"Anaconda?" Nathan said.

Tonto rubbed his chin again. "Anacondas are rare. To attack a man—*very* rare. But yes. Anaconda. Big anaconda."

26

"Let's take a chance and see if anyone hears us," Hawley said. He pointed his rifle at the river and fired off three quick shots, each one throwing up a tall plume of water.

He twisted the rifle sideways and pushed three fresh cartridges through the loading port. Then he rested the rifle butt on his hip, the barrel pointed skyward, and cocked his head to listen.

Nothing, Nathan thought. *Silence. Where are they?* He glanced around and realized there was no way he and Tonto had lost the trail. It simply ended, less than two miles downriver from where they had found the grave.

And the trail didn't end in the river. No, it ended right where he stood, in the weeds and grasses.

So where did they go?

Three shotgun blasts shook a cloud of white egrets out of the trees a hundred yards behind them, and they turned to watch as the flock flew a circle, and then returned to their nests.

"That's got to be them," Hawley said. Mark coaxed the mules around and they started back along the riverbank just as Arthur stepped out of the trees, waving both arms, his shotgun raised in one hand.

When he saw them turn back, Arthur stood and waited, hands on hips. As they neared he walked out to greet them. Tall and gangly, almost aristocratic, he greeted Hawley with a formal handshake, a curious look on his angular face.

"What happened?" Hawley asked, as the others gathered around. "Give me the postcard version."

Arthur bowed his head. "Frankie's dead. You saw his grave back there? Okay, then. That was Frankie. One of the mules ran off, and Scott's laid up with fever. And you—I could ask you the same thing. You're alive."

"Yes," Hawley said.

"Everybody thought you were dead," Arthur said.

"Yeah. So I heard. Everybody except my friend Nate, here."

"Well..." Arthur rubbed the side of his face. "I guess we owe you an apology."

"Maybe we just need to focus on what's going on right now," Nathan said.

The moment they entered camp, Hawley's anger and impatience seemed to drain from him. He stood over Scott as he writhed in what appeared to be the throes of a malarial nightmare. Hawley's shoulders slumped, his hands fell to his sides. He shrugged his pack off of his back, swung it to the ground, and leaned his rifle against it. Then he turned to Arthur. "Maybe you can tell us the full version now."

They gathered on the river's bank and watched as Tonto dragged a fishing line against the lazy flow of the dirty green water. When Nathan saw him bait his hook with berries, he thought he must be crazy. Minutes later, as he watched him haul out his third straight piranha, he couldn't help asking, "But don't piranhas eat meat?"

"There are many kinds of piranha. This kind eats berries."

Arthur jerked his chin toward Tonto. "He's a good guy to have around. I couldn't catch a thing in that river. Now I know why. Maybe we shouldn't have left you."

"Yeah," Hawley said, "maybe you shouldn't have."

"I don't regret having left because of you, Charles. Look, I'm glad you're alive, but it could just as easily have gone the other way. Sorry, but you've got to put your personal feelings aside. I believe Scott made the right decision under the circumstances. Had our positions been reversed, you might have done the same. No, it's just that there's strength in numbers. If we had stayed together, Frankie might still be alive."

Hawley turned and gazed across the river. After a moment's silence, he said, "Okay, we told you what happened with us, now it's your turn."

Arthur picked up a flattened stone from beside him and skipped it across the water. Tonto gave him a look and raised a hand.

"Sorry, Tonto. I wasn't thinking," Arthur said. He shrugged one eyebrow, then turned back to face them. "Scott came down with fever almost as soon as we left you. It really slowed us down, but we kept going as best we could. It was Frankie's turn to lead, and I was in the back with the mules. One minute Frankie was sauntering through the groundcover, the next minute it exploded at his feet and this monster anaconda wrapped him in its coils. Before we could do anything, the snake dragged him into the water. We couldn't shoot out of fear of hitting Frankie, and once in the water we couldn't keep hold of him *or* the snake. It was grab the snake, get hit by its tail; grab Frankie, everything spins and you get thrown into the water; pick yourself up and clear your eyes, find the snake's head, and something coils around your legs, sweeps you off your feet and drags you under. Half of the time, I didn't know if I was fighting for Frankie's life, or for my own." He bowed his head in his hands and slowly rocked himself, as if to make the painful memory go away. "In the end, I grabbed my knife and stabbed and cut anything that squirmed. The snake took off, but by the time we got Frankie back, he had drowned."

He stared across the water, his eyes filling with tears. "You know, he was a good guy. He was my friend."

Hawley drew his forehead into deep furrows. "We're all sorry to lose him, Arthur. What happened next?"

Arthur gazed past Tonto as he pulled in his fifth fish, his eyes focused on oblivion. "During the fight and confusion, both mules ran away. I found one, but the other took off for places unknown. I couldn't follow him, because I had to get back to take care of Scott. We tried to continue on, but Scott was overcome by his illness. When we realized he was in no condition to travel, we backtracked to this bend in the river. With the nesting egrets, we figured at least we'd have a steady food supply."

"His fever should break, like it did with Mark. But look," Hawley said, with a meaningful glance in Mark's direction. "We're just trying to survive now, okay? So I've got to ask where Frankie's gun is."

Arthur waved a hand upstream. "In the river. The anaconda caught everything in its coils. Frankie, his pack, his gun—all dragged into the water. The only thing he left on dry land was his hat." He shook his head sadly. "We lost a lot to that snake. Frankie, a mule, two rifles. Heck, Scott and I almost died out there as well."

"Did you say you lost *two* rifles? Why two?"

Arthur sighed, picked up another stone to throw, caught a warning look from Tonto, and let it roll harmlessly from his hand. "I dropped my gear before I ran into the water. Scott took his rifle with him, thinking he'd shoot the snake. He got thrashed, thrown, and dragged under before he could get off a shot. On one of his dunks he lost his rifle fighting for air. You're free to go search the river, if you're brave enough. We didn't even try, knowing the snake was still out there. We were happy just to have survived."

"I'll go," Mark said, jumping to his feet.

"You've never fought an anaconda," Arthur reminded him.

"Whoa, slow down," Hawley said, holding up a hand like a traffic cop. "Those guns are ruined by now. And the last thing we need is to lose another member of our team." He scanned their faces for a moment. "Jeekers," he said. "We started out as twelve. Now half of us are dead. Wogan, Hugh, Duke, our two Indian guides—and now Frankie."

Arthur shook his head sadly and got to his feet. "If we don't want to add one more name to that list, we'd better go check on Scott."

Nathan scanned the scenery, and was immediately struck by the incongruity of something so beautiful and serene being so completely deadly. Flat and somnolent, the khaki green river flowed so slowly the current was almost undetectable. The forest, alive with exotic flowers and the chirps and whistles of brilliantly colored birds, beckoned visitors to explore its abundant treasures.

And yet both hid a myriad of death traps and terrors.

Which one of us is next? Nathan wondered. *"Does somebody else have to die?"*

27

"Pops? You okay?"

Nathan raised his eyes from the living room carpet. The video camera stood to one side, staring at him coldly, the red record light its only sign of life.

"Pops?"

As if rousing from a daze, Nathan honed in on the source of the interruption. His oldest son, Martin, walked over and hit the camera's pause button.

"You okay, Pops? You stopped talking."

So much of it was still vivid in his mind, after all these years. A picture was burned into his mind of Scott Campbell lying in the still, suffocating air of the forest, sweating his bedroll wet.

"Sorry, son."

"If it's too much, we can continue later. Or not at all, if you don't want to."

"No, no. I want to finish. It feels good to tell it. Turn the recorder back on."

Martin gazed at his father with concern. The older man's face looked tired and drawn.

"Okay, Pops. But only if you're sure."

"I'm...just turn it on, okay?"

28

At first, they assumed Campbell's fever would pass, as it had with Mark.

The first sign that he was suffering from a different illness was when he complained of intense headache and bone pains. Within twenty-four hours, the bone pains became crushing, and a pinpoint rash blossomed all over his body. In their ignorance, they treated him with penicillin and aspirin—*lots* of aspirin. It was the only analgesic they had, and in desperation they doubled the normal dosage.

Years later, doctors would learn that aspirin's anti-platelet action could save the lives of heart attack and stroke victims. They also learned, however, that it would exacerbate the lowered platelet count brought on by dengue fever—better known as break-bone or bone-crusher fever. The consequences were often fatal.

At the time, nobody knew any of this—not Hawley, not Arthur, not Nathan, not even the doctors back home. So when Campbell bellowed in pain, they fed him aspirin. Then they watched him bleed to death, never understanding why.

It started with a nosebleed. Two hours later, he vomited swallowed blood that had collected in his stomach. The stinking, partially digested horror puddled on the ground, as black, thick and congealed as coffee grounds. Within minutes blood started to drip from his eyes, nose and lips. Those drops turned to rivulets, but it wasn't until he bled from his skin that Campbell went into hemorrhagic shock. His skin rash burst out through his pores, and his entire body took on the ghastly appearance of a bloody sponge being squeezed from within.

After Campbell died, they were too scared to touch him, even to pull his body to where they could dig a proper grave. As they had done with Frankie, they piled rocks on him where he lay. Then they broke camp and fled downstream, as if running from the devil's work.

Each team member went through the routine of his duties, dragged into a collective silence by the undertow of horrors they had witnessed. Nathan couldn't clear his mind of the image of Campbell's dead body, enshrouded in a rust-colored crust of dried blood, like an ancient mummy subjected to some bizarre preservation ritual. He doubted anybody tasted their dinner that night, and judging from the looks on their faces, all went to bed expecting to die in their sleep.

Arthur, Mark and Hawley disappeared into the two tents they still possessed. Nathan resigned himself to a sleepless night, and volunteered to tend the fire with Tonto. Anyway, he felt safer under the Indian's watchful gaze than he did sharing a frail tent with his brother.

Twenty minutes later, Hawley and Arthur emerged from their tent. Without so much as a yawn or a rubbing of eyes, they joined Nathan and Tonto around the fire. They exchanged nods silently, sat and stared into the swaying flames, as if seeking to divine their future. Nobody voiced what all were thinking—that they were doomed. With so many of their team members dead, they all seemed to sense they were on a collision course with their own mortality.

Eventually they began to speak, reminiscing about home, friends, and family—even food. Hawley and Arthur passed around pictures of their wives and children. Nathan shared a photograph of his parents on the night of their 25th wedding anniversary. Somehow these reminders of their lives back home slightly soothed their worries. After an hour, they left Nathan and Tonto to tend the fire and returned to their tent.

In the morning, Tonto and Arthur ventured upstream to track down the renegade mule. Nathan and Hawley sat side-by-side, dangling fishing lines in the lazy river, hoping to hook their lunch. The three remaining mules grazed the undergrowth that lined the narrow strip of riverbank. Tied together and hobbled, Nathan was certain they were going nowhere fast.

"Hawley, I've got a bad feeling," Nathan said. "We've lost seven—it's almost as though we're not meant to make it out of here alive."

"Yeah? Well, I don't believe in fate," Hawley said. "Even if I did, I wouldn't believe it's my destiny to die here. Especially not after living through what I lived through."

Nathan watched the flashes of iridescence in the depth of the river flit past, and wondered why the fish weren't biting. Last night, Tonto had practically plucked them from the river with his hands. He tried to think of something to say, but Scott's frightful death left him empty inside. He watched a white egret stab minnows from the river a hundred yards downstream.

That's the Amazon. Death and dread one minute, elegant beauty the next.

As Nathan watched, the water around the egret exploded. A black caiman snapped its jaws shut on one of the bird's legs and, in a flurry of feathers and churning water, dragged it under.

Yup, Nathan concluded with a deep sigh, *that's the Amazon for you.*

"Man, I've got to get out of here," he said.

"We've all got to get out of here," Hawley said.

"Do you have any thoughts?"

Hawley gazed at the tree line across the river, some fifty yards away. "I can't tell you what I'm going to do, but I can tell you what I'm *not* going to do." He nodded toward the forest and said, "I'm not going back into those woods. That's for sure."

"So, you're going to…"

Nathan's next words were jerked from him by a powerful yank on his fishing line. *No nibbles from these guys,* he thought, as he reeled in the thrashing piranha. The muscular, snub-nosed fish with the enormous underbite was instantly recognizable. He swung the eight-inch specimen onto the bank and clubbed it to death before removing the hook. For six weeks now he had fished piranha, and each time he pried their gaping mouths open their interlocking triangular, blade-like teeth fascinated him. This was the first herbivorous piranha he landed, however, and he was surprised to see the teeth were no less imposing. He wedged the fish's mouth open with a stick before wiggling the hook free. He had learned the hard way that even a dead fish can bite reflexively.

Better to bite a stick than my finger.

Hawley landed a fish beside him and went through the same killing routine. Together they stood, plucked seeds from a riverside bush, and re-baited their hooks. "You were asking what I'm going to do," he said. Reading Nathan's nod, he tossed his hook into the river and sat down on the bank again. "We'll have no shortage of food if we stay by the river. I figure we can hike downstream. Sooner or later, we're sure to happen upon a village, or a fisherman in a boat."

"If we follow the river, we'll lose our compass heading, which we know takes us back. We'll get even more lost than we already are."

Hawley shrugged. "I'll take my chances. We know where the river goes; all rivers dump into the Amazon, eventually. But we don't know where that compass heading takes us. We've been getting killed ever since we lost our guides. I'm not following their heading any more, and I'm not going back into those woods. That's all there is to it."

"Huh." Nathan gazed up at the azure blue sky, streaked with fingers of mist as the morning breeze teased vapors from the treetops. He allowed his thoughts to drift among the cricket calls and bird songs. "I hate to break up the group again."

As he spoke, a pair of scarlet macaws broke from the cover of the treetops, flew directly across the river, and disappeared as silently as the sun when it sets.

29

"The mule is dead," Tonto said as he stumbled into camp late that afternoon.

He dumped a bloodstained, partially loaded mule pack to the ground at Hawley's feet, tottered over to an exposed tree root and sat down heavily. He arched his back over the root, using it as a fulcrum as he stretched out the knots in his muscles. His face screwed up in pain as he let out a long, much–needed *"Aaargh…"*

Arthur strode into camp as straight and tall as ever. Nathan couldn't help but reflect that, despite the half-full mule pack balanced on one shoulder, his jungle comportment was no different than if he was strolling the halls of academia.

"It's a bit unfair, I'm afraid," Arthur said, motioning to Tonto's pack, as he lowered his own to the ground. "His load was a good deal heavier, but he wouldn't let me help him out, or even redistribute the weight more evenly. Where is Mark?"

"Never got out of bed," Nathan said. He reached out and turned a fish with a stick, watching it sizzle in a pan set over a bed of red-hot coals. "He's been there since last night, just staring. Won't talk, won't eat or drink." When he looked up and caught Arthur's concerned gaze, he said, "It's okay, he'll snap out of it. It happened once before, when he got the phone call telling him our mother had died."

"I thought your mother is still living."

"She is. It was a prank call. You know how they go: 'Hello, Mr. Jones, this is the county sheriff's office. I'm sorry to tell you this, but there's been a terrible accident. We'd like you to come down to the coroner's office and identify Mrs. Jones' remains….' Like I said, you know how it goes. But Mark didn't. He thought it was for real. He only stumbled to his feet, hours later, when he saw Mom walk into his room."

"He'll snap out of it," Hawley said. "He'll have to."

Nathan nodded. "What happened to the mule?"

"Jaguar," Tonto said, twisting his torso first to one side and then to the other, wringing a few grunts and groans from his lungs. "Mules are strong, but stupid. And slow. Jaguars are fast—and clever."

"We jettisoned all the soil samples and superfluous gear," Arthur said. "We only brought back what we could carry: Food, trade goods, medicine."

"Well, I've got some good news," Nathan said, removing the sizzling pan from the burning coals. "Small flocks of scarlet macaws flew overhead all morning, then flew back in early afternoon. It looked like a mini-migration."

"The way of the red macaw," Tonto said, suddenly sitting up and paying attention.

"Exactly what I thought," Nathan said. "There's only one problem."

"What's that?" Arthur leaned over the pan and gave the food an inquisitive sniff.

"I'm the problem," Hawley said. "I'm not going."

30

"Perhaps this will change your mind." Arthur said, as he emerged from the tent he shared with Hawley. He unfolded a crude survey map, laid it on the ground, and they squatted around it. "We aren't traveling completely blind. Wogan marked our progress and test sites, correlated with the tagged soil samples. Campbell rescued this map when Wogan died, and I took it from his backpack when he passed on."

He traced their semicircular path, and Nathan could clearly see that the shortest route home took them directly over the river and two mountain ranges beyond. "Scott led us downriver not because it was the right direction, but to find a safe crossing," Arthur explained.

"That might be the shortest route back," Hawley said, "but the river is the path of least resistance. The route will be longer, but easier going. Food and water will always be close at hand, and we'll have a better chance of meeting up with helpful natives. Where we are now, we're closer to civilization."

"Natives near civilization aren't always more friendly," Tonto said. "Some hate white men more."

"Like I said, I'll take my chances." Hawley copied the map freehand into his notebook, paying particular attention to the network of rivers.

"We saw before how splitting up weakened our chances," Arthur said.

Nathan considered the options, and shot an inquiring look in Tonto's direction.

"I'll follow the guide's advice," Tonto said. "The way of the red macaw."

Nathan felt torn between keeping the group together and following his best judgment. "Mark and I will stick with Tonto," he muttered, though uncertainty weighed heavily in his chest.

"Well, I'm sticking with the majority," Arthur said. "Sorry, Hawley. I hope you change your mind. If not, you'll have to go it alone."

"So be it. But I'll be damned if I'm going to go back into those woods again." Just saying the word *woods* seemed to give him a shiver. It was easy to read the fear lines on his face.

Nathan suspected all of them shared Hawley's fear. Entering the forest meant leaving the relative safety and abundant food supply of the river behind.

The first time the rainforest turned to jungle, Nathan had felt on the verge of panic, as if he was being smothered. Not being able to see more than a few yards in any direction was more than disorienting; it brought a realization that danger lurked everywhere you walked. Like Hawley, he shivered at the thought of returning to that closed, claustrophobic world.

But unlike Hawley, he didn't consider the river a better option.

"We'll miss you," Nathan said.

"Chuck," Hawley prompted him with a sardonic grin.

Nathan nodded. "We'll miss you, Chuck."

Hawley nodded back, and stood to shake hands all around.

"Let's hope we meet on the other side," Hawley said.

For a moment their eyes met, and Nathan felt a bond pass through their hands and between their eyes. Hawley must have felt it as well, because he looked down in embarrassment and turned away.

31

Nathan waited with the others on the riverbank as they watched Tonto wade into the river. He turned when the water was at his waist and called back to them, "This place seems good."

Arthur called back, "Is it shallow all the way across?"

"I don't know," Tonto said as he waded back to them with a big, yellow-toothed smile. "It's good because nothing tried to eat me."

Nathan looked down at his khaki safari clothes and wished he had some kind of body armor. Back home, swimming fully clothed would make him the laughing stock of his friends. Here, it was frail protection. He had heard too many "stripped to the bone" horror stories to trust Tonto's assurance that it was the wrong season and conditions for a piranha attack. Anyway, the clothes really would only protect him against the smaller nuisances. To piranhas, clothing is nothing more than the paper wrap on a sandwich.

"How are you feeling?" Nathan glanced at Mark as they tied improvised blousing ribbons around the cuffs of their pant legs and shirtsleeves. Mark's face was haggard, but he had risen on his own for breakfast. That was roughly an hour after Hawley shouldered his pack and disappeared downstream with one mule in tow, taking his share of food and trade items—and, company man that he was, all of the remaining soil samples.

"I'm okay," Mark muttered. "I'll be a whole lot better...well, when this nightmare is over. That's all."

Arthur passed a halter rope to Tonto, and then followed him into the river, pulling the remaining mule. When they got waist deep, they lay down in the water, held onto the pack harnesses, and allowed themselves to be pulled. The mules did not so much swim as plow through the water, trailing their masters by their sides like tug boats trailing boat fenders. The first clambered out on the other side. As he regained his footing, Tonto re-grasped the halter rope, led his charge ashore and tied him to a bush. When he turned around, he found Arthur's mule had swum full circle and retreated to the familiar shore. Arthur, unable to steer, had trailed along helplessly.

Hands on knees, Tonto bent over in laughter as Arthur stood, spluttering and wiping water from his eyes. Nathan chuckled. Mark, standing immediately beside him, did not even crack a smile. Nathan's easygoing, goofy brother, like Campbell before him, had changed—maybe permanently.

Nathan shouldered his pack and elbowed Mark. "Come on, bro. It's our turn."

As they waded in, Arthur's mule swam straight across and dragged his master into shallow water.

Tonto took the halter rope while Arthur stumbled ashore, his feet slipping on the slick, loose rocks of the riverbed.

"Race you," Nathan said when they got knee deep.

"I'm not racing *you*," Mark said, without a trace of a smile. "I'm racing Frankie's anaconda."

Mark took a few running steps, threw himself into the river and thrashed his way across. Nathan looked both ways, as if checking for traffic on a roadway, but only saw smooth water.

"It's not what's on the surface that kills you," he muttered. Then he dived in and struck out for the opposite side with strong, measured strokes.

32

When they regrouped on the opposite river-bank, they discovered the blousing ribbons had done their job. Arthur and Tonto had both picked up leeches on their hands. Tonto carried two of the black, gelatinous creatures stuck to his bare back. When Mark and Nathan stripped, however, they didn't find any.

After building a fire, they burned the parasites off using a hot brand. The ugly things writhed, but still had to be plucked off with their fingers. Then they waited for their clothes to dry where they had draped them on the bushes.

The moment they entered the forest, Nathan understood the emotions that had driven Hawley to venture off downstream on his own. The still air and high humidity pressed in on him, but the foreboding shadows and dense foliage shouted a thousand threats. Every rustle in the bushes was a cannibal stalking him; every *whoosh* of a bird in flight was a poisoned arrow flying straight for his chest. Shadowy masses of brush became jaguars poised to attack, and every vine was a deadly snake—until proven otherwise.

After two hours, Nathan eased into the routine and felt his jumpiness wane. The others seemed calmer as well. As he had ever since his illness, Mark plodded along listlessly, as if marching to his fate.

They followed the raucous cries of the scarlet macaws when they could hear them, and their flight path when they could see their small flocks through the forest canopy. By mid-afternoon they realized they no longer knew if the birds were coming or going, so they stopped and made camp.

The next morning they resumed their trek, ever deeper into the forest. By late morning, Nathan knew they were getting closer to their goal. Not only scarlet macaws, but a wide variety of birds all flew in the same direction. In addition, a troop of spider monkeys sped past in the forest canopy, over one hundred feet above the forest floor.

The forest changed as Nathan sensed their group was approaching their destination. The cries of wildlife intensified, as if a huge battle for supremacy was being waged directly ahead of them. The trees thinned, and then melded into a palm forest. Each palm rose to the relatively modest height of twenty-five yards, and stood balanced upon a peculiar cone of stilt roots. An exotic array of plants seemed to have found the palm to be a convenient host. Ferns, orchids, mosses, and an assortment of flowering plants adorned the roots and tree stem alike.

"*Cashapona*," Tonto said, pointing to one of the larger palms. "We call it 'walking palm.'"

Nathan stopped in his tracks. Thinking anything could be possible in this phantasmagoria of wonders and horrors, he stared at the stilt roots. "Does it really walk?"

"No."

"Oh. But then, why do you call it..."

Tonto shrugged, and strode past him.

After a hundred yards, they stepped from the forest onto a narrow strip of riverbank. Across the wide expanse of murky green water, a reddish-grey cliff rose forty yards straight up, and spread a hundred yards along the opposite riverbank. All around them, flocks of parrots of all sizes and colors screeched and squabbled in the tree tops, as if strategizing their assault on the clay lick in front of them. The cliff face crawled with pockets of color, each pocket comprised of a single species of parrot. Spider monkeys and peccaries scrambled in the thin undergrowth at the base of the cliff, stirring up clouds of butterflies from the damp mineral flats.

"Now what?" Nathan said, gazing on the riotous scene in front of him.

A pair of eagles swooped out of the sky, wings swept back in power dives. The monkeys and peccaries shot into the forest undergrowth, and the parrots exploded in clouds of color that streaked into the forest canopy and disappeared.

The smallest of the pair, the male, flew directly into a flock of scarlet macaws. He snatched first at one, then at another, missing both. The larger female rose with her prey, a green parrot, jerking spasmodically in her talons. The victorious eagle flew to the top of the cliff and landed on its edge. She stabbed at her meal with her beak and tore into its flesh, sending a shower of green feathers fluttering down the precipice. The male eagle flew a circle and then, with a shriek of frustration, disappeared over the treetops.

"Harpy eagle," Tonto told them.

Nathan stared, stunned at the size of the grey and black bird. Roughly twenty pounds in weight and three feet tall, with a six foot wingspan, the eagle looked to him to be almost as large as an American condor. "Why harpy?"

Beside him, Tonto shrugged.

"Greek mythology," Arthur said, stepping forward. "That's one of the world's largest raptors. An adult's talons can measure five inches long. They're so powerful, they can carry off sloths and monkeys half their weight."

"So, why 'harpy'?"

Arthur tilted his head back and bounced on his heels, stroking his chin thoughtfully.

Nathan kept a straight face, but couldn't help but laugh on the inside. Here they were, in the middle of a rainforest that was doing its best to kill them, and Arthur seemed to be preparing a small lecture.

He's going to make a great professor if we survive this, Nathan thought.

"According to Greek mythology, Harpies were winged eagle-like spirits. They snatched the souls of the damned—and dragged them down to the depths of Hell."

"Great," Mark said from behind them. "It's not enough that half the animals here can kill us. Now there's one that can snatch away our souls as well."

33

"Look," Arthur said. "We've been camping here for two days, and so far we've seen nothing but wildlife."

Nathan furrowed his brows. "What do you suggest?"

"Well," Arthur replied, stretching out Wogan's map on the ground between the four of them, "according to this map, if we continue straight, as we have been going, we'll come out close to Coari in a week or so. From there, we can take a boat downriver to Manaus."

"The scale on that map could be way off. And you don't know where we are, exactly," Nathan said. "It could be a three-days' hike, it could be three weeks. The guide said to come here."

"He said to go in this *direction*. He said to go in the *way* of the macaws, not to the *place* of the macaws. He didn't say to sit and wait here. This might be nothing more than a waypoint, a marker to show we're going in the right direction."

"Tonto? Mark?" Nathan swung in their direction.

Mark shrugged. He had been staring as if hypnotized at the same spot on the clay mountain across the river for an hour. "If we sit here, our rations will run out. Then we'll be down to living off of fish and parrots. Anyway, I'm tired of getting pooped on."

Nathan glanced at their tent, which was liberally splattered with parrot guano, and sighed. None of them had escaped the twice-daily bombing run unscathed. The major migration had not yet descended upon them this morning, but in another hour the forest would turn into a clay-eating, parrot-pooping madhouse.

"Tonto, do you know this place?" Arthur circled the area of the rainforest that lay between their rough position and Coari on the map. Tonto shook his head. "Okay, then," Arthur said. "Let's vote."

Thirty minutes later, as they shrugged their backpacks on, Nathan asked, "Tonto, why did you vote to leave?"

The Indian pointed at the river. "Men are like water. If they sit, they go bad. We'll only stay fresh if we keep moving."

A mile downstream, they found the river shallow enough to ford without getting in over their waists.

Four hours later they stood at the crest of a small mountain range, the sun at its apex. Their gradual climb had led them to a sheer cliff-face that afforded them a view of the forest ahead. The only feature that broke the vast, undulating green canopy was a ribbon of smoke rising through the trees at the edge of a wide river. Other than that, there were no signs of human settlement for as far as they could see.

"A village," Arthur said, as he took a compass heading toward the smoke trail.

"Question is," Mark said, as he shifted nervously on his feet, "Are we going to be safe, or are we going to be shish-kabob?"

They arrived at the edge of the village clearing in mid-afternoon. Crouching unseen in the thick undergrowth at the clearing's edge, Nathan didn't notice anything out of the ordinary. The men appeared to be returning from fishing, the women occupied with the sundry duties of village life. Children, as usual, ran around naked and unrestrained.

"What do you think?" Arthur said.

"Beats me. Tonto?"

"Let's just jump in there and get it over with," Mark said. "I'm tired."

Tonto squinted his eyes as he scoured the village for detail. "No metal weapons. No machetes. No guns...maybe no trade."

"You think it's safe?" Nathan watched Tonto's facial features closely, reading for signs.

Tonto shook his head. "I don't know."

"Okay," Arthur said, "Let's fall back and regroup."

They slowly let the plant leaves they had swept aside for a view fall back into place. Once they were sure the villagers could not see them, they retreated and gathered in a circle.

"You're in the most danger," Tonto said, pointing to Arthur. "If they don't like white men, they might kill you quick. Me next. They might think I'm a scout for their enemies. You two—" Tonto nodded to Mark and Nathan, "Who knows? You'll probably be brand new to them."

Mark rubbed his cheek with his fist. "Well, I'm not going to be the big toe the group dangles into the village to test the water."

"So what do you think we should do?" Nathan asked, speaking in Arthur's direction. "Go in one by one and see what happens? Or go in all together?"

"Strength in numbers," Arthur said.

"Okay then. Let's do it," Nathan said.

Mark and Tonto kept quiet, so they got up as one and strode toward the clearing, their two pack mules in tow.

34

Two days and three villages later, the group followed their native guide through a lowland swamp, the mid-morning sun at their backs.

The professor's pretty smart, Nathan thought, with a glance at their elected leader's narrow back. Arthur had negotiated with each village leader for safe passage. Not only that, but for the trade trinkets they still had to offer, Arthur had negotiated for each tribe to provide a guide to the next safe village in the direction they were headed—the village chain back to civilization.

They eased out of the swamp and started to climb a shallow grade of forest floor. Nathan noticed that every few steps, the guide would glance nervously to both sides and scan the bushes.

"Tonto," he whispered over his shoulder. "Why's the guide so nervous?"

Tonto shrugged. "You want me to ask him?"

"No—not yet. You're sure he's friendly, right?"

"Sure, he's friendly." The Indian skewed his eyes and face to one side in thought, and then said, "You think he's making an ambush?"

"Could be."

"No. No ambush," Tonto said with an emphatic headshake. "If he wanted us dead, he'd kill us near his village. Whatever he's worrying about—it's something else."

Ten minutes later, their guide's skittishness was becoming more and more obvious. Nathan was just about to tell Tonto to find out what was wrong when he heard a low singsong voice off to their right side, barely audible above the normal jungle chatter.

What the...

"Mark, Arthur," Nathan called in a harsh whisper. When they turned, he jerked a thumb in the direction of the sound, which deepened as they listened.

Their guide shifted uneasily on his feet and peered into the forest, as if hoping to penetrate the foliage.

As they waited, the song intensified into something distinctly human, and took on a plaintive quality.

Arthur nodded in the direction of the song and drew his lips into a smirk. "Considering our luck lately, maybe it's a marooned Siren. You know, the mythical sea temptresses who lured sailors to their deaths with their seductive voices."

Nathan shrugged his M1 off of his shoulder and into his hands. "Very funny. Whatever it is, we should probably check it out. Agreed?"

Nathan turned and led the others in the direction of the song, his rifle at the ready.

Nathan snuck forward until they came to the edge of a clearing. Crouching down, he could see where a rock wall on one side rose ten feet before it rejoined the forest. Under the ledge of layered rock gaped the menacingly dark slit of a cave's mouth. Opposite the cave, a young woman twirled in private abandon to the rhythm of her song, her sinewy arms undulating, as if buoyed by the current of her chords. Her grass skirt, ornamental body paint and brown complexion marked her as an indigenous Indian, but her tall, slender frame seemed at odds with the stocky build typical of the natives.

"Maybe she's waiting for a lover," Nathan whispered, feeling strangely overcome by embarrassment. "We should either greet her or leave."

As he spoke, a huge jaguar silently slipped from the forest and stood on the stone ledge overlooking the clearing, one front leg cocked, the huge spotted paw hovering inches from the ground. The woman gazed up and went rigid. Nathan saw her chest heave, the cords tighten in her neck. Even at this distance, he felt he could see her eyes darken with fear.

The imposing beast craned its neck in her direction and sniffed the air. Then, in a movement that seemed more fluid than feline, it flowed down the rock face and crouched in the low groundcover. The tip of its tail twitching, it slunk in her direction, as if fearing she would bolt and run.

Nathan could tell she was frozen in terror. He raised his rifle, sighted, and fired just as the jaguar lunged. He watched in horror as the animal's head disappeared from his rifle sights as it leapt toward its victim, fangs bared. He remembered his father's hunting stories of deer "jumping the bullet,"—but just then the jaguar's hindquarters entered his rifle's sights. A pink-orange puff of blood and fur blew from the beast's hips and the animal spun a quarter-turn in midair. It landed facing him, propped up on its two front legs, its hindquarters flattened on the ground as if they had been kicked out from underneath it. Glaring straight at Nathan, murder in its eyes, the animal drew back its lips and bared its teeth. Nathan fired into the center of the most vicious snarl he had ever seen, and the animal crumpled to the ground.

Locking eyes with the woman through the leafy cover, he rose up and broke through the foliage. She stood as still as a tree, every muscle in her body drawn tight. Her deep, dark eyes stared past them, as though unseeing, and her lips quivered uncontrollably.

Tonto tried to calm her in a variety of languages and dialects. Mark tugged at the rifle in Nathan's hand. "The jaguar—it's still breathing."

"Finish it off," Nathan said, releasing his grip on the Garand without even looking around. He heard a crash in the bush behind him and turned to see their guide racing off into the forest, in the direction from which they had come.

Now what's that all about?

"Forget him," Arthur said. "We'll sort this out first. Then we'll backtrack to the village and arrange for a new guide."

Tonto connected with one of his dialects, and color seemed to infuse the woman's pale lips. Her eyes slowly focused on his face. Then her legs gave way and she fell to her knees. They lifted her to her feet just as the rifle exploded behind them.

Nathan held her at arm's length. He turned to see Mark smiling for the first time in many days, with one foot on the dead beast's chest. Striking a pose with the rifle braced on his hip, angled toward the sky, he asked, "Anybody care to snap a photo?"

Mark's smile faded as a ring of Indians stepped through the foliage from all sides, war weapons in hand, encircling the clearing at the tree line.

The woman took a step back. Nathan's hands slipped from her shoulders and fell to his sides.

Dropping her face to the ground, she muttered a few words that Tonto strained to hear.

"The Suypari," he said. "Her tribe."

35

"Impressive shot," Arthur said, as they followed the Suypari Indians back to their village.

"Yeah," Nathan said. "A split-second sooner, it would have blown the jaguar's brains out. A split second later, and it would have missed completely."

"Not only did you save a beautiful woman's life, but she's the chieftain's daughter to boot. I'm telling you, that was a million-dollar shot."

"What I can't figure is what she was doing out here, all alone," Nathan said, nervously scratching behind one ear. "And why does everybody look like they're in shock?"

"They're sure giving Mark a lot of attention," Arthur said. "That should be *you* up there."

Nathan glanced ahead to where the Suypari huddled around Mark, disarmingly emotionless. He would have expected them to laugh and smile like children, jockeying for position closest to the hero. Instead, they hovered an arm's length away, occasionally reaching out to tentatively touch the rifle Mark still carried. They seemed drawn by its power, but afraid it could harm them. In fact, they seemed to be daring one another to touch it, as a test of bravery.

"Nah," Nathan said. "Let him enjoy the hero-worship. He's not objecting to the positive attention, and he hasn't had much of that in a long time."

Up ahead, Tonto hung back from where he had been talking with the main party. He swung alongside Nathan and Arthur as they drew near. The three bunched together, aware not only of the main group ahead, but of the flanking party, including the chieftain, immediately behind them.

Arthur tapped the shotgun nestled in the crook of one arm. "They let us keep our weapons. Do you think we're safe? Or do they not understand guns?"

Tonto hesitated, and then nodded. "I think we're safe. Maybe. There's something that doesn't feel right." He nudged Nathan, and took the halter rope for the lead mule from his hand. "They seem...not straight. I think they might be hiding something." As he spoke, he slipped Nathan's survival rifle from his shoulder and handed it to him. "Take the gun, Kemosabe. You have no gun right now."

"Something doesn't feel right," Nathan repeated, as he shouldered the rifle. He barely felt its weight after having lugged the heavy M1 Garand around. "I know what you mean, Tonto. I've never seen so many poker faces in one place at one time. They don't seem overjoyed she survived, and they don't seem relieved the jaguar's dead. They look like zombies, in shock, emotionless. What's wrong with these people? The guide brought us here because he considered the Suyp-ari to be safe, right? But then he ran away in fear. Now, what's up with that?"

All three of them fell silent in thought. As they swung around the splayed prop roots of yet an-other forest monster, Tonto said, "I'll try to find out."

36

"That's not a village," Arthur said. "That's a town."

Nathan stood and stared. There must have been thirty huts. There were also twenty longhouses or *maloka*, the traditional communal dwellings built to shelter a group of relatives rather than a single family. It was by far the largest settlement they had seen in the Amazon since they left Coari, seven weeks before.

The clearing spread from where the structures occupied an elevated plateau, above the wet-season flood line. From there, the village sloped up a shallow incline to the edge of the forest. A hundred feet away the river coursed along one side of the village, and a coffee-colored lake protected the other.

Between the village and the forest lay animal pens, a flattened arena, and a wide cultivated field, tended by women wielding primitive farming tools. Without looking, Nathan knew what he would find in the field: manioc—a staple root used to make tapioca cakes—yams and potatoes, plantains. Some tribes cultivated corn and even peanuts.

As they watched the settlement from their vantage point, where the incline entered the woods, two natives ran forward, shouting and waving their arms. The closest natives gathered around them to receive the news. After a moment, the circle burst outward, each native running in a different direction. The wave of information fanned out through the village until, when news reached the farthest sides, the entire population raced from their huts, houses, and fields. They massed on the village edge facing them until the Suypari chieftain shouldered his way between Arthur and Nathan and stepped to the front. He raised an empty hand, and on his wild, warbling cry, the natives surged forward to meet them.

The chieftain took the lead, with Mark behind him, and they strode through the channel the natives formed, heading into the village.

"Well, now, this doesn't seem too bad," Arthur said, as he followed them down the indigenous version of a red carpet treatment.

Nathan couldn't help but notice that among the emotionless faces, a few appeared amazed. Others appeared to project animosity—even hatred.

"The biggest, but not exactly the warmest reception we've ever had," Nathan muttered to himself. To him, the people seemed restrained, even afraid. Instead of reaching in to touch their skin and clothing, these people actually edged away from them as they passed.

The chieftain led them to an empty hut and motioned with a heavily tattooed arm for them to enter. Nathan admired the leather band on his bicep, adorned with a wicked-looking array of killing teeth and talons. Other Indians carried the mule packs into the hut, and then led the animals to where they could graze. As they entered, Nathan was struck by the springiness of the reed floor mat and the overwhelmingly musty odor, despite the window and door cutouts.

After a few minutes, natives delivered bamboo tumblers of guarana juice, a popular stimulant, and leaf platters filled with baked fish and manioc. Then they left, gesturing to the cotton and palm-fiber hammocks that lined the walls, upon which to rest.

"Hey, Nate," Mark said, patting the M1 that lay beside him. "Do you mind if I hold onto this for a while?"

"Well, let's see," Nathan said, rubbing his chin thoughtfully. "I figure there are probably about three, four hundred natives here, maybe half of them of fighting age. So it would be about two hundred of them up against eight shots in that gun, if we went to war. Nope, I don't think it's going to save anybody's life. Just give it back to me when we leave, okay?"

"Thanks, bro. The natives are crazy about it."

Arthur lowered a bamboo tumbler from his lips and opened his mouth to speak, but Nathan hoped he wouldn't. He could imagine what he was going to say. Mark didn't need to be reminded that he was hijacking Nathan's glory—and a reminder would be pointless anyway. How could Nathan convince the natives that *he* shot the jaguar, when they found Mark standing over the carcass with the smoking gun, maybe even saw him deliver the final bullet?

Leave it. Let Mark enjoy his moment in the sun.

Nathan waved Arthur into silence while Mark gazed down into his leaf platter. As an afterthought, he said, "Bro, that's a semi-auto. Every time you pull the trigger, you send a bullet down the barrel, which right now is pointed at my left foot. You remembered to put the safety back on, didn't you?"

"Oh, shoot!" Mark sloshed guarana juice as he hastily lowered his tumbler to the mat beside him. Lifting the rifle, he clicked the safety back on.

Arthur rolled his eyes, clasped his hands together and shook them at the heavens, mouthing a pantomimed prayer.

Nathan leaned forward, motioned for Mark to pass him the rifle. He jacked all the rounds from the magazine and handed it back empty.

Then he cocked his head. *It's quiet out there* had been a standing joke between him and Tonto. But now he realized it really *was* too quiet outside. A village this size should generate a great deal more ambient noise. Standing, he peered out the two cutout windows, and saw nobody through either one.

Weird. "Hey, Tonto," he said. "Where is everybody?"

The Indian stood and looked around. "Four guards outside doorway. I can't see anyone else."

Sure enough, four guards stood outside the hut, two facing in, two facing out, all wearing belt weapons and carrying bamboo-tipped spears.

Tightness pulled at Nathan's throat. "Are they keeping others from coming in, or keeping us from going out?"

"Only one way to know for sure," Tonto said.

"After you."

Together, they turned to leave, but the inward-facing guards stepped directly into their path. Their blank stares and expressionless faces seemed warning enough, but they lowered their spears in case the message was not clear.

"Oookay," Nathan said, holding up his hands in surrender as he back-stepped into the hut. "Tonto, what do you say? That idea of taking a nap sounds pretty good right now, don't you think?"

37

"Maybe we can shoot our way out," Mark suggested.

Once again, Arthur rolled his eyes and pantomimed a prayer. "Mark, how do you expect to shoot your way out of a village that is flanked by a river on one side, a lake on the other, and filled with hundreds of warriors?" He tossed his hands in the air and let them flop back limply into his lap.

"In my village, this means one thing," Tonto said. "The elders are meeting to decide what to do with us. Everybody else is waiting in a big circle for their decision. When they decide, they'll tell us."

"What's to decide?" Nathan shook his head. Since he had met these people, nothing seemed to make any sense. "We saved the chieftain's daughter. How can there possibly be a bad angle to that?"

Arthur stroked his chin. "Tonto, do any tribes here still practice human sacrifice?"

Tonto thought for a moment, and then said, "You mean the girl?" When Arthur nodded, Tonto said, "That's crazy. Everybody knows God doesn't accept a sacrifice without flowers in her hair and covered in honey."

Nathan glanced into Arthur's shocked eyes, and then snapped his head in Tonto's direction. "You're kidding, right?"

The native flashed his big, yellow-toothed smile. "I'm a big joke."

"Joker."

"Yeah." Tonto's face turned serious. "Actually, sacrifice isn't common. Usually, when there *is* a sacrifice, it's a baby or a man. The victim is held on the ground. They cut out the heart and pass it around. I've never heard of a woman being sacrificed."

"I think you're reaching," Nathan said to Arthur. "Remember, she was singing. That's not something a person does when facing death."

Arthur shrugged. "Maybe you were right. Maybe she was waiting for her lover."

"Out *there*? And by *herself*?" Mark said. "He's got to be one very special guy."

"Maybe he's not from her tribe," Tonto said. When everybody turned their eyes in his direction he shrugged. "It happens."

"Okay, okay," Mark said, jumping to his feet. "Back up." He pointed to Tonto. "You said they'd decide. Decide what? What'll they do to us?"

Tonto lay down on his side on a reed mat, his head propped in one hand. "Well, let's see. I'd say they'll welcome us, kill us, or send us out of the village. What else is there?" He dropped his head onto the pillow of his arm and closed his eyes.

Tonto's the most sensible one here, Nathan thought. *What else can we do?* He crawled into a hammock and stretched out to sleep. As he laid his head on his backpack, a huge roar exploded from the direction of the village arena, as if a stadium full of fans went wild over a winning goal.

"What was *that?*" cried Mark.

"A decision," Tonto said, without opening his eyes. "They're either going to welcome us or kill us. Nobody celebrates throwing people out of the village."

38

Nathan watched as the mass of natives flew toward them at full sprint. The young men in the lead jostled and shoved, as if trying to knock the others out of the race. The guards jumped aside to allow them to pass, and the leading contestants scuffled briefly at the doorway.

Arthur shouted, "Hey!" and pointed at a fourteen- or fifteen-year-old, the clear winner. All scuffling stopped. The youth puffed out his bare chest, devoid of tattoos or decorations save for a single leather chest-band, and proudly shouted out a lungful of words.

Tonto, at his feet by the door, turned to the room.

"Good news. He says there's going to be a big party—three days—for the hero." He gestured to Mark. "I guess that's you. After the party, everybody gives thanks to God. Then we can stay or go—our choice."

"Yeah!" Mark jumped up, his round face aglow. Then he stilled and, head down, glanced abashedly at Nathan.

His cocker spaniel look, Nathan thought. He smiled indulgently at his brother. "Hey, bro—there's no going back now," he said. "Just order your servant girls to drop a grape in my mouth every once in a while, okay?"

Mark jive-shook his brother's hand and said, "Thanks, bro. You're the best!"

"We need to give the messenger a gift," Tonto said.

They glanced at the youth in the doorway, his happy eyes shining, a silly, expectant grin over-stretching his face. "He's waiting for a gift," Tonto said. "That's why they raced. You get a gift for good news."

"He wants a gift? I've got a *great* gift," Mark said, as he rummaged through his backpack.

"It should be a knife," Tonto said, stilling Mark's hands. "A knife makes a boy feel like a man. Make him very happy. We should give him a knife, and give the chief a machete."

Nathan pulled a hunting knife from the mule pack that contained their trade items. He slid the gleaming blade from its leather sheath as he stepped toward the youth, angling the flat blade to catch the afternoon sun as it peeped through the doorway.

When the mirror finish flashed the sun's reflection across the youth's face, he stepped back in surprise, shielding his eyes with his hands. Nathan couldn't resist giving a demonstration. He plucked a dry palm frond from the overhanging thatched roof and shaved it into thin strips in front of the crowd's eyes.

Re-sheathing the knife with the whisper of polished steel against hardened leather, he grabbed the awestruck youth's hand by his wrist and slapped the prize into his open palm. The bedazzled youth's face, now pale and sweaty from a near-faint, struggled against tears to toughen with manhood. Conquering the quiver in his lips, his eyes expressed more than appreciation to Nathan; it was unworthiness and eternal gratitude and dreams beyond his imagining. Then he stripped the knife from its sheath, turned, and with a shout held both high in extended arms for all to see.

At first the crowd, unused to iron implements and completely ignorant of polished steel, emitted hushed murmurs of admiration. Then, as the youth played the sun's reflection across their faces, they stepped backward, as he had done, and fell silent, subdued by a miracle they had never even thought possible. Shouts arose, and then the teen descended into the crowd to show off his prize. The people crowded around, reaching in to touch and grasp the miracle blade as he passed.

Tonto, standing beside Nathan in the doorway, turned to the other two, who stood watching over their shoulders.

"They think he holds the sun in his hand," he said with a grin almost as big as the youth's. Glancing back as the crowd pushed and shoved to touch the knife, he muttered, "I think there will be many cut hands today."

It means so little to us, but so much to them, Nathan thought. With a pang of guilt he remembered Tonto's rusted pot-metal knife, and was struck by the Indian's reserve. He had never asked for anything, even though he must have lusted after the trinkets they had dispensed over the past seven weeks. And then, when Mark had borrowed his M1 Garand, Tonto had freely returned Nathan's survival rifle. *We have a lot to learn from these people.*

Nathan turned in the doorway and slapped Mark on the shoulder. "Bro, you need to wash up and change clothes. You're the guest of honor at the party tonight—and you can't go looking like that. Tonto, maybe you should go teach that kid the way of steel before he ruins it. How to sharpen it, keep it oiled before it turns to rust, tie a lanyard to it so he doesn't lose it in the lake—that sort of thing."

Tonto stepped from the hut and shouted back over his shoulder as he ran after the crowd, "Also—I'll try to get the answers to a few questions."

"Whatever happens," Arthur said as he watched Tonto disappear into the crowd, "we need to give that man his money—and whatever trade items we have left over when we get back."

"*If* we get back."

"Yes," Arthur said with a sigh. "If we get back."

39

The next twelve hours passed in a blur of communal dance and feasting.

It was like a mini-Carnival, but without the parades and alcohol. Fillets carved from pirarucu fish, a river monster that grows up to ten feet long, were served on platters of broad leaves, guarana was consumed until everybody had caffeine jitters, exotic fruit and juices flowed as if someone had hit a jackpot on a cornucopia.

Whenever Nathan felt the urge to slip away to get some rest, the *mirim*, or chieftain, would start another dance. That would pump everybody up for at least another hour.

By the next morning, the villagers had all slipped off to harvest fish and food for the next night's feast.

"Man," Mark said, as they bedded down in their hammocks to sleep the morning away. "Now *that's* what I call royal treatment!"

"That's what I call exhausting," Arthur said. "Get some rest."

"How can I sleep?" Mark said, jumping to his feet and walking a tight circle around the hut's center pole. "I feel like I've been made king for a day."

"For three days," Nathan said, as he watched him pace. "And you *can* sleep, because if you keep us awake, Your Majesty, we're going to kill you, all right? Hey, Tonto, what's that amazingly beautiful song?"

"That's the wirapu'ru. It sings for ten minutes at dawn, every day for two weeks. Nesting season only. Its song is so beautiful, when the wirapu'ru sings, all the other birds listen."

"The way things are here in the Amazon," Mark said, "something will probably eat it."

As if to fulfill his prediction, the bird's song ended abruptly.

Tonto shook a finger at them. "Like I said. Ten minutes at dawn. Show's over."

Arthur propped himself up on one elbow and yawned. "Tonto, you didn't tell us. Did you learn anything from the villagers?"

He nodded. "The girl's name. U'Yara. Her name means 'lady of the water.' She's the chief's favorite daughter."

"Anything else?"

"This tribe, the Suypari, have a killing feud with their neighbors. A Xuraquit village. They plan to execute two captives soon. That's all I know."

After pondering the new information for a moment, Arthur eased himself down to lying on his side. Mark settled into his own hammock. Nathan tried to put the new information together with the little they already knew, but like a lullaby, the soft snores that grew around him joined forces with his fatigue to lull him into a deep sleep.

He woke with a start, lying on his back, Arthur's face hovering inches above his own. "Shh." Arthur lowered the finger from his lips.

Arthur glanced at the others, oblivious in their slumber, despite the sunlight streaking into the hut through the window cutouts and between the slats. "Nate," he whispered, "do you remember how we were thinking that girl, U'Yara, might have been waiting to meet a lover? And then Tonto suggested her lover might be from the other tribe?"

"Uh-oh," he said, quietly drawing himself up to sitting, his legs dangling off of the hammock.

Arthur glanced back at the others. "Yeah. Uh-oh is right," he whispered. "If she was waiting for her lover, and he's from the tribe they have a killing feud with, that explains how these villagers found us so quickly. We shot the jaguar and then they appeared within minutes, remember? Even though their village was a thirty-minute walk away? They appeared quickly because they were in the vicinity—looking for her."

"And she's the chief's favorite daughter," Nathan mumbled. "That makes it worse. She was bringing shame not only on her father and his family, but on the whole tribe."

"Exactly. If the jaguar had killed her, it would've erased the chief's shame."

"But we saved her and kept his shame alive. Great!"

Mark snorted in his sleep.

Tonto's lids flew open and he stared at them with the eyes of a wild animal, ready to jump into fight or flight, whichever the situation required.

Arthur held out an open palm to him, and then repeated his "shh" gesture. He pointed to where Mark lay softly snoring.

"That explains why they weren't overjoyed when we saved U'Yara," Arthur whispered. "Secretly, the whole village wished her dead."

"Right." Nathan ran a palm over his hair, and noticed it came away wet. "That also explains why they held a pow-wow to decide what to do with us—welcome us as heroes, or kill us for having preserved their shame. Huh. No wonder the guide got spooked and ran away like that."

In the corner, Mark snorted himself awake. He abruptly sat up. Rubbing sleep from his eyes, he squinted past a sunbeam that streaked in between two of the wall-poles.

"Hey guys," he said, "ready for another party?"

The three of them surreptitiously exchanged worried looks while Mark slipped from his hammock. He stood and stretched, fists at thrown-back shoulders, chest puffed out.

"Yessir! Maybe today they'll fill my pockets with diamonds and marry me to the king's daughter!"

40

After going through his morning ritual, Mark left to scout out party preparations at the village center.

Nathan explained his and Arthur's suspicions to Tonto.

"So what do you think, Tonto? Should we tell my brother?"

"If everything's the way you think it is," he said, thoughtfully, "When the party is finished—we leave."

"Somehow," Arthur said, "I'm not sure it'll be that easy. Nate, do you remember the shaman? How you pointed out the ugly looks he was giving Mark last night? How does that figure into this?"

The shaman. Covered in tattoos and body paint, his face pierced and studded, he looked like the living definition of a South American shaman. Nathan had been the first to notice the man's malevolent glances at Mark during the celebration.

Was it jealousy? Maybe. Hatred? Quite possibly. But why?

Perhaps the shaman had voted for execution and had been overruled by the majority of elders. Whatever the reason, having the shaman among their potential enemies gave Nathan chills.

The celebration resumed in early afternoon. A fertility ceremony was followed by a dance that seemed to celebrate the warriors' fighting abilities. Men and women each formed concentric circles that rotated in opposite directions. Tonto explained that this symbolized the opposition of their natures. The outer circle of women sang words of praise and encouragement, to symbolize the importance of their nurturing and support not only in wartime, but also in daily life. The men took turns dancing in the middle with their weapons. When one warrior finished, another would break from the inner circle and take his place. Each warrior took a turn in the center, performing his dance of manhood and battle-worthiness with gymnastic-style stunts as proof of strength and dexterity.

Mark remained the focus of attention, being pulled into every dance alongside the chieftain. It wasn't until he was pulled into the center of the circle in this dance, however, that Nathan felt a change in the villagers' mood. Yesterday, the dances had all been lighthearted, and Mark's lack of coordination and silly approach to the festivities was tolerated, even received with good humor. Today, however, the ceremonies were more somber and symbolic.

When Mark bumbled his way through a weapons dance with his rifle, planting the barrel in the ground and vaulting, as he had seen other warriors do with their spears, or swinging it overhead like a club and even assuming various shooting stances, he looked—unfortunately—comical.

The tone of the women's singing became more subdued, as if they didn't know whether he was mocking their tradition. The men's dancing became less vigorous, as if they were stunned by the unexpectedly poor performance of the ceremony's "hero."

When Mark returned to the inner circle, he changed places with his brother.

Nathan gained the attention of a warrior beside him. He motioned to the man's spear. The native handed it to him with both hands, looking him directly in the eyes, as if honored to grant the loan of his weapon.

Nathan stripped off his shirt, revealing his tightly muscled body. He bunched the fabric together and tossed it to one side. Then he strode solemnly into the center of the circle.

Nathan held the spear in one hand with the shaft tucked along the back of one arm, the bamboo tip peeking out from above his shoulder. The Suypari, subdued by Mark's lackluster performance, fell silent, the men nominally bobbing their heads and bouncing on the pads of their feet.

Without warning, Nathan spun into a series of advanced *bo* staff *kata* he had memorized in his *ju-jitsu* classes back home. He felt his body loosen as he spun, lunged, planted and struck, flowing from one blow or parry into another. He lost himself in the fluid movements that a body in motion less performed than *became*.

As he transitioned into the showiest *kata* he knew, Nathan felt a collective excitement spur him on. The drums and women's voices grew to a fever pitch. The circle of men pounded their feet and jumped in excitement, raising their own voices. The other warrior dancers fanned out to give him room, and stood still as they watched in amazement.

For a moment he felt alone, as he had in the dojo, in the parks, in the school gymnasium where he had practiced after hours. It was just him, the staff that had become an extension of his own body, and the energy that flowed from one to the other and then back again.

Lost in his movements, Nathan leveled a battlefield of enemies. Planting his feet as solidly as a statue, his toned arms turned to stone. The tip of his spear hummed as it vibrated with the force of his final blow in the empty air.

Men and women alike erupted with a great shout and stamping of feet. Nathan looked up to find both circles arrested, his audience awestruck. As solemnly as he had entered, he strode to the inner circle and handed the spear back to its owner.

The native jumped into the arena, sprinted a tight circle with the weapon held high, as if displaying a trophy, and then started his own warrior's dance. Nathan took his place and both circles started rotating again, as the pitch returned to a normal level.

"Masterful, bro," Mark said, from where he jostled beside him. Nathan detected a hint of jealousy, perhaps hurt in his brother's voice, but when he turned to face him he was not struck so much by the puppy-dog sadness in Mark's eyes as he was by the intensity of admiration in the chieftain's face. Even the shaman by his side seemed begrudgingly impressed.

"Sorry, Mark," he muttered. "Didn't mean to upstage you. It just...kind of came out, you know what I mean?"

"It's cool, bro."

But Nathan could see in his brother's eyes that, deep down inside, being one-upped was—even if he'd grown used to it after years alongside his more gifted brother—anything but cool.

41

Tonto took their group aside before the next event, which was more a contest than a dance. Together with one of the Suypari men, he explained the point of the exercise.

"It's a test of manhood," he said, after listening to the villager's explanation. "It's called turtle...not fight, exactly—but a word like fight..."

"Wrestle?" Arthur said.

"Mmm...maybe. Turtle wrestle. A man has a turtle, and the women try to take the turtle. The women always win. Always. So the test isn't who wins. The test is how long it *takes* the women to win."

The villager, looking very serious, rattled off more explanation, and Tonto said, "Four women fight—wrestle—one man. They pull, pinch, tickle. If that doesn't work, they hit, kick, bite, scratch, tear. Anything to get the turtle."

The villager added a few words and Tonto laughed. "He says it's like being married. Women fight for what women want. And she will always win." The villager burst into a wide smile, tapping his chest, forehead, and then pinching a flexed bicep.

"Test of heart, mind, and muscle," Nathan said. I get it. "You show your manhood, the woman show their womanhood."

Tonto listened to a last few words of advice from the villager, then translated: "Good man sometimes marries good woman. If they want. This is how this tribe works."

Nathan, Arthur and Tonto sat together behind the positions of honor, which were reserved for the chieftain, shaman, and Mark. Nathan noticed a few strands of grass sticking from the barrel of his M1 rifle, as Mark held it upright, like a royal scepter. He remembered his brother having jammed the barrel into the ground to vault with when performing his version his warrior's dance, and realized with concern that the barrel might be plugged with dirt.

With an inward groan Nathan realized he was betting against his brother's competence, but since the gun wasn't loaded, it was less of an issue. It would have to be taken care of soon, though. Hopefully, Mark would clear it himself and prove him wrong.

Each of the turtle contestants was young, presumably single. *So this really is a proving ground for marriage,* Nathan realized. *How...inventive.*

Nathan noticed a few other things right away—the first being that none of the young village men opted out of the contest. He imagined to do so would be seen as an act of cowardice.

One at a time, each man took up his position at a line drawn in the dirt facing four women, who were clumped together ten yards away. When the chieftain shouted a command, the man would charge at the women, cradling the undoubtedly baffled turtle in his arms like a football. Sometimes he would break through the women's ranks, but usually they would manage to trip or tackle him. The men who broke through would immediately turn around and charge again, as a show of bravery and determination, *until* they got tackled. Rarely did any man break through more than once.

After the women got him on the ground, it seemed to be a simple contest of how long he could hold out against their tricks and torture before he gave up the turtle.

The women would then wrestle between themselves, and whoever ended up with the hapless reptile would run around the encircling audience, displaying the animal as though she had caught the bride's bouquet at a wedding. Then a new man and quartet of women would be brought in, and the fun would start all over again. In many ways, Nathan felt the battle was as much between women as it was between the sexes.

He was surprised at the brutality of it, however, and made a few mental notes. The first was that the men did not give the women any quarter. They slammed into them with as much force as they could muster, without consideration to them being the supposedly frailer sex, which it appeared they were not—or at least, not by much. These women withstood the full assault of the man's charge without flinching, and frequently gave him back as much as they got.

So, never retreat, no holds barred, suffer the women's tortures as long as possible before surrender, but in the end always give them what they want—yup, he thought with a smile, *if that's what marriage is all about in this tribe, I'm better off single.*

When the turn eventually rotated around to their group, Tonto and Arthur both gave it a try for fun—despite being married men. Tonto was tackled on the first pass but held out manfully against the women's assault, winning a round of cries and foot stamping from the audience at the end of his torture. Arthur surprised Nathan by breaking through the women's line twice before being tackled and wrestled to the ground. He curled up into the fetal position, and in a moment of sheer amusement, the women tickled the turtle away from him.

Mark stepped forward next, and Nathan watched in consternation as he first sidestepped, and then turned and ran when the chieftain gave the command to engage. Apparently, Mark thought he was being clever—but unfortunately, the tribe wasn't getting the joke.

The women chased him in a circle within the limits of the ringed audience. Eventually, they split up and cornered him—then stripped him of the prize in a matter of seconds.

Mark strode back to sit in his privileged position, apparently oblivious to the chieftain's stolid look of disapproval, as well as to the embarrassed hush that had fallen over the villagers. He glanced over his shoulder, a what-didja-think-of-that grin on his face. "Took them a while to catch me, didn't it?" he said.

Nathan chose his words carefully. "I think you may have missed the point of this contest, bro."

"Huh? What do you mean? Nobody else avoided them for as long as I did."

Nathan felt an elbow nudge his ribs, and looked up as Tonto pointed toward the chieftain. "*Mirim* wants you next."

Nathan stood and obediently strode into the center of the arena, head down.

42

When he raised his head, he faced four Suyp-ari women of varying height and build. In the middle stood U'Yara, a sly smile on her full lips. All four crouched, wearing grass skirts and body paint, bracing themselves against his opening charge.

When the chieftain gave his command, Nathan shot forward, cradling the turtle in one arm. He jumped and spun as he threw himself between U'Yara and another woman, and exploded out the other side. Instead of turning immediately, he sprinted a half-circle and then tore back at them. Driving himself through their line, twisting and turning against their slapping hands, he felt the tug of nails, but there were no folds in his tightly muscled body to get a grip on. Again he burst out the other side, circled, and rushed them. As he passed through, one of the women kicked her leg out and he felt himself tumble in midair. He instinctively curled up, rolled to his feet, and raced off with the women in pursuit.

Every time he turned and faced them, they were more divided, and he could run through their defense using a combination of footwork, dodges and spins. He would straight-arm when necessary, or finesse his way past with face-pushes or head-twists that left them disoriented—but which would have pulled penalties in a football game back home.

Each time he looped around, drawing them after him. Then he would turn suddenly, face them again, and race through their ranks. Just as he saw them panting for breath, a large woman tripped him as he flew past, and a second woman jumped on his back as he tried to roll out of his fall. He stood under her weight and spun, and the woman on his back swung her feet into his tripper's face. Dropping to one knee and hunching his back, he rolled her off his shoulders, turned and ran. On his next pass, they punched and kicked as he raced by, but he avoided the full force of their blows by spinning away from them. With each successive pass, he noticed that the strength behind their blows waned. First one woman, then another, hung back from running after him on his loops around, until on one turn he found all four women standing where he had passed them, chests heaving, sucking air. Two of them crouched to the ground, two stood, one with hands crossed on her abdomen. U'Yara stood with hands on hips, her face flushed from heat and exertion.

Raising both hands as if to salute the audience and call an end to the contest, Nathan strode forward. He stopped in front of U'Yara, lowered his arms, and extended the turtle to her in one hand.

Her eyes went wide, the flush in her cheeks deepened, and the village fell silent. The other women rose from crouching and drifted to her side.

"Go ahead," he said, with a nod in her direction. "Take it." As he spoke, he realized that whatever else she may have been, U'Yara was without doubt one of the most beautiful women he had ever seen. She raised her hand halfway, hesitated, and then bashfully glanced at where her father stood swaying on his feet, in front of the reed mat he normally sat upon.

The chieftain craned his neck for a better view, not wishing to miss a detail of this moment. Behind him, U'Yara's mother clasped her hands together in the crook of her neck, a gleeful expression on her face. The chieftain bobbed his head twice in a rare show of eagerness.

One of the women beside U'Yara whispered what sounded to Nathan like words of encouragement. She raised her arm and delicately took the turtle from him. Then, her face bowed so low that she seemed to be looking at her feet, she mumbled a few incomprehensible syllables to him.

"Huh?" Nathan said. "What's that?"

She raised her face to meet his, and repeated the words. He said it back to her, she nodded and said it again, this time more clearly and with what Nathan thought sounded like great reverence, and then bowed her head again. He turned to walk from the field, unable to suppress a smile. Glancing back, he saw the poor turtle stick its head out for the first time since the game had begun. It took one look at its tormentor and immediately retracted back into its shell again.

Nathan looked up as he left the field and noticed that the Suypari chieftain's normally emotionless face held the hint of a smile, and his eyes twinkled with something he couldn't quite read. *Mirth? Mischief? Happiness?* Whatever it was, it seemed to be a positive step, given the shaky series of events that had led up to this point.

The chieftain stepped forward and grabbed Nathan by both arms. He turned him to face the arena, and shouted out a command. The villagers exploded with shouts and foot-stamping, the chieftain said a few more words that sounded laudatory in nature, and after another round of wild applause, Nathan stepped through the circle to rejoin their little group.

"Well done," Arthur said, as Nathan slipped his khaki shirt back on. "Unless I'm wrong, I saw a healthy dose of running back in that play."

Tonto leaned away from Nathan, cocked his head and gazed at him through narrowed lids, as if trying to figure what other secrets he was harboring. "What did that girl say to you, Kemosabe?"

"She thanked me...I think."

"What word? What *word* did she say?"

Nathan repeated it—and Tonto nearly fell over laughing.

"What? What did I say?"

"What did *you* say?" Tonto literally rolled on the ground laughing, arms crossed on his gut. After he was able to compose himself slightly, he said, "It's not what *you* said, it's what *she* said." He pushed himself to sitting, grabbed Nathan by both hands and said, "That word doesn't mean 'thank you.' It means 'my husband.' Congratulations, Kemosabe. You think Mark messed that test up? At least he's still single. *You're* married."

For a moment it didn't register. All Nathan saw was Tonto's wide, laughing eyes. All he heard were words that didn't make sense. Then all the pieces fell together, and the realization made his head spin.

"Married? Me, *married?*" He was about to jump up when he remembered Tonto's previous jokes, and shook a finger while giving him a sideways glance. *"Tonto..."*

"Wait, wait," Tonto said, wiping his eyes. "I'll check." He turned and conferred with a squat warrior, heavily decorated with jungle souvenirs and looped chest bands, who sat by his side. The warrior leaned forward and gave Nathan a friendly shoulder-punch that was easily understood in any language: 'congratulations.'

"No. I was right," Tonto said in a voice that sounded strangely distant to Nathan's ears. "You're married. Feast and wedding dance tonight. Private dance later." Then he started laughing again.

43

"Okay," Nathan said, after they regrouped at the hut, "maybe what Mark said the day we got here *is* right." He clapped his hands together into a tight clasp and shook them as he paced the tiny floor. "Maybe we *can* shoot our way out of this."

Tonto couldn't keep the smile off of his face. "You gave the girl the turtle, Kemosabe. The man *never* gives the girl the turtle. Well...rarely. Why? Because that's their invitation to marry. She looked at her father, took his permission—and accepted. She called you husband. No way out for you now."

"Annulment, perhaps?" Arthur asked hopefully from where he leaned against the window cutout.

Nathan snapped his fingers and pointed at Tonto. "Annulment. The marriage isn't consummated." When the native stared at him with a blank face and empty eyes, he said, "You know, we didn't...Can't I cancel the proposal—the offer?"

Tonto shook his head. "I'm pretty sure if you cancel, you die. Big shame for the father. Chief's daughter not good enough to be a wife? He'll kill both of you." Tonto glanced around the dim interior of the hut. "Maybe...probably he'll kill all of us."

Arthur pushed off from the wall, grabbed Nathan by the elbow and shook, as if to wake him from a daze. "Nathan, you can't say no, but you also can't stay here. Staying here will kill you someday, as surely as a thrust from the *Mirim's* spear would." Nathan met his eyes, and knew he was right.

"Okay, so you're with me, Nathan?" When he nodded, Arthur dropped his hand to his side and said, "Go through with this. Not just for your life, but for all of our lives. She's young, beautiful. You can do this. In the end, one way or another, I promise I'll get you—all of us—out of it. I *promise*."

"It's...*marriage*," Nathan said. "I'm nineteen. I'm not ready for this."

Nathan turned to the doorway, but Tonto stopped him. "Kemosabe, you're going to your wife. Wash your face. Change your clothes. You can't go looking like that," he said, repeating the same admonishment Nathan had given his brother just yesterday. "Anyway, the wedding dance is in two hours."

44

The Suypari chieftain greeted them at the door of his longhouse, and then led them to where U'Yara was seated on the reed floor. A flock of sisters and friends encircled her as they prepared her wedding clothes for the upcoming ceremony. Unlike Western tradition, there didn't seem to be any social taboo regarding the groom witnessing the bride's preparations.

A pair of girls stained U'Yara's nails with concentrated berry juice. Another wove flowers into fine braids that flowed in a row down one side of her elegant face. Behind her, her mother laid out jewelry composed from forest treasures—rare leathers and strips of exotic furs, colorful feathers and iridescent beetle wings, beads of colored hardwoods, turtle and snail shells. Lastly, a tattooed woman body-painted elaborate designs down her arms and onto the backs of her hands, in a manner similar to the henna art of the Middle East.

The sight of all these elaborate preparations gave Nathan more than cold feet; he felt a chill that went straight to his heart. And yet, the sight of U'Yara mid-transformation, as she beamed a smile at him entering the hut, partially thawed that chill. She looked even more beautiful than he had remembered.

After exchanging greetings, Arthur puffed out his chest like a preacher. Nudging Tonto, he said, "Tell her that in our culture, a holy man counsels the prospective couple, to ensure they understand the significance of their union."

U'Yara nodded bashfully, so Arthur continued. "Our great warrior, Nathan the Jaguar-hearted, has chosen me to convey his hope to honor her for as long as he is with her."

"For as long as he is with her." Clever wording—that is the issue, isn't it? Nathan thought, as he glanced around the hut. A toddler sat in the near corner, one hand draped along the back of the family's pet sloth, which didn't seem to pose any risk of escaping. Or at least, not anytime soon.

When Tonto translated Nathan's alleged title of "Jaguar-hearted," all of the women's eyes jerked in surprise, and the chieftain, who stood to one side, snapped his head in Nathan's direction. As Tonto continued to speak, the ladies returned to their duties. When he finished, U'Yara's smile, combined with a titter of laughter from the attending ladies, signaled the message was well received.

"Tell her that I, Arthur the Cloud-faced, wish you the best of health and happiness. However, just as today brings her the Jaguar-hearted, tomorrow may take him away." As Tonto translated, the woman's smile did not falter. Her shy but hesitant "yes" seemed too easy, so Nathan leaned forward. "What did you really say?"

Tonto turned at him, eyes wide with a mixture of hurt and surprise. Then a smirk invaded his lips. "I'm a translator, not a liar. What Cloud-face said, I translated."

"You told her I might go away? And she understood?"

"I didn't say you'd go away. 'Go away,' in their language, means you leave, on purpose. She wouldn't understand this idea. She *does* understand that the Creator might take Jaguar-heart away. That's the way of the Creator, life, and jungle. Many go to hunt, go to war—they never come back. Some disappear in jungle. Only the jungle and the Creator ever know why."

"What would she do if I disappeared?"

"I'll tell you—but I won't ask her. That's a dangerous question."

Nathan twirled a hand in the air impatiently, and Tonto said, "One or two months with no husband—she'll marry again. Unless the jungle takes her before it takes you."

Nathan scanned the faces in the room, from the bemused smiles of the women and wistful admiration of U'Yara's mother to the cool, unreadable calm of the chieftain.

Arthur winked down at where he crouched beside Tonto, in front of the women as they worked. "All settled, then?" he said, grabbing the lapels of his open safari shirt as he puffed out his chest and bounced on his heels, like a self-satisfied country judge.

Nathan turned to Tonto. "One more question. What happens if she remarries, but then I return?"

"A woman can have only one husband," Tonto said. "If there are two husbands, they have to fight to the death." He paused in thought, his chin pinched between thumb and forefinger. "So...if she loves you, she'll want to be very sure before she remarries." Tonto paused. "If she loves you—really, really loves you—maybe she'll wait three months before she marries again."

45

Two o'clock. In the morning.
What do I do now?

Nathan raised his gaze from the luminous dial of his wristwatch. He stood, gazing through a small aperture in the palm fronds that covered the doorway. He could see a glow from the fires at the communal arena. A few natives dragged their shadows through the night as they traversed the village.

Behind him, U'Yara coughed delicately.

Not a "cough" cough—but an "I'm over here" cough.

Everything that had happened in the last six hours had been a mystery to him, but Tonto had explained. It had started with a series of symbolic dances. Then a feast that seemed to last forever.

Next, the chieftain presented his daughter to Nathan. She placed a dozen seeds in his hand, symbolic of the beginning of a fruitful union. As the seeds symbolized new life, transition and growth, so the couple transition to a new life together, hopefully to foster a powerful, upright lineage.

Then Nathan lifted the woven cloth veil from U'Yara's face, symbolically transporting her from the blind innocence of childhood to the clear-sighted maturity of adulthood. Through her role as wife and mother she would see and learn new realities, of which she had been ignorant as a child.

The shaman drank a potion he claimed would transport him into the spiritual world, where he could align the spirits of the married couple and repair defects in their auras. Nathan had to fight to keep from rolling his eyes, but was impressed by the man's physical changes as he lay before them. After thrashing in what Tonto explained to be the throes of combating evil spirits, the shaman revived drenched in sweat and frothing at the mouth. Fighting the lassitude of whatever psychedelic he was obviously tripping on, he staggered to his feet and proclaimed victory over the demons—the union purified in the spiritual world.

Next, all that remained was to complete the physical union. After exchanging gifts with the chieftain and his wife, Nathan and his bride were escorted by the crowd to the small, windowless hut he now stood in. Constructed of green palm leaves and perfumed with strong resinous oils, it symbolized a fresh beginning. The lack of windows was intended to emphasize their focus on each other.

As Nathan stood and stared through his peephole, his mind swarmed with thoughts of morals and consequences. A rustling sound behind him drew close. An arm snaked around his torso and pulled.

Outside, the tempo of the drumbeat grew, the voices of the singers rose, building to a crescendo that ended in a round of shouts and foot stamping. After a moment of silence, the singing began, barely audible at first. The drumbeat coaxed the melodious voices higher, beginning the slow climb to what Nathan knew would be yet another crashing crescendo, symbolic of...

He turned and allowed himself to be drawn into the center of the room.

The music would continue all night.

46

Nathan woke the next morning to joyous voices raised in song—not from the direction of the arena, but from all around their little dome-shaped hut.

What's missing here? he wondered.

He rose and quickly dressed, then went to push aside the palm branches that covered the doorway. U'Yara hooked one of his arms with her hand and held him back. Standing, she rolled up the reed mat they had slept on and handed it to him. She gestured first to the mat, then to the doorway.

"Um...Take this outside?" he asked.

As if to be sure he understood, she took the mat back, motioned to the doorway, and then placed the rolled mat in his hand again, exaggerating her movements.

"Oh. Give it to them?"

She shrugged and motioned to the doorway. He pushed the branches aside to find his new mother-in-law at the head of a phalanx of U'Yara's sisters. The rest of the village women surrounded the hut, swaying with the rhythm of their song.

That's what's missing, he thought. *There are no drums. No men.*

He felt a slender hand encircle his wrist from behind, and push the rolled mat forward. U'Yara's mother turned to face the crowd as it drifted around from the sides of the hut to gather in front of her. As she unrolled the mat, the women went quiet and stared. Then all shouted and stamped their feet as one. Nathan followed their eyes to the pink stain that showed through the back of the mat.

He turned to his wife with a smile, unable to hide an odd feeling of pride that swelled in his chest. At the same time, a klaxon screamed in his mind, flashing warning lights into his thoughts.

There's no going back now.

"Kemosabe! Kemosabe!"

Nathan jerked his eyes to the side, where Tonto stood well behind the women, waving his arms. "Kemosabe, you go back inside now. Mother take daughter away."

After the women left, Tonto led him back to their guest hut. As they passed one of the longhouses, Nathan glanced in through one of the cutouts and saw two warriors lying, bound in fetal positions on the ground. Both men wore genital slings and colored cloth arm and chest bands, their ears and noses studded with trumpet-shaped snail shells.

"The Xuraquit prisoners," Tonto said. "Never mind them. They're dead men, for sure." He nudged Nathan, and then continued, "Now pay attention. On the first day, mother takes daughter. Makes sure you treated her right—didn't hurt her."

Nathan gave him an indignant look, and Tonto shrugged sheepishly in response.

"We have a saying: Trust, but check. Anyway, you get the girl back tonight, if mother thinks you're a good man. If she thinks you're a bad man, then you have to make an apology—this involves a big talk, gifts to family. But I'm sure that won't happen here."

Nathan looked at him but didn't say anything.

Yeah. That's hardly the problem.

The moment Nathan entered their hut, he felt a chill from his brother, who sat propped against one wall. The others felt it, too. Arthur nudged Tonto and motioned him toward the door. They excused themselves on the pretense of wanting to make preparations for leaving at the end of the next day's celebrations.

Nathan faced his brother. He saw his lower lip quivering and realized he was close to tears.

Well, after what I've done, he's got good reason.

Nathan threw out his arms. "I'm sorry, Mark. I didn't mean to steal your thunder. But what do you want me to do? What's happened—I can't take it back."

"I could never keep up with you," Mark said. "You always had the shine, I was always stuck in your shadow. Even now, you're not stealing *my* thunder; you're only taking your own back.

It should have been your celebration to begin with—remember? I should have never taken the credit. I didn't deserve it."

Nathan slid to the floor beside his brother, his back to the wall, and thumped Mark's knee with a fist. "Look, bro, you don't want it. Tomorrow, you and Art can leave. I can't. I'm stuck here. I'll be fishing their waters, fighting their wars until I'm killed—or until a miracle sets me free. Is that really what you want for yourself?"

As Nathan spoke, something small and furry rustled in the walls of his thoughts. Whatever it was, it sent chills down his spine. It was as though he could hear its teeth gnawing—but couldn't understand what it was trying to get at.

He suddenly became aware Mark had just spoken. "What?" he said. "I'm sorry, I blacked out on you there for a sec. Can you say that again?"

Mark sighed. "I *said,* you're just so good at *everything*. Back home it was always, 'How was the game today, Nathan?' 'Okay, I guess. But I only scored two touchdowns.' Or, 'How'd the tournament go last night, son?' 'All right, Dad. I took first place in sparring, but I had to settle for second in kata.' Now all this. As long as I'm with you, I'm never going to be anything but a screw-up. Sometimes…sometimes, Nathan—I *hate* you for it."

"Hate? Aw, come on, bro. It can't be all that—"

"No," Mark said, his facial muscles twisting his features into something ugly and unfamiliar.

He pushed himself unsteadily up to his feet. "I said it...and I mean it. I've had all I can take for one lifetime, Nathan. When we get back home...*if* we get back home, I...I—don't want to see you anymore."

Nathan felt his circuits overload. In the last week he had witnessed more death and carnage than most adults experience in a lifetime. He had just married a beautiful woman he would one day have to abandon. He was locked into a world he neither understood nor desired. Escape would be next to impossible. Staying was a death sentence.

Nathan's mental gears were burning a clutch trying to pinpoint how any of this was his fault—and then Mark picked this time to allow his jealousy to slip the chain of rational thought? For a few seconds, his brother's words left him speechless. Then his emotional wolverine smashed through the gate and exploded onto the scene.

After a couple of minutes of sheer rant, Nathan caught himself. He froze with his finger pointed directly at his brother's chest. He was so enraged, he couldn't even remember what he had said.

Mark stared back at him. "Is that all, man? And did you expect that tirade to make me feel better about you?"

Mark bent and picked up the M1. Nathan saw the dirt plug in the gun's muzzle. He opened his mouth to call Mark back as he marched out the door, but then thought better of it.

I'll deal with it tonight, he thought. *Things will have calmed down by then.*

By the time Nathan stepped outside, Mark had disappeared. Tonto strolled over and said, "The whole village heard you shouting." He nodded to a clump of natives standing around, openly curious to see how the show would end.

"Come on, Tonto," Nathan said. "Let's go for a walk. I need to calm down."

"I have better idea," Tonto said. "Let's go fishing."

47

Nathan glanced at Tonto as they slid along the bank of the lake in a long dugout canoe. The fishermen in the stern scanned the coffee-colored water for a good spot. Nathan had learned that the bark of a local tree leeched tannins into the water, rendering it dark and bitter. What he didn't understand was how the fishermen could read a good fishing spot from a bad one in such murky waters. He tried to focus on the fishing, to dull the edge of his worries, but uneasiness kept creeping in.

"Tonto," he said, "where are the nets? The fishing lines?"

Tonto shook his head, and pointed at a ceramic jar cradled between one of the fishermen's feet. "Indians fish with this, or with a bow and arrow."

The two native fishermen conferred between themselves. The one closest to them lifted the lid on the pot. He cast doses of its slimy, gray contents into the water. Then he waited. A pungent vinegary odor wafted down the length of the canoe. Nathan pinched his nose.

"What the heck *is* that?"

After a few efforts at clarifying what Tonto was trying to explain, Nathan learned the natives fermented *huaca* with clay in ceramic jars. When they added this mixture to still water it depleted the oxygen, creating a temporary dead space. About the time Nathan grasped the principle of what they were doing, dead fish started rising to the surface.

The fishermen jumped into the water and harvested the suffocated fish by hand. Nathan grabbed those within reach and placed them at his feet in the bottom of the dugout.

After two hauls and a visit to one of the tribe's fish traps, the canoe rode low in the water from the weight of two pirarucu they had speared. Each was around five feet long and weighed over sixty pounds.

One fisherman sorted through Nathan's catch and threw a few overboard. Then they turned around and headed back to the village.

"They don't eat fish without scales," Tonto said. "Local custom."

The trip took less time than Nathan had expected. He spent the rest of the morning and early afternoon touring the village with Tonto, familiarizing himself with everything he needed to know in order to adapt to his new home. He knew he would be losing his greatest asset when Tonto left, but he couldn't ask him to stay.

Outside of some kind of escape attempt, Mark and Arthur were Nathan's only hope of ever being rescued and returning to civilization. If they got lost, or died, Nathan would live out the rest of his days in the jungle. And since they had a far greater chance of reaching Coari with Tonto by their side, he would have to face village life alone until help arrived.

Nathan found the marital hut empty, as he had expected. He returned to the men's hut with Tonto. Arthur napped in one of the hammocks, but awoke when they entered, the reed mat crackling underfoot.

"Have you seen Mark?" Nathan asked.

"Not a sign of him." Arthur swung one leg to each side of the hammock and sat up, his legs dangling, balanced in the cradle of its woven mesh. "I'm worried about him. People do strange things under stress. And I'm sorry to say this—but I don't think your brother is all that stable."

Nathan lay back in his hammock. He cupped his head in one hand and gazed up at the thatched roof. "Let's hope he doesn't do anything rash. Tonto, do you think you can find him?"

Tonto immediately headed out the low doorway.

Nathan felt his fatigue pull at him.

"Everything okay last night?" Arthur said.

"Mmph. Yeah. Great."

"No problem with the language barrier?"

"Universal language, Art. Tonto would've been in the way."

"Get any sleep?"

"Snatches. Trying to catch up now, buddy. If you can just...give me a few..."

As Nathan drifted off, the last words he remembered hearing were, "Huh. Must've been all right then, after all."

48

Nathan believed some dreams are precognitive, while others are a product of the dreamer's obsessions. He didn't know which was the case that afternoon, but he jerked himself awake after dreaming of shooting his M1—and having it blow up in his face.

He could still feel the powder burn of the explosion, the stabbing pain of the shrapnel. Stranger still, he vividly remembered looking down on his own corpse, his face blown away to the bone. He ran a tremulous hand across his nose and mouth, felt the healthy flesh, and realized it had only been a dream.

"Awake, Kemosabe?"

"What? Oh, yeah. Whew. Bad dream." Nathan sat up and gazed at Tonto silhouetted by the late afternoon sun in the open doorway. "Everything okay out there?"

"Everything's fine. The ceremony's starting now. You go, you eat, you dance—you get your wife back." Tonto winked. "Then you dance again. In the hut."

Nathan rubbed both fists into his closed eyes and yawned. "What about Mark? Where's he?"

"He went hunting with the men."

"Hunting. That's not a bad..."

A terror shot up Nathan's spine and exploded at the base of his skull. In one movement he swung from the hammock and to the floor. Tearing open his backpack, he rummaged inside frantically.

"The loose bullets!" he said. "Where are the loose bullets? The ones I took out of the rifle when I loaned it to Mark?"

Tonto shrugged.

"Tonto, quick. Where is Mark now?"

Startled by the outburst, Tonto replied softly, "Don't know. If he's back from the hunt, maybe he's at the ceremony."

"Follow me!"

Nathan flew out the door and raced toward the arena, kicking dirt with each step. A drumbeat started to build. Flutes and women's voices joined in song—and as he neared the corner of the last longhouse a massive gunshot erupted.

The village fell silent.

Nathan stumbled to a stop and dropped to his knees in the dirt. "Oh God, no!" He bent forward, his head in his hands, just as a second gunshot rocked the village.

What the...? He raised his head in wonder. *A gun can't blow up twice!*

Nathan jumped to his feet again. He found his knees wobbly but working. Stumbling around the corner of the longhouse, he spotted Mark standing in the middle of the arena, Arthur by his side. He lowered Arthur's shotgun from his shoulder and handed it to him. Then he picked up the

M1 Garand and sighted along the barrel, aiming at a ceramic pot fifty feet away.

For an instant, Nathan's voice caught in his throat. Then he sucked a bucket of air and yelled, *"Stop!"* at the top of his lungs.

Mark lowered the rifle an inch and glanced in his direction. Then he raised it again, firmly tucking his cheek against the stock, as if determined not to let his brother upstage him again.

Nathan ran forward yelling, "Stop, Mark! *Stop!* You'll kill yourself!"

Twenty yards away and closing, he could see Mark's finger tighten on the trigger. He knew he would never reach him in time. At that moment Arthur, confusion etched into his face, laid his hand on the barrel and pushed the gun down toward the ground.

Mark swung the rifle to one side and turned on Nathan as he raced into the arena.

"Stop? Stop? Who do you think you're talking to, Nate? I'm showing our hosts our firepower, and you're blowing it!"

"Put the safety on."

"What?"

"Put the safety on."

"Who do you think you are to give me orders? You're not better than me, Nate, though you may *think* you are...."

"Give me the gun, Mark." Nathan stretched a hand toward him. "Please. Just give me the gun and we'll talk about it."

"There's nothing to talk about," Mark stepped back, holding the rifle behind him.

"Mark, do you remember the Indian's face after the shotgun exploded in his hands?"

Mark cocked his head, but Nathan could read the fear in his brother's eyes. "Is this some kind of trick?"

"No trick, Mark. Do you remember how he blew off one hand and half of his face?" He nodded at the rifle. "Now give me the gun."

Mark brought the M1 forward and looked at it hesitatingly. "I don't see any...Oh, the heck with it. I don't even know what to look for." Nathan stepped close, clicked the safety on without taking the gun from his brother's hands, then turned the barrel up and pointed at the clog in the muzzle. "*That's* what you look for. *That's* what would've blown your face off."

Nathan watched as his brother paled. Mark's eyes widened and beads of sweat broke out on his brow. He pulled the rifle from his limp hands. Mark's eyes rolled up into his head, and he crumpled to the ground in the boneless collapse of a dead faint.

49

"You saved my life, bro."

"I'm sorry," Nathan said. "I should have told you sooner. I was hoping you'd clean the bore without me having to tell you. I never thought you might raid my backpack for the bullets."

"If we had seen anything worth shooting when we were out in the forest…"

Nathan saw the full horror of what might have been dawn on Mark's face. "Deep breaths, bro. Put your head down between your knees."

Nathan glanced at where the chieftain and the shaman sat, whispering together as they looked on. They had moved Mark to his privileged position beside the chieftain. Now, the drums and dancing were suspended until he could rejoin the ceremonies. In the meantime, the natives picked up potshards left over from the shotgun demonstration.

When Mark straightened again, he had regained his color.

Nathan rubbed his chin in thought. "Look, bro. Everybody has some special gift. You just haven't discovered yours yet. When you do, all of this will be a bad memory, and the doors of opportunity will open for you."

"You sound like my career counselor in college—but thanks."

Nathan was worried by the cold looks the chieftain and the shaman gave Mark. But there was nothing to be done about it. "Look, bro," he said. "I've got to sort out this rifle and collect my wife. Are you going to be all right?"

Mark nodded.

"Do me a favor, then. This is your last night in the spotlight, try to forget everything that's happened and enjoy the rest of the ceremony. Deal?"

They shook hands, and Nathan stood, rifle nestled in the crook of his elbow.

"I probably won't be back tonight. But we'll get together in the morning, okay?"

Nathan glanced at the dyed cotton mat the Suypari chieftain had given Mark to sit on. Stained with the fruit of the *achiote* tree, the mat had originally been red, but had faded to a pinkish orange.

With a mental crash, the rat Nathan had heard scurrying around in the walls of his mind earlier that day now jumped out and bit him. His head swam for a moment. He took a step backwards, one hand to his brow.

"You all right, bro?" Now Mark was the one who looked concerned.

"Yeah," Nathan said. "I just got up too fast. I need to talk with Arthur for a minute, but then I'll be off. Have a good time, okay?"

Nathan glanced at where Arthur sat beside Tonto. He motioned for both of them to follow him as he started walking away from the arena.

"What's up?" Arthur asked.

Nathan drew the two men alongside him as he strode through the village. "Something's wrong," he said, quietly. "All along, we assumed U'Yara was in the jungle waiting for a lover's tryst."

"Yes," Arthur said. "Yes we did."

Nathan turned and faced them. "Arthur—last night was her first time. I felt it, and this morning I saw the...the evidence. The whole village saw it, for that matter. Well, the women did, anyway. So what does that mean?"

Arthur shrugged and crossed his arms on his chest. "No idea. Maybe she went into the jungle to meet him for the first...no, that doesn't make sense."

"No, it doesn't. If she were waiting for their first tryst, how would the Suypari have known they were having an affair, and followed her? You never get caught the first time. The first time, or *times*, might set off the alarm bells. If you're going to get caught, it always happens *after* that."

Arthur shook his head. "Sorry, I'm clueless. Does it matter? We're leaving tomorrow."

"We *hope* you're leaving tomorrow. The chieftain and the shaman look at Mark like he's a side of beef they plan to butcher. So yeah, it might matter...it might matter a *whole* lot."

Nathan stood, tapping one foot on the ground.

"Okay, let's do this: Arthur, you go back and keep an eye on Mark. Tonto and I," he slapped his friend's back, "we're going to go have a chat with my wife."

50

Standing at the cutout door of the chieftain's hut, Nathan scratched his head.

"Are you telling me I could see her *before* we married—but now I can't see her *after* we married?"

Tonto turned from talking with U'Yara's mother, who filled the doorway, an amused smile on her face. "As you Americans say: 'Uh, yeah. That's exactly what I mean.'"

"So, I have to eat first? After the feast, I'll get her back?"

After rattling off some more words, Tonto said, "After the feast, you'll find your wife in the marriage hut. You have to eat first. It will give you strength, and..." Tonto tried to suppress a smile, but it burst through and exploded into a full grin. "And full stomachs slow husbands down."

Nathan nodded. He gazed west thoughtfully, toward where the setting sun was sweeping its spectrum of colors through the prism of the horizon. "Slow and steady wins the race."

"What?"

Nathan sighed. "It's just a saying. Okay. We've got a few minutes before nightfall. Let's clean this rifle, go eat, then dig up whatever demons this sleepy little town is hiding."

An hour later, after having been practically force-overfed, Nathan excused himself and rose for the third time in twenty minutes. This time the chieftain did not pull him back down to the feast. All of the men in the village stood and chanted traditional good wishes until he was well past the corner of the closest longhouse.

"Okay, Tonto," he said. "Let's go over this one more time. Now, exactly *how* do I tell my bride that I thought she was a jungle tramp when I married her? Without getting killed and eaten, that is."

Tonto laughed. Then he repeated the words again.

"And *that* means?"

"Why were you in the jungle the day we met?'"

Nathan repeated the sentence until he got it right. By then, they had arrived at the little hut. Overlapping palm fronds blocked the doorway, which had stood open all day.

"Stay here and wait for the answer," Nathan said. Then he hitched up his belt and said, in his best John Wayne accent, "All right, Pilgrim, watch ma back, 'cause I'm a-goin' in."

Tonto slipped to one side of the hut as Nathan parted the fronds and squeezed through. Before he could speak, a pair of soft hands snaked out of the darkness, clasped both sides of his head and pulled him into a clinch.

For the next hour, the sounds that filtered through the thatched walls were completely incoherent, but vibrant with meaning.

Nathan eventually stepped from the hut and stood in the darkness, staring at the star-sprinkled sky. He felt, more than heard, Tonto slip up beside him.

"Sorry, Kemosabe," Tonto said with a grin, "I couldn't translate that."

"I won't say things are going badly," Nathan said. "But I'm no closer to getting answers. What was that question again?"

Armed with the right words, he stepped back into the hut. He intercepted the hands that reached for him. Then he dropped to his knees, her hands in his. His heart pounding hard enough to bruise his ribs, he repeated Tonto's words.

Even in the darkness, he could see her head bow to the ground. Wordlessly, she stood. She took his hand, and then led him outside.

"Stay with me," he called to Tonto, as she pulled him down a trail beside a line of longhouses. Nathan was surprised when she passed her family home, the chieftain's hut. He was even more shocked when she grabbed a burning brand from a communal fire and entered the longhouse belonging to the shaman and his extended family.

At first, Nathan thought the interior matched that of the other longhouses. The walls were lined with hammocks, and the floor was covered with reed mats, and various and sundry weapons and personal effects. But when U'Yara led them to the far end, the flame of her brand illuminated a treasure of earthenware pots and dried gourds filled with mysterious herbs and potions. Animal furs, bones and teeth were arranged beside leather pouches that contained the more precious tools of the shaman's spiritual trade.

U'Yara held her burning brand up to one of the walls, and Nathan sucked in a breath. Scrawled down the length of each vertical pole was a story, painted in primitive images.

"Tonto," Nathan said. "Ask her what these mean."

Tonto spoke with U'Yara, and then explained that each story followed a hero from his or her victories in battles and hunts, through spiritual ascension to an invariable conclusion—sacrifice to the village god, the jaguar.

The last in the series of pictographs showed the chieftain's daughter offered as sacrifice for her rare beauty.

U'Yara, standing straight and proud, spoke a few words, her voice the whisper of the wind in the trees.

Tonto leaned forward from where he stood behind them, a burning brand held high in his hand. "She says the Suypari give the best to their god. It's a great honor to be chosen."

For a moment, Nathan's imagination was filled with visions of the sacrificial orgies of the Aztec and Mayan Indians.

His mind started to juggle vapors. A fountain of nausea rose from his gut, and he felt himself sway on his feet. The next moment, it passed.

Nathan shook his head. He locked eyes with U'Yara, but spoke out of the side of his mouth to Tonto. "Why was she singing?"

After a brief exchange, he said, "She wanted to face death without fear, like a warrior. To die showing fear is to die twice: once in body, once in honor. The chosen one must not shame self or tribe."

"And they took a *jaguar* for their god?"

"She says the jaguar is the master of sky, earth and water. He kills on land, in the water, in the trees. Nothing can beat him."

Nathan stepped back and waved his torch over the rest of the shaman's wares, as if searching for answers in the man's potions. "This isn't good."

"Nathan, look here. This is *very* not good."

Nathan turned to where Tonto swept his torch over a series of pictographs painted down the opposite wall. Each story featured the same elements—a celebration, three moons—and a violent death by the shaman's blade.

The final story in the series began with an image of a man in Western clothing standing over the dead jaguar. A power stick in his hand radiated lightning. The unfinished tale ended with three moons—and the paint on the third moon looked like it was still wet.

"Oh God, oh no...They think Mark killed their god!"

Tonto grabbed him by the arm. "Kemosabe, don't panic. We have to think, find a solution."

"They think Mark...all along this celebration has been nothing more than his final dinner! That's it, isn't it? Ask her! I need to know for sure."

Tonto asked. U'Yara answered calmly, an innocent, child-like grin on her face. The light of the flame in her hands danced across her exquisite features.

Tonto turned back to Nathan. "She says it's a great honor to be chosen."

51

Nathan bolted from the shaman's longhouse. Tonto was at his heels, rifle in hand.

"Nathan, stop! We have to think."

Nathan broke into a run. "I'm done thinking, Tonto. There's only one thing that will save Mark. That's *me*. If we try to blast our way out, we'll all be killed. There are too many of them. We'll never even make the tree line. Let's just hope we're in time."

The drums and singing told Nathan the celebration was still in full swing—but he felt a change in the tempo of the drums, in the mood of the song.

Nathan rounded the corner of the last longhouse in a sprint. He saw the shaman and Mark together in the center of the arena, as if for an award ceremony.

Warriors dragged the pair of bound Xuraquit prisoners into the arena and threw them to the ground at the shaman's feet. The drums stilled.

The arena fell silent as the shaman raised both hands, as if to make a proclamation. Mark stood facing the chieftain, looking uncertain about what was going to happen next.

Nathan shot into the arena and skidded to a stop in front of his brother, just as two warriors took places flanking Mark, one on either side.

The shaman stared at Nathan and lowered his arms in surprise, as if he had jumped onstage uninvited and snatched the emcee's microphone out of his hand.

Nathan grasped Mark by one shoulder, gripping his rifle—his insurance—in the other.

You've only got one shot at this, make it good.

"Bro, listen. I need you to trust me again, okay? Our lives depend on it."

Mark's awkward smile faded to sober attention. Out of the corner of his eye, Nathan saw the shaman shift his feet impatiently—then noticed the stone knife that hung from his neck on a braided leather thong, over-decorated with beads and feathers. A ceremonial knife, if ever he had seen one.

"Look, Mark. I just checked out the shaman's house. These people worship the jaguar—and they think you killed their god. These past three days may seem like a celebration, but it's all been part of a religious ritual. You took their god's life. Now they're going to take yours."

Nathan half expected Mark to faint again, but he just felt his shoulders droop slightly, as if his last dream had been taken away from him. Then he drew himself straight again. Nathan saw something set his brother's jaw and fix his gaze in a way he had never seen before. He struggled to read the look. Bravery. In his brother's face.

"What do you want me to do?" Mark asked, with a quick glance at the condemned prisoners.

"There's only one thing you *can* do. You've got to tell them I killed the jaguar, not you."

Glancing over his shoulder, Nathan saw a cluster of four warriors surround Arthur, where he sat behind the chieftain. Arthur smiled first at one—but when he looked to the other side and saw he was surrounded, he reached for the shotgun he had laid on the ground beside him and started to rise. One warrior held him down with a hand on his shoulder.

Another one pulled the shotgun away from him.

This isn't going well.

"But if I tell them that—" Mark started to say.

"Just tell him the truth," Nathan said. "Let Tonto translate."

At the far side of the arena, U'Yara stood illuminated by the torchlight, the expression on her face puzzlement itself.

"I can't do that, bro." Mark twisted a sad smile and clenched his teeth. "If I say that, they'll kill *you*."

"Mark. Don't argue with me. Just do it."

The two warriors edged closer to Mark's side. When Nathan glanced over his shoulder he found another two had snuck up behind him. They were just teenagers, but well muscled.

Reflexively, Nathan raised the rifle to cradle it against his chest. The shaman stepped closer, and he realized they were almost out of time.

"Tonto," Nathan said, his voice breaking with the panic he felt rising inside of him, "tell the shaman *I* killed the jaguar—not Mark."

"Don't do it, Tonto," Mark said. He took Nathan's hand in both of his.

"Tell Mom and Dad I'm sorry I was such a mess-up all the time. Tell them I love them and... and I'm sorry it didn't work out."

Nathan reached behind him, grabbed Tonto by the arm and pulled him forward. "Tell him!" he shouted, nodding at the shaman. "Tell him I did it, tell him Mark says *I* killed the jaguar. Tell him anything!"

"And I'm sorry I said I hated you, Nate," Mark said. "You know I didn't mean it."

Nathan glanced again at U'Yara. She could do nothing. As he gazed across the arena to where she stood, he saw the soft concern in her face, the love in her eyes. He realized with a shock that she didn't *want* to save his brother—not because she wanted Mark to have the honor of being sacrificed. No, he realized, his heart punching fists into his throat, her reason was far more selfish. From the first day, she had chosen him over Mark, knowing full well he was the one who had taken the jaguar down.

The teenagers' hands pinned Nathan's arms and pulled him back at the same time the other two warriors grabbed Mark.

The shaman looked inquiringly at Tonto, who rippled off some words, the tone respectful but firm.

The shaman nodded, as if satisfied. Then he thrust his arms skyward, shouted a proclamation and spun around, stripping his stone knife from the sheath at his neck. The warriors threw Mark to the ground and pinned him on his back while the two teenagers dragged Nathan away.

Shocked by their strength, Nathan shouted and thrashed, but like a fish in a net, his efforts only tightened their hold on him. His arms frozen in their grasp, he couldn't even lower his hand to the trigger.

The shaman fell to his knees. He pounded his knife into Mark's chest with an overhead thrust, and tore downward. Mark's scream woke the forest—and a chorus of startled birdcalls and outraged monkey howls drowned out his last dying moan.

The shaman stood, jagged stone knife in one hand, his other hand raised to the heavens. Bloody rivulets streaked down his arm as he held Mark's still-beating heart aloft. The crowd went wild with shouts and foot stamping.

Nathan relched. Shock tripped a switch in his brain and his limbs fell limp, as if the shaman had torn out his own heart. Feeling as though he were a human automaton, with all fuses blown but one, his eyes scanned the insanity around him and settled on the one individual who shouted and stamped her feet with greater enthusiasm than any other.

U'Yara.

52

Nathan felt the rifle slip from his hands, pulled free by the warriors who held him tight. He stared at his brother's bloody heart, pumping air in the shaman's fist, and was struck by the finality of death. The moment it happened, all hope was lost. Seconds before, he was prepared to plea, bargain, or fight. Whatever it took.

Now, there was nothing.

A wave of energy surged through him and blinded him with anger. Stepping and thrusting both hands forward, he drew the two warriors who now held him by his wrists off-balance. Reversing his movement, he stepped backward while wind-milling his arms overhead, breaking their grip on him while at the same time spinning them around to face him.

Nathan leapt into the air with a double-kick, the balls of his feet smashing under each warrior's chin. Their mouths snapped shut with the clack of teeth crashing together, their heads flailed backward, and they tumbled to the ground un-conscious. Nathan dived between them, rolled out into a crouching spin-kick. He caught both of the shaman's legs above the ankle and toppled him. Gasps and shouts broke out in the arena as he launched himself upon the shaman as he lay stunned on his back, his breath knocked out of him. Nathan clamped his hand around the shaman's knife-fist. With a powerful twist he forced the chiseled stone blade to point at the man's tattooed throat. Unable to release his grip on the knife or to resist Nathan's weight behind the blade, the shaman's eyes opened wide as the blade inched closer to its target.

Nathan was suddenly aware and shocked that no warrior had rushed to the shaman's defense. The entire audience seemed paralyzed, rooted in their places. The only sound Nathan heard was the shaman's raspy pant and the blood pulsating in his ears.

Nathan's primal bloodlust boiled within him. He bore down on the blade to drive it home—just as two warriors in his peripheral vision broke from the crowd and lunged forward.

The shaman's chest heaved, and with the blade still inches from his neck, he squeezed his eyes shut...and *screamed!*

Nathan leapt from the man's chest and to his feet, as if thrown by an explosion. The shaman screamed again, his eyes still shut in terror, the knife in his hand hovering above his throat. As his scream died down, he seemed to regain his senses. His face suddenly stilled. His eyes opened a slit, and then snapped open fully.

Nathan scanned the arena; saw the shock on every face. The closest warriors hadn't just halt-

ed in their tracks, but were back-stepping, as if re-
pelled by an abomination.

Nathan turned his back on the shaman and
took two steps before he heard the shaman's wild,
animal-like yell. He glanced over his shoulder0 in
time to see the man rise to his feet and leap at his
back.

Nathan spun and stepped into the charge.
He dodged quickly to the side, catching the shaman's outstretched arm with his own arms. Twisting backward and down, he felt the man's arm
break with a snap, his shoulder pop from its socket.

Once again, the only screams in the arena were the shaman's, this time a high-pitched
squeal that formed an image in Nathan's mind
of a stuck pig. The man's momentum carried his
feet forward at the same time Nathan drew his
torso backward. He flipped in mid-air, pounded
his back to the ground, and skidded to a stop in
a cloud of dust. Nathan stooped and plucked the
stone knife from the ground in a backhand grip
as the shaman rolled over and tried to push himself up. His broken arm buckled from under him,
but he caught himself with his good arm. With a
chest-deep growl he launched himself at Nathan
once more.

Nathan sidestepped, tripped him, crouched
and slashed twice with the knife as the shaman
went down.

Slanding, he flipped the knife in the air and
caught it in a forehand grip. Then he picked up

his rifle from where it lay beside one of the unconscious warriors. Glancing back, he saw the shaman struggle to stand, despite the hamstring cuts in both legs. He flopped back to the ground with a hiss, his eyes projecting curses and murder.

Nathan ignored him as he strode toward the spot where Arthur sat. He pointed the knife at the warriors who crouched around him. Silently, they drifted away and Arthur stood, reclaiming his shotgun from the ground beside him and clicking the safety off.

Nathan turned. The chieftain stepped past him into the middle of the arena. Standing over the crippled shaman, the chieftain raised his arms. The flames of the many fires danced the length of his dark limbs.

Arthur stepped to Nathan's side as the chieftain shouted a proclamation. The two men exchanged a look that needed no words. It was the end of the line for them, their eyes seemed to say. In the next moment the crowd would rush forward to carry them to their deaths.

Nathan wasn't going out with a fight. He leveled his rifle at his hip.

The chieftain finished his proclamation. The entire tribe dropped to their knees and prostrated in the visitors' direction.

It was unreal. Nathan felt—as Arthur surely did as well—that he must be dreaming. His feet flowed beneath him as if striding under their own volition, and Nathan crossed the arena and strode through the crowd. As he passed Tonto, U'Yara lifted her head from the ground and muttered some words to him.

"Kemosabe," Tonto said. "That means…"

"I know what it means," Nathan muttered in disgust. "It means 'my husband.'"

53

"What on earth happened back there, Tonto?" Arthur lit the Coleman lantern and suspended it from the center pole of their hut as Nathan threw himself into a corner and, emotionally exhausted, cradled his head in his hands.

As Tonto explained, Arthur crouched just inside the doorway with his back to the room. He peered intently into the darkness, his shotgun gripped in both hands.

Nathan wiped his eyes on his shirtsleeve. Choking on the words, he mumbled, "What did you tell the shaman, Tonto? What did you say before he killed Mark?"

"The truth."

"Don't play with me." Nathan shook his head. Silent tears streamed down his cheeks. "He cut Mark's heart out and looked *happy* about it! Now what did you *say*? I want the *words!*"

Tonto stood and strode across the small floor and crouched in front of Nathan. He stared into his distraught friend's eyes. "I told the truth. I said Mark was ready to go to God. I said you were ready to go to God. I said you wanted to go to God instead of Mark."

"Oh, God...Tonto," Nathan said. "You didn't tell him I killed the jaguar?"

Tonto laid hands on both of Nathan's shoulders. "If I'd said that, he would have killed you both. It wouldn't save Mark. You'd die for no reason."

Nathan stuffed the heels of his hands into his eyes. He felt his chest heave. He tried to hold back—but his cries came out in great shuddering sobs.

Tonto swung around to sit beside him, one hand on his shoulder. "Much sadness in the Amazon," he said. "The rainforest cries every day."

When Nathan's sobs passed, Arthur turned from his vigil at the doorway. "Tonto, where does this leave us? Nathan crippled their shaman. Will they come for us next?"

Tonto shook his head. "I think not."

"Why?"

Tonto rubbed this head where his straight black shoulder-length hair formed a natural part down the middle. "The Chief made an announcement before we left. He said the Suypari have a new shaman. That's why they bowed to you," he said, turning toward Nathan.

Nathan's jaw slackened and his eyes went wide. "Wait, wait. No, you don't mean..."

"They believe you take the strength, you take the qualities of the man you kill. You're the shaman now."

Nathan pushed himself up straight in the corner. "But I didn't kill him."

"You *more* than killed him. A warrior wants a good life—or a good death. To be injured is bad. To be a coward is worse than death. You made the shaman scream before he died."

"He's *not* dead! I *didn't* kill him!"

"Visitors!" Arthur shouted from the doorway.

Tonto glanced out the doorway. "Stand up," he said. "Put down your gun. Don't worry."

Nathan forced himself to stand. He made it to the doorway.

The chieftain strode into the light. His steps were purposeful, and the crowd fanned out behind him.

Closing the gap between himself and Nathan to inches, the chieftain's cold, emotionless eyes seemed to bore into Nathan's skull. Then, with bloodstained hands, he draped something around Nathan's neck.

Nathan raised a hand to hold it—and stared down at the shaman's beaded sheath suspended on its decorated thong of braided leather. The chieftain motioned to the ceremonial stone knife Nathan had laid on the reed mat beside his rifle. Then he turned, clapped his hands—and the gathered crowd exploded with gleeful shouts and foot-stamping.

"Just because you didn't kill the shaman," Tonto said, "doesn't mean the shaman isn't dead."

54

An hour later, the sounds of drumbeats and chants drifted in from the arena. Nathan fingered the ceremonial stone knife hanging at his chest.

"Mark...screamed," he said, quietly.

"No shame in that," Tonto replied. "Everybody screams at death. But the shaman screamed *before* his death. *That's* shame. He screamed even when you jumped off him, no longer any danger. That's a big, *big* shame. Then he attacked you from behind. There's no word for how big a shame *that* is. If you killed him—maybe that would have saved his honor. But you left him to live with shame. That's worse than death. The Suypari won't accept his shame upon them. They *had* to execute him."

Tonto's logic made sense. So much so that it scared him. He never would have understood any of this eight weeks ago, before embarking on this nightmare.

"Why do I have to be the shaman?" Nathan said. "He must have had an apprentice or someone trained to take his place." But even as he asked the question, the warped logic of the jungle was making the answer clear.

"Kemosabe. You defeated their shaman and two warriors, lightning-quick. The Chief needed to choose a new shaman. You're married to his favorite daughter. Jungle law."

Nathan wondered how he could possibly return to the arena tonight, as Tonto had explained he must. For reasons none of them knew, the chieftain required it.

"Art, you carry my gun. If I have it in my hands, I don't know what I might do. Tonto, you take the two survival rifles. And guys? Whatever happens tonight—we've got to stick together."

Tonto and Arthur nodded their agreement with grim faces.

"All right, then. Let's go."

At Nathan's special request, conveyed through Tonto, Mark's body had been removed. But Nathan couldn't help but stop and stare for a moment at the shaman's head, stuck on the end of a ten-foot pole. The grisly display was intended to remind the Suypari of the price of dishonor.

Nathan's heart rose up and choked him as he approached the arena. He stared straight ahead as he traversed it, fearful the sight of blood would light the fuse on his emotions. He stopped in front of the chieftain and mumbled the greetings he was required to offer. Tonto saved him by translating the traditional phrases in full.

Then the chieftain stood and spoke, hands pressed into the small of his back, belly pushed out like a little child.

"The Chief says they knew your greatness this morning, when you shouted at Mark. He killed the jaguar, but you shouted at him. Showed power over him. Then, when you took the rifle from Mark this afternoon, he fainted—so they knew you took his power. But when warriors took the rifle from you tonight, you fought with bare hands like a demon. Your strength is not in a rifle, not in a weapon. Your strength is in *you*. Jaguar-hearted, most powerful warrior—good shaman."

Nathan took a deep breath and stared the Chief in the eye. "Tell him he's a blithering idiot, a pagan heathen—and I'll see him rot in hell for killing my brother."

Tonto spoke, and the chieftain's face lit up at whatever lies he had conveyed.

The Chief raised a hand, and the two warriors who had restrained Nathan during Mark's sacrifice ran forward. They bowed and presented Nathan with their weapons.

"It's an apology," Tonto explained. "Weapons are a warrior's most valuable possessions. If you keep them, it means you don't trust them, never want to see them again. That's worse than death. They'll be cast out, and die alone in the forest. If you return the weapons, you accept their apology. For the rest of your life they'll protect you—even die for you."

Nathan turned cold eyes on Tonto.

"Take wise way, Kemosabe. Take the weapons. Admire them. Then return them. Make these men your warriors."

Nathan took his time. There was nothing he would have liked more than to condemn these men for having contributed to Mark's death. As they bowed before him, he could sense their fear. But Tonto was right. These two young men had been strong enough to hold him. Having their allegiance could be helpful.

Nathan handed the weapons back. Each warrior fell to his knees. They kissed his feet, and then withdrew.

The chieftain motioned to his family, grouped together behind him. U'Yara stepped forward, head bowed in humility, holding her younger sister by the elbow. Together they slipped in front of Nathan, where U'Yara presented her sister, then stepped back.

Tonto said, "She is offering her sister—she accepts that you will marry again."

The chieftain rattled off something. Tonto said, "Powerful warriors need many wives."

Nathan glanced at U'Yara, who stood with downcast face, a frown twitching at the corners of her lips. Whatever warm feelings Nathan had felt toward her had died completely the moment she led the celebration of Mark's death. Two wives would only compound his difficulties.

"A jaguar only has one wife," He said dryly.

Tonto smiled and translated this honestly.

The chieftain beamed, then nodded. U'Yara smiled triumphantly as she coaxed her sister away, whispering what Nathan imagined to be words of false sympathy.

As he watched the girls rejoin their family group, two warriors shoved the pair of Xuraquit captives to the ground at Nathan's feet.

"Nathan, I'm sorry," Tonto said. His words were suddenly distant, as if he wished he could be anywhere else. "It's the...duty of the shaman. Take enemies' powers. Nathan—you're expected to execute these prisoners."

The warriors pushed the bound prisoners down to their knees. They yanked their heads back by the hair, exposing their throats.

Arthur edged up beside Nathan. "Nathan, no matter what you do—they're dead men. Unfortunately, if you don't act as the chieftain's executioner...I don't think it will go well for us."

"Why are they fighting?" Nathan asked, his mind wrestling for control over his emotions.

"What?" Tonto said.

"The Suypari and the Xuraquit. Why are they fighting?"

"They hate each other."

After a series of exchanges, Nathan learned the feud had lasted for as long as anyone could remember. Nobody knew how it started. They just carried it forward, duty-bound. So many men had died on both sides that mothers frequently murdered newborn daughters due to the imbalance between the sexes.

Nathan looked out over the expectant faces of the tribe. They were waiting for him to commit cold-blooded murder. He was suddenly, overwhelmingly sickened at the thought of conforming to yet another brutal jungle rule.

Trying to survive by following the tribe's customs had forced him into a marriage he didn't want. It had killed his twin brother. It put them all at the mercy of a tribe who could turn on them at any moment.

Enough. They had given him the most powerful position in their tribe, next to the Chief. It was time he used that power.

On his own terms.

"As shaman, this is my medicine," Nathan said. "Send these men back to their tribe to report what they witnessed here tonight. The new shaman of the Suypari is the most powerful shaman in the Amazon. He wishes to be known by all the peoples of the jungle—the Xuraquit as well as the Suypari. If they follow this command, the Suypari shaman will let their women have their husbands, and let their men live long enough to see their children grow. As bond to this trust, our chieftain will give a daughter to their chieftain as a wife— and he will do the same to ours. These marriages will bind our truce. If the Xuraquit do not accept the terms," he said, reaching over and taking his M1 Garand from Arthur's hand, "the Suypari, led by their new shaman, will visit them with the wrath of our weapons. Every man, woman, and child of the Xuraquit will die!"

As the last words of Nathan's proclamation were translated, Nathan raised the heavy rifle, sighted—and exploded the shaman's skull. The head jumped from the post that held it, landed twelve feet away, and rolled to a halt in a pile of animal dung.

The Suypari shouted and stamped their feet in approval of this show of raw power. Even in death, the enemies of their new shaman were not safe!

Nathan slipped the ceremonial knife from its sheath and cut the prisoners' bonds. They rose tentatively, then fell on their knees and bowed to Nathan.

"Tell them to go," Nathan said. "Tell them to go back to their village without delay and share the wishes of the Suypari shaman!"

Tonto translated, and the men rose and took a few wary steps, as if expecting to be struck down in trickery. Then they turned and ran like unleashed spirits through the channel the villagers opened in their circle.

"One more thing," Nathan said, turning to Tonto. "Tell the chief to arrange a guide to take you and Arthur to civilization. Tell him you're spreading the fame of the Suypari's new shaman. Tell him anything that will work. I want you to leave as soon as possible."

"I'm staying with you, Kemosabe."

"No, Tonto. You go. If Arthur doesn't survive, I'll never get out of here. He's my last link to civilization. If you want to help me, you'll help him."

Tonto hesitated, and then did as Nathan had asked. There was a hushed murmur among the crowd, but all were now apparently too awed to question their new shaman. The Chief nodded his head in agreement.

As they walked back to the hut, Arthur said, "Nate, there's something...something you should do tonight. I know it'll be hard, but I've talked to Tonto...and it really should be done."

"I'm not going back to her."

"Look, Nate, she sees the world differently from us. To her, Mark is in spiritual paradise now. She loves you. She has done her best to protect you. If you want to survive until I get back with a rescue party, you'll keep peace in your new family. Just say you'll think about it."

"I'll think about it."

"Okay, now listen up." Arthur stopped outside one of the longhouses and put a hand on Nathan's shoulder. "If I make it back, I'll come fast— and we'll need to leave fast. We're on water here, so I'll try to come by speedboat or helicopter. With this lake, I might even be able to land a pontoon plane. However I arrive, you have to be ready to leave immediately. No hesitation whatsoever. Can you do that? Because if you can't, tell me now. I'm not willing to take a chance on getting speared or shot full of arrows waiting for you to get your act together."

Nathan shook his head. "Don't get cold feet on me, Art. If I don't get out of here, no matter what they think about me right now, someday *my* head will be stuck on a post."

55

Nathan spent the night balled up in a corner. For reasons he could not understand, his heart would not allow him to grieve as deeply as he wanted, or as deeply as he thought he should. Had the shock of their expedition's many losses hardened his heart? Agonizing over the loss of death—even the death of his own brother—seemed a civilized luxury to him now. In the Amazon, you simply lived until you died.

Whatever the reasons, Nathan realized something had dampened his emotions. His lack of grief compounded his feelings of guilt. With a heavy heart, he bade Arthur farewell the next morning, along with Tonto, their Suypari guide, and one mule. Arthur wanted to travel light, so he took only the barest of essentials.

"My French teacher tells me to say *au revoir*," Nathan said. "Unlike good-bye, it implies that we'll see each other again someday."

"I don't know much about French," Arthur replied, "but number one, I'm not superstitious. Number two, 'good-bye' is the contraction of the Elizabethan English 'God be with ye.' So I'll stick with good-bye. Now remember, Nate," he said, "when you see I'm back, you drop whatever you're doing and jump aboard. If you hesitate, I might just take off again to save my own skin—and you'll have missed your only chance."

Nathan didn't know what to say to Tonto. The man had become, at least on this expedition, his best friend. And surviving with the Suypari would be even tougher without a translator.

Tonto seemed to understand that their bond was beyond words. He simply held out his hand, and Nathan grasped it in his. Then Tonto turned and the small group headed toward the jungle.

Whatever emotions Nathan had bottled up to get through last night's events, they burst from their bonds as soon as he saw Arthur and Tonto enter the tree line. He kept a stone face until he reached his hut. Once inside, he broke down and spent the rest of the day grieving.

U'Yara delivered him meals, but he turned both her and the food away. That night, Nathan tossed and turned more than a hammock allows before it gets fed up and evicts its tenant.

After having been dumped onto the floor twice, he went for a walk. In his utter aloneness he felt himself pulled toward the marital hut. At first, he heard nothing. But as he neared, the sound of a woman struggling to suppress her sobs reached his ears.

He turned and retreated to his own hut, beating his hands against his thighs. Tears streamed down his face. He spent the rest of the night fighting nightmares that struggled to outdo the terrible reality he was living.

The next morning, Nathan finally ate. That evening, he allowed U'Yara to join him for dinner when she brought his meal. She reached for his hand; he withdrew. Later, when he no longer could bear the dark silence and tortured attempts at sleep, his feet carried him where his heart hated to go.

Nathan stood outside the marital hut for an hour as the muffled sobs from within chipped away at the ice in his heart. As his cold anger thawed, something snuck forward from a shadowy corner in his conscience. It whispered that losing his brother shouldn't cost him his only comfort in this village—his wife.

It's not her fault. She didn't know what she was doing.

With trembling fingers, Nathan rustled the palm frond door. The sobs went silent. He pulled the fronds aside and squeezed through. For a moment he stood in the dark. Then he felt her in front of him, the warmth of her breath mingling in the still air with his.

A picture of Mark appeared in his mind, almost upending his conflicting emotions and sending him to the brink of despair. Some protective part of his mind had mercy on him, and shuttered past regrets behind present needs.

Slowly, delicately, as if seeking to capture a dream that at any moment could slip away, he reached out, and found her there.

56

Three days later, Nathan returned from yet another failed attempt at distracting himself from his grief. His fishing boat was still a hundred yards from shore when he saw the crowd gathered in front of his hut. He jumped from the bow the moment the natives ran it aground, and ran to see what the commotion was about.

The crowd parted when they saw him, and Nathan found Tonto sitting in the doorway, a big, yellow-toothed smile on his mud-streaked face.

"Where's Arthur?" Nathan blurted out, fearing the worst.

Tonto stood and shook his hand. "I left Cloud-face with another translator. We traveled three days and found another translator. He knew the way to Coari. Another six-day walk from there."

When Tonto saw Nathan's questioning glance, he shrugged his shoulders and said, "The tribes are at war. You have to go around them. So I left Arthur—and came back for you."

"You were only gone five days," Nathan said.

Tonto waved a hand in the air. "No mule. No Arthur." He laughed. "The Suypari guide and I made it back in two days."

Nathan was opening his mouth to ask why he came back at all when Tonto said, "I was worried,

Kemosabe. If the Xuraquits send a messenger, how could you make peace without a translator?"

He was right, of course—as usual. Nathan realized all he had been able to think about lately was Mark. "If Coari is six days' walk from where you left him, then Art should be back in four or five days—depending on how long it takes him to charter a boat or a helicopter."

"That sounds about right," Tonto said. "Meanwhile, we need to keep you alive."

An hour later, as Nathan mapped Tonto's journey according to his description, a cry went up in the village. Together they stepped from the hut to see two Xuraquit warriors standing at the tree line, their hands empty of weapons.

Tonto looked at Nathan. "Looks like I have good timing," he said with a smile.

As the two warriors approached, the line of villagers advanced cautiously, wary of an ambush. Even at a distance, Nathan could see the messengers were the same warriors he had freed.

Things were touchy, but the Suypari sat the two Xuraquit warriors down and fed them. After they had eaten, the men conveyed their chieftain's willingness to uphold the truce, and invited Suypari representatives back to their village to settle the deal.

Everybody realized the invitation could be a trap. They looked to the chieftain and their new shaman for advice.

"We'll keep these two as hostages," Nathan said. "Tonto and I will go to their village."

The chieftain fidgeted, obviously uncomfortable with the idea. Two warriors was not a fair trade for his prized shaman. Nathan did some rough calculations. One day of travel each way to the Xuraquit village, half a day for negotiations... he should be back in plenty of time to meet Arthur's rescue party.

"Kemosabe, this is risky," Tonto said. "There's a real chance it could be a trap."

For a moment, U'Yara filled Nathan's thoughts. Tribal feuds knew no bounds. He had heard the natives' stories of what happened to women taken captive. If he was going to desert U'Yara, he would at least give her the parting gift of peace.

"Tonto, I know it's risky, but just breathing in this place is risky. I want to get home...safe and sound, sure, but..."

Tonto raised a quizzical eyebrow.

How could Nathan explain? What had he—or anyone—accomplished on this expedition? Nothing. Not one single thing. Most of the group had not even managed to come out alive. In every way imaginable, it had been an utter, unmitigated disaster. Maybe, by doing this one thing, Nathan could give this whole horrible experience some kind of meaning. And maybe—just maybe—it would ease his nagging guilt.

"I want to see the killing stopped. I've seen enough meaningless death on this trip for two lifetimes. I wish I could give the job to someone else—but I don't see how one of the natives can pull it off. So...are you with me?"

The next day, they arrived at the Xuraquit village. Their Suypari guide faded into the forest. Then Nathan and Tonto broke through the tree line and entered the clearing.

Nathan never could get used to the tumultuous, onward rush of natives—but he was becoming more comfortable with consigning himself to his fate. Within moments, they were surrounded and taken to the chieftain.

Although the natives were naked except for genital slings, the chieftain reclined on a jaguar skin, his elbow resting on the stuffed head.

Oh, great, Nathan thought. *I think I have an idea why they're fighting.*

Still, Nathan was surprised at the eagerness with which the chieftain negotiated. Having passed through the village, he had some understanding as to why. He estimated there were four women to each man. The attrition rate among the men must have been great, for many women seemed to have assumed traditionally male duties. He had spotted several carrying hunting and fishing gear. He assumed from these observations that the Xuraquit were not the main aggressor in this feud.

Nathan explained the ties of intertribal marriage in the same way he had conveyed the concept to the Suypari chieftain. The consenting daughters would each become a chieftain's wife—a status she could never hope to achieve in her own village. By creating good will in her new family, she would bring peace and tie the tribes together, bringing great honor upon herself and her family. The tribes would be stronger together than they ever would be at war. Past losses must be forgiven if future gains were to be won.

The chieftain took only ten minutes to consult with his shaman and the few surviving elders. As with the Suypari tribe, Nathan noted that almost none of the villagers, men or women, appeared to have passed their fiftieth birthday. The few elders all appeared to be between forty and forty-five, the population culled by the many threats they faced on a daily basis, never cheating death long enough to achieve old age.

When the chieftain returned, he posed only one condition: He wanted to see Nathan's warrior dance. The two captives Nathan had released had not witnessed the dance—but apparently they had related the abundant praise they heard from the Suypari.

Nathan nodded his assent. Then he turned to Tonto and spoke quietly. "If anything happens to me," he said, pointing to the survival rifle in Tonto's hands, "blow the chief's brains out."

The Indian grinned and, without fanfare, clicked the safety off. "Life with you is interesting, Kemosabe. Short, maybe—but interesting."

Borrowing a spear, Nathan entered the communal arena where the villagers had already gathered together.

Scanning the silent, attentive crowd, he saw nothing but anticipation in their faces. No malice, no hatred; just smiles and curiosity.

Why the heck are these people killing one another? As part of a pagan inquisition?

Nathan laid his rifle on the ground within reach, but beyond the limits of his footwork. Relaxed by their evident benevolence, he started his kata, limber and smooth. As his body slipped into the familiar rhythm, he felt the energy carry him faster, through the spins, jumps, swoops and lunges. He felt his speed peak—when a whooshing sound he had heard only once before in his life, but swore he would never forget, swept past his face.

A native screamed behind him. Still, Nathan spun through his routine, his body following the pattern by muscle memory alone.

As his eyes swept the arena, he saw the archer standing by the chieftain's side as he notched another arrow, and a half turn later, the impaled villager whose chest had caught the arrow meant for him.

If I hadn't lunged just at that moment...

A burst of adrenalin sped Nathan into a ducking spin as another arrow whooshed by, its feather fletching tickling his cheek as it passed. A villager grunted as he fell, his leg impaled.

Then Nathan saw the chieftain snatch the archer's bow with a look of disgust on his face. Nathan cycled through a parry-blow combination and spun into his final sequence, just as the chieftain notched an arrow and drew the bowstring to his cheek.

Unsure whether they were shooting to kill or merely testing his nerve, Nathan completed his routine by planting his feet and freezing the weapon's sweep mid-arc, holding it flat at eye level and pointing directly at the chieftain. As Nathan sighted along its length, the arrow struck the spear tip and glanced off, shearing off a sliver of wooden shaft and one feather of its fletching. The deflected missile whizzed past, and Nathan found himself staring beyond the chieftain's empty bow, into his amazed face.

Nope, shooting to kill.

He dropped the spear and snatched the rifle at his feet. In one movement he sighted and fired. Flame leapt from the muzzle. The deafening blast shattered the air and a water gourd suspended from a sapling beside the chieftain exploded, showering him in spray and husk fragments.

The entire tribe cowered to the ground, the chieftain included, although he was the first to straighten up.

Huh, Nathan thought as he strode toward him. *No reticence about showing fear in this tribe. And they test you with arrows, not with jaguars.*

Nathan squared himself with the chieftain, less than two feet between them, his rifle pointed straight at his chest. Nodding at the gourd remnant swinging from the sapling beside him, Nathan said, "That would be your head, if I had wanted it."

Tonto edged closer, his own rifle at the ready, and translated. The chieftain split a grin and dropped his bow.

"Xuraquit make truce with Suypari," he said. Then he pounded a fist against his chest. "And Jaguar-head become friend of Jaguar-hearted."

57

As they followed their Xuraquit guide back to the Suypari village, Nathan glanced back at the chieftain's daughter they were entrusted to deliver in marriage. Her straight hair hung like a closed umbrella around her head; even her bangs reached her chin.

"You're sure she accepts this marriage?"

"Sure, she accepts." Tonto shrugged. "But it really doesn't make a difference. Accept or not—it's her duty."

"How does she see through that curtain of hair hanging over her face?"

Tonto shrugged. "Xuraquit custom. Her husband will cut her hair at the wedding, so she can see. Means he opens her eyes to a new life."

Riiight.

"Tonto, by the way—why didn't you shoot when you saw them trying to kill me?"

"Why didn't you stop dancing and grab your rifle?"

Good question.

"I...I don't know. It seemed like the right thing at the time. Okay, I get it. That's probably your answer as well. Right? Yeah. Well, the thing is...I felt if I stopped, their arrows would kill me for sure."

Nathan halted in his tracks and watched as the Xuraquit warrior interrupted their hike to grub a root. He had noticed the Xuraquit had no agriculture, completely relying on the forest for their sustenance. On the other hand, they seemed somehow happier than the Suypari. More open in their emotions. They felt no shame in showing fear, no restraint in their laughter. When they weren't shooting arrows at him, they seemed more genuine than the Suypari.

The warrior dropped the root into a pouch slung around his neck, then grunted at them as he headed off into the forest again.

"Kemosabe," Tonto said, as they followed, "How did you catch that arrow with your spear?"

Nathan shrugged his shoulders and sighed. "It just happened. You know, Tonto, things here—sometimes they make me feel immortal. Other times, I feel like this place will crush me like an insect. Mostly, I feel like I'm going to die. I'm basically past caring. I don't know which would be worse—dying, or having to explain Mark's death to my parents."

"You've seen too much death, too fast. You're not thinking straight."

As if I'll ever be able to think straight again.

Nathan fingered the chunks of rock strung on the necklace the Xuraquit chieftain had given him as a peace offering. He absent-mindedly wondered what it was made of. His father took the family to the Smithsonian National Museum of Natural History in Washington D.C. once while on vacation. The mineralogy display had been so exhaustive he became bored by the monotony of unique and unusual crystals. He had eventually tuned out as he strolled through. Even so, he was sure he would have remembered something this striking.

The natives explained they found the rocks only in one place—in a riverbed at the base of an extinct volcano. The stones seemed to be composed of a pink metal—pink with a tinge of rose-gold—laced with ribbons of white. It was so exquisitely beautiful Nathan half expected it to bite. After all, most things of beauty in this jungle seemed to either bite, sting or suck blood.

Huh. I wonder what Professor Gwyn Wogan would've made of this?

58

The next few days flew by. The captive Xuraquit warriors departed with one of the Suypari chieftain's daughters. Two days later, in a show of supreme trust, the entire Xuraquit village arrived unannounced for an impromptu day of celebration and trade. Both chieftains greeted one another with their newlywed intertribal wives by their sides. Both young women were heavily decorated with the treasures of the forest, as if competing to show which chief had honored the other's daughter more.

When he saw the villagers converge, Nathan was immediately struck by the imbalance of numbers. The Xuraquit numbered less than a third of the Suypari. They must have put up a magnificent fight to not have been wiped out.

On one hand, Nathan was thrilled to see the two tribes coming together peacefully. On the other hand, it couldn't have happened at a worse time. Arthur was due back at any moment. In anticipation of this, he and Tonto never left one another's side for long.

To warn all to keep the peace, he wore his ceremonial stone knife everywhere. To honor the Xuraquit chieftain, he also wore his precious gift of "blood-stones." When they greeted each other for the first time, Chief "Jaguar-head" cocked his head at Nathan and ran his finger along the line of eight chunky stones.

Can he count? Nathan wondered as the chieftain raised questioning eyes in his direction. But then U'Yara stepped to his side, the missing bloodstone hanging from her neck on a beaded thong. She had refused the full necklace Nathan had offered two days before, upon his return. Explaining that only the shaman could wear a chieftain's gift, she had exchanged it for the one stone Nathan had slipped from the string he now understood he had to keep for himself.

The Xuraquit chieftain smiled in understanding when he saw U'Yara adorned with the final stone. In the manner of his people, he lightly punched Nathan's shoulder, then his own.

As evening neared, it became obvious to all that their one-day celebration would turn into a marathon. Women competed in their own dances, as well as in culinary arts, as they prepared the evening feast. Men competed in games of strength and endurance. When it came time for the warrior dances, Nathan stripped two machetes from their sheaths for a double-sword kata.

He pointed to where the chieftains sat together with their families and announced, as Tonto translated, "No arrows this time."

Chief Jaguar-head broke into a huge grin and leaned into the Suypari chieftain to explain. Nathan watched as his eyes went wide with wonder. Neither he nor Tonto had the immodesty to share the story upon their return, but he was pleased to see the tale told, certain that with the chieftain's embellishments, it would become legend. Then he launched into his kata, leaving the audience stunned. No warrior ventured into the ring for the next half-hour out of respect and—Nathan hoped—out of fear their performance would disappoint in comparison.

That night, as the celebration continued, Nathan left the Coleman lantern ablaze at the end of a pole outside his hut as a beacon to rescuers. He realized his reserve of fuel wouldn't last another five days at this rate. But he figured that if he wasn't rescued by then, he would take his chances and escape into the jungle. Especially now that Tonto knew the way.

The next night, the activities only increased. Nathan stood by the lake's edge and prayed for Arthur to see his light.

"Something's wrong, Kemosabe," Tonto said.

As always, he heard it first, Nathan thought, as the sounds of celebration turned threatening. He spun and bolted toward the arena, rifle in hand, stone knife beating cadence against his chest to his quickening foot-treads.

He arrived to find the tribes divided into two masses. Each faced the other across the arena with weapons bared. In the middle of the arena lay the prone body of a Suypari villager.

Nathan's presence stilled the menacing gestures and silenced the shouted threats. He stooped over the still form. He realized he didn't have to check a pulse to verify the man was dead. The haft of a bone knife protruded from his skull like a blunt horn, as if he had been gored.

Nathan walked to the Xuraquit chieftain, who stood at the head of his people.

"Who did this?"

When he had identified the guilty man, Nathan traversed the stilled arena to the Suypari chieftain. After a number of passes, he was able to bring the two chieftains over the body of the deceased, in the center of the arena.

"If the two of you want peace for your tribes, you have to accept my medicine." He stared at the Xuraquit chieftain. "Your numbers are few. If you fight, you will be wiped out." To the Suypari chieftain he said, "Do not be deceived. The Xuraquit are strong. If you go to war with them here, they will kill two or three Suypari for every Xuraquit killed. This is how they have survived your feud to this day. Even if you win, what remains of your tribe will only fill one longhouse."

"But he..." Jaguar-head said, pointing to the dead man. He fell silent the moment Nathan raised a hand. "Everybody here has blood feud," Nathan said. "Everybody has a reason to continue the killing. The reasons don't matter. All that matters if whether you want the happiness peace brings, such as we have enjoyed these past few days—or if you want to spend the rest of your lives awash in blood and suffering." When he saw he had their attention, he went on, "This is my medicine for this disease: Each chief will execute any murderer from his own tribe. And he will execute this warrior in front of the offended tribe, to show his humility, justice, and commitment to peace. No man desires the disgrace of being executed by his own chief, especially in front of the offended tribe."

The Suypari chieftain opened his mouth to speak, but Nathan cut him off. "In addition, the murderer's family will be transferred to the offended tribe. They will not live among their own people, praising his honor after he is executed. Instead, they will curse his memory for making them leave their tribe. Knowing these humiliations will restrain your warriors' hands and end the killing."

Both chieftains stared at the ground in silence. First one, then the other, shifted on their feet, reminding Nathan of the tethered mules' dance. He glanced to the crowds at each side of the arena, and saw that each tribe anxiously awaited its chieftain's decision. With the curious apathy that had crept into him since Mark's death, he realized that any moment now, this arena would erupt in battle or the celebration of justice.

Jaguar-head grunted, then raised his gaze. "I call my warrior?"

The Suypari chieftain's stone face twitched with an uncharacteristic grin, which he quickly suppressed.

Jaguar-head met his warrior a few paces away from them. As he spoke, the warrior first bowed his head respectfully, then straightened abruptly. With a few more words, coupled with glances back at his tribe, the expression on his face melted from shock to resignation.

No way out for you, Nathan thought.

Dropping his weapons to the ground, the warrior allowed himself to be led into the small group. The others stepped back as the warrior knelt to the ground, facing his death honorably. Nathan raised his arms in the manner of making a proclamation, and declared his remedy. As Tonto translated the transfer of the murderer's family to the offended tribe, the warrior glanced at his chieftain in hope. Finding his leader's dark eyes resolute, he hung his head in shame.

Justice was meted out swiftly. It caught the condemned man unawares as he raised his head again. At that moment, the Xuraquit chieftain's knife slashed, and the condemned fell to the ground in his death throes, blood gushing from his slit neck.

A wail went up from the warrior's wife and family. Through their cries, Nathan heard the drone of what could only be a single-engine prop plane. The sound skirted the clearing. Then the red and green navigation lights broke from the edge of the trees as it circled over the lake. Nathan shrugged his rifle off of his shoulder and into his hands. He thrust it straight into the air and fired the wilderness distress signal of a volley of three shots, the foot-long blades of flame stabbing the darkness. The plane circled once more. Nathan shot off another volley, and then watched as it banked into a turn in the direction of civilization. As quickly as it appeared, its lights blinked out over the treetops on the other side of the lake.

Only then did Nathan realize the village had fallen into a stunned silence. Both chieftains and a number of men crowded around him.

"Was that Arthur?" Tonto murmured.

"No, Tonto," Nathan said, as hope swelled in his chest, "That was an *angel*."

Tonto nodded. He turned and translated, and word spread through the crowd that the shaman's justice had been visited by a heavenly host.

As Nathan strode from the arena, the two tribes slowly melted together once again. U'Yara drew up to his side and slid her hand into his. She whispered, "My husband," and Nathan felt his heart tear from the strain upon it.

59

"Unless I'm off my mark," Nathan said, as he reloaded his rifle in their hut, "he'll be back for us at first light."

"Where are you going now?"

Nathan turned in the doorway, rifle in hand. "Anything you want to take, keep it with you at all times. The two survival rifles are yours. Also the trade items. Wogan's money belt. Anything else of value."

"And for you?"

Nathan fingered the bloodstone necklace and the shaman's ceremonial dagger that hung around his neck. "I just want to get out of here alive." He glanced out the doorway, then back at Tonto. "I have one last night with U'Yara. Then I'll never see her again. Make sure you wake me at sunrise."

"Kemosabe, your heart bleeds. But she would die in your world. You would die in hers. You no have choice. You must go."

Nathan nodded. "Come and get me if there's any more trouble at the celebration. Stay awake, okay?"

The next morning, Nathan left the marital hut just as U'Yara was waking. Incredibly, the inter-tribal celebration was still in full swing, as Tonto had explained it would be for a full three days and three nights. Sleep, it seemed, was a luxury and not a necessity for these natives.

Nathan sat with the two chieftains. He was pleased to find no residual animosity from the previous night's altercation. U'Yara brought food, and they shared what he expected to be their last breakfast together. Every bite stuck in his throat. When he washed it down with their bitter water, the food sat like a lump in his gut.

In the early morning light, U'Yara's beauty was so intense Nathan averted his eyes out of fear that his commitment to depart would falter. Together they laughed at the children's comical attempts at warrior dances during their turn in the arena. Then, two hours after sunrise, he heard the sound of a rotor, and jumped to his feet.

A passenger helicopter swung a circle around the village, and then hovered directly overhead. Tonto jumped to his side as the villagers ran out with their bows and arrows. Nathan stepped into the middle of the arena, hands raised, and shouted them back.

When the warriors lowered their weapons, the helicopter descended to hover a foot off the ground. Nathan saw a helmeted figure seated beside the pilot, waving frantically for them to board. The powerful rotor whipped up a stinging dust cloud that pushed the villagers back, hands and arms covering their eyes.

Nathan stepped onto the landing gear skid and jumped aboard, then turned and pulled Tonto into the seat beside him. "Where's Arthur?" a voice shouted from up front. Nathan whipped his head around and stared into the man's steel-grey eyes. His mental synapses flickered for a moment, then fired. With a shock he realized the front-seat passenger was Hawley, not Arthur.

"Just kidding," Hawley shouted, fighting to make himself heard over the roar of the rotor. "He's the one who told me where to find you." Hawley gave the pilot a thumb's-up, and Nathan felt the g-forces press him down into his seat as the helicopter shot up into the air. Then the cabin tilted forward, and the village started to slip away behind them.

His throat cramping, Nathan watched it disappear under the forest canopy. He knew he would regret leaving. Maybe for the rest of his life. At the same time, he was certain this was better than waking up one day to find his neck replaced by a ten foot-long wooden pole.

Hawley turned in his seat, reached back and slapped a hand into Nathan's open palm in a tight clasp. Then he handed him a headset communicator, and motioned for him to slip it on.

"Boy, I bet you've got a story to tell," he said, as he ran his eyes over the ceremonial dagger and bloodstone necklace.

"Still calling me 'boy,' are you?"

When he saw Hawley throw his head back and heard his laugh, he glanced around him, then said, "And you've still got me riding in the back of the bus, don't ya?"

Hawley shot him a smile from his eyes and said, "Do me a favor, Nate. Stow that rifle before you stage a revolt."

Somehow his words hit just right—the way Scott Campbell's verbal jabs used to do—and Nathan broke down in laughter. He knew he was reacting as much from stress release as from anything funny having been said. But at that moment he needed to unload, and it came out in great guffaws. Tonto caught the infection, without even knowing what words had passed under the roar of the helicopter's engine and swirling blades. All together, the three of them rocked the cabin with laughter as though they were returning from a raucous party—rather than escaping near-certain death.

60

Martin had entered the room earlier, and had become enthralled by his father's story. Now he noticed Nathan had stopped, and seemed to be staring outside through the living room window.

"Do you want to take a break, Pops?" his son asked.

Nathan was noticing how everything was white outside, except for dark patches where evergreen trees poked through the blanket of snow. A whistle of wind swept a dusting of flakes off the rooftop of the Trenton, New Jersey home and swirled in front of the window, as if a harbinger of a fresh snowfall.

"What happened to Tonto? And U'Yara? And Arthur? Do you want to say a little about all that?" Martin asked, gently.

Nathan shrugged. "Tonto and U'Yara? Yes. I'll get to that. Arthur ran into Hawley in Coari. Dumb luck? Destiny? However it happened, he sent Hawley back for us." As he spoke, Nathan got up from his recliner, walked over to the fireplace, and lifted the lid of a heavy wooden box that rested on the mantle.

He pulled a beaded, braided leather thong from the box, complete with beaded sheath and ceremonial stone dagger. Stripping the dagger from its sheath, he held it up close to the video camera, displaying the rusty brown streaks on the stone blade. "I never cleaned it," he said. "The last things this dagger cut were Mark, the shaman's legs, and the leather thongs that bound the Xuraquit prisoners I released. These brown streaks," he said, as he ran his finger along them, "mostly, this is Mark's blood. This is the blood that saved my life."

Nathan never could look at the artifact without choking up. He quickly buried the dagger in its sheath and laid the assembly on the mantle. Then he removed a layer of cloth from the box and raised a chunky necklace of seven stones.

"I had to give one stone to the company for analysis—but they let me keep the rest." Once again, Nathan held the necklace up to the camera.

"What is it, Pops?"

He took it back and held it up, running one finger over the rock matrix. "The white ribbons are common quartz. The red stuff is a rare earth element—one of those rare elements only found in one or two places in the world. Now, don't get all excited," he said, noticing the excitement in Martin's eyes. "It's rare, but that doesn't make it valuable. Forty-five years ago, when we discovered hemosiderhonium, as we named it, we couldn't find any industrial use for it. Anyway, the discovery belongs to ADR Chemical, since they sponsored the trip."

"So what's it used for now?"

"ADR Chem found a use for it in the light filters for dye lasers," Nathan said. "Just a tiny bit augments the laser efficiency many fold. At the same time, believe it or not, the soil samples Hawley brought back showed silicone dioxide, calcium carbonate, and *alluvium*." He clapped his hands together and rubbed them conspiratorially.

Nathan stared at him, expectantly.

"In other words, dirt."

"*Riiiight.* Listen, Pops. This can't be easy. Maybe you should take a break and tell the rest tomorrow. You know—the story about what happened after you returned?"

Nathan nodded his head.

"Tomorrow. That's a good idea, son. I could use some rest. If you think this part of the story takes a lot out of me, just wait until you hear the rest of it."

61

"Let's see…After returning from the Amazon…"

Nathan had exchanged his commercial interest in geochemistry for a more sincere and abiding fascination with social anthropology. His nearly forty-year teaching career at Princeton was enlivened by his research, all of which he performed in the field during summer vacations and sabbaticals.

From the cannibals of Papua, New Guinea to newly discovered tribes in Borneo and Micronesia, and all the way back again to the indigenous South American Indians, Nathan's ventures into primitive societies had become legendary—not only in his family, but in the academic world as well. He had returned many times to the Amazon. But he had never been able to bring himself to return to the Suypari tribe. Certainly a woman as young and beautiful as U'Yara would not have remained single for long, and he did not relish the idea of having to fight her new husband to the death. Even if he were victorious, he would just have to leave her again anyway.

Over the years he tracked the destruction of the Amazon. He was horrified by the obliteration of tribal lands by shortsighted conglomerates blinded by lust for profits gained through indiscriminate logging, gold mining, oil exploration, and slash-and-burn farming. Each had far-reaching negative consequences. Amazonia was not just losing trees; commercial development risked irreversible damage to an ecosystem rendered fragile by its many keystone species—species upon which entire subsystems depended. Fifty years of industrialization could leave nothing but polluted wasteland.

Many times, Nathan had wondered about U'Yara and the Suypari, but he never summoned the courage to revisit. Then, six months earlier, he had spotted an exquisite bloodstone necklace in a display case at a museum gift shop. The pamphlet that came with the necklace explained its origin in the Amazon. The moment he read the card, he knew he had to return.

If the world had discovered the humble treasures of the Xuraquit, civilization was standing at the Suypari's doorstep, ringing their bell.

Nathan wanted to be there when they opened the door.

62

When Nathan realized he had to return, his first phone call was to Hawley. They never forgot each other's birthdays or holidays, and each knew the other's children by name. Hawley had even stood by Nathan's side the day his wife died of cancer.

"About the Amazon and the Suypari tribe..." Nathan said.

"Yeah?" Hawley's voice had roughened from age and emphysema, but still carried an edge.

"I'm going to go back."

"I'm going to hang up."

"No, seriously," Nathan said, "I want you to come with me."

"And I want *you* to go to hell."

"In one week."

"In your dreams."

Nathan hung up. He was pretty sure that when he called back in a few hours, Hawley would be packed and ready to go. The poor man had one foot in an assisted living complex and the other foot in his son's house—and he hated both options.

He'd go.

63

Nathan stopped in the Brazilian city of Manaus just long enough to catch a connecting flight to Coari. From the air he gazed down on the Amazon River as it snaked off into the distance in both directions, through over two million square miles of rainforest. Although it was a thousand miles to the Atlantic, the massive river was already seven miles wide.

Manaus hosts the "meeting of the waters." To Nathan, it was one of the most impressive sights in the world, where Peru's caramel-cream *Rio Solimões* merges with Venezuela's coffee-colored *Rio Negro*, running side-by-side for miles like two flavor ribbons in a giant confectionary.

When he landed in Coari, a half-forgotten but still-familiar depression returned. The destructive impact of industrialization upon indigenous people lowered Nathan's spirits, no matter where he saw it. When Professor Wogan used Coari as a jumping-off point for their ill-fated expedition in 1965, Coari was little more than a dirt-water town. Since then, the petroleum industry had catalyzed phenomenal growth. As usually happened, the conglomerates raped the land, stripping the indigenous people of their livelihoods. Pollution and habitat destruction forced the natives into the cities out of desperation. Lacking marketable skills, they were lucky to get the most menial of jobs. Many fell victim first to alcoholism, then destitution. Nathan was always dismayed to see the Indians, a once proud people who lived in harmony with nature, reduced to drunken beggars and prostitutes.

Nathan picked up a message at the reception desk when they checked into their hotel, and a smile lit his face. Two hours later, he sat in the mezzanine restaurant.

Hawley's late, he thought, checking his watch.

Nathan motioned the waiter for a second mineral water. He checked his watch again, remembered how difficult it is to keep to a schedule in South America. Hawley's note had contained exceptionally good news. He had managed to track down Tonto—and Tonto had agreed to come along. He was picking him up—along with, as he put it, a surprise.

I wonder what that'll be.

Nathan wondered what Tonto would be like now. Nathan was 65, and the Indian must have been about 10 years older than him. Mid-70s? That was a very old man in this part of the world. He must've taken good care of himself. Regardless of the condition he was in, it would be exciting to see his old sidekick—a man who had saved his life more times than he could count.

Just as Nathan's thoughts started drifting to the past, Hawley strode in his direction. His steps were surprisingly straight, strong, and purposeful. Behind him, an older but still strong-looking Tonto guided a taller, younger, and considerably more svelte version of himself by the elbow.

Tonto's daughter—or granddaughter?

Nathan rose and shook hands with Hawley. Tonto threw his arms around Nathan and gave him a big hug.

"Kemosabe! You haven't changed a bit," Tonto said.

"Really? Thanks," Nathan said. "Neither have you."

"Actually, I'm kidding," Tonto laughed. "You've changed a lot."

Nathan returned the laugh. "You too, I'm afraid."

"Kemosabe—"

"You know what?" Nathan interrupted, "Maybe it's time you called me Nathan."

"Okay, then—Nathan, I want you to meet my granddaughter, Karintha."

64

After dinner, Nathan sat with Hawley and staged their expedition.

Nathan, Tonto and Karintha would head off by motorized longboat the next morning. A helicopter had been a nice luxury for their rescue forty-five years ago—but back then ADR Chemical was footing the bill. Hawley would stay behind and handle logistics for anything they'd need—and coordinate help if necessary. Two heart attacks and frequent angina made him more of a liability than an asset in the field.

Traveling by boat, it would take most of a day to reach the Suypari, assuming they hadn't moved their village, but it would offer greater mobility and could be kept at the ready for an emergency getaway.

"Satellite phone?" Hawley asked.

"Two," Nathan said. "Also backup batteries and a solar charger."

"GPS?"

"Check. Two again."

"Water purifier, MRE's, malaria pills…"

After they crosschecked their lists of essentials, Tonto took his granddaughter to arrange transportation and to purchase the few supplies they had not brought with them. Every one of Hawley's seventy-four years had drawn fatigue lines in his face, and he retreated to his room to curse the vagaries of old age.

After relaxing over his third cup of coffee, Nathan wandered over to the hotel gift shop. He picked up a three-foot-long blowgun.

Tourist stuff. The real ones are seven to eight-feet long, completely handmade, and the bore is so straight you can see daylight through the far end.

Nathan picked up a dart and tugged strands from the cotton wadding.

Real darts are made from bamboo slivers or palm needles, and the plug is made of silky fibers found in Kapok seedpods—not drugstore cotton.

Nathan looked around at some of the other items on display—and the memories came flooding back.

Real bows are taller than a man. The arrows are six-foot-long works of art. Each one is made from three pieces of wood bonded together. The fletching is natural bird feather angled to induce torque during flight.

Nathan's mind flashed memories of Hawley taking a shot through the arm, and of arrows whizzing past his head during his warrior dance in the Xuraquit village—one so close the fletching tickled his cheek.

Suddenly, he wasn't sure he wanted to be here.

He wondered what he would do if he met U'Yara.

Not many Suypari live to their sixties. At least that's how it used to be.

As Nathan swung his gaze over the over-priced souvenirs, it only deepened his melancholy. He knew each item, even the less authentic items, was bought from a native for a fraction of its resale price.

Hawley walked up behind him. "Couldn't sleep," he said. "Too many memories coming back."

"Yeah. Me, too," Nathan said.

"Bad ones, mostly."

"I'm with you there," Nathan agreed.

"So, really, Nate—why come back? You've got a great life in the states. This was probably the worst experience of your life. Same for all of us lucky enough to get out. Why?"

Nathan shook his head thoughtfully. "Wish I had a better reason. I've been curious about the Suypari since the day I left, to tell you the truth. But this new industrial application for hemosiderhonium was a big trigger for me—it might save the Xuraquit. Once they understand hemosiderhonium isn't found anywhere else in the world, they might be able to live off of it. With a little luck, they won't need to sell their forest to slash-and-burn farmers or lumber companies to survive. They can preserve their tribe—and a piece of the Amazon along with it. So...I guess that's the main objective."

"Hmmm…" Hawley said. "That's…mighty *charitable* of you."

"Give me a break, old man. Why did *you* come along?"

"Simple reason," Hawley said.

"Oh yeah? What's that?"

Hawley stopped when they reached the elevator and jabbed at the button. "Because you asked me to."

The doors in front of him slid open with a *ping*. The two aging men stepped inside.

"So if anything goes wrong," Hawley said, and looked Nathan dead in the eye as the doors slid shut, "don't blame me."

65

The next morning, Nathan stepped from a battered taxi and strode the marina until he found Tonto and the two motorized longboats he had chartered. Tied alongside a weathered wooden pier, one boat already rode low in the water from the bundles of provisions.

"Let me make sure I have this right, Nathan," Tonto said, as he stepped into the nearest vessel, "Are we planning to be in the field for a week—or for a month?"

"I always travel heavy," Nathan said. "It's one of the ways I've stayed alive."

He patted one of the three waterproofed bundles that lined the belly of the longboat. "We've got MREs for regular meals. freeze-dried foods if we have to hump it overland. Water purifiers and sterilization tablets. A full spectrum of antibiotics and antifungals, topical, oral and parenteral, complete with intravenous lines and solutions. Tents. Mosquito nets and sprays. Trade items, communication and locator equipment, dry clothing in zip lock bags..."

"And guns," Tonto completed the list.

"Yes," Nathan said. "Unfortunately."

In fact, Nathan was slightly embarrassed by all the armament he was carrying. But long experience had taught him it was always better to be safe than sorry. Two 40-caliber Glock semi-automatic pistols, one in a pancake holster in the small of his back, the other stuffed into the side pocket of his grey tactical pants. A 22-caliber Beretta semi-auto in an ankle holster, and a .44 Magnum derringer in a specially sewn inside pocket of his safari shirt, completed the hidden arsenal.

Despite all the firepower, Nathan understood that the trick was more in knowing when *not* to shoot than when *to* shoot. Tonto still carried the battered survival rifle he'd given him so many years before. Nathan motioned toward a bundle behind him. "I've got 12-gauge shotguns for both of us."

"Thanks, Kemosabe—I mean Nathan. That was thoughtful of you. But I have a sentimental attachment to this rifle."

"Well," Nathan said, "Karintha might be able to use one of mine."

Tonto laughed. "Oh, sure," he said, settling cross-legged into the boat. "She could use it just fine. But she's pretty much her own firepower."

The guides pushed the two longboats into the river, dipped the long propeller arms into the water, and fired the outboard motors with a yank of their ignition cords.

Shouting to make himself heard above the racket, Nathan said, "The perfect weapon is one that's good for hunting, but that we can also use for self defense if the watermelon hits the pavement. When we arrive, we promise to give our guns to the chieftain when we leave. That way he'll protect us during our stay. The snazzier our guns are, the greater the likelihood someone will kill us for them."

"Another reason I like my old rifle," Tonto said.

Karintha knelt in the bow, back arched and chest thrust forward. Her arms were braced on hands that straddled the bow point as she split the onrushing air with her aquiline nose and supple teenaged frame.

Like a sailor's dream of a ship's masthead.

Her long black hair streamed behind her in tendrils, completing the fantasy. Nathan threw his gaze overboard, past Tonto's living masthead of a granddaughter, and over the miles of river to the dark sliver of forest on the other side.

66

The tributary opened onto a finger-shaped lake. They ran its length, and from there zigzagged along a maze of rivers, trying to match GPS readings with Hawley's map coordinates from their 1965 rescue. Eventually, they shot from the mouth of a small tributary into a medium-sized lake.

The river guide swung the boat into a quarter turn—and Nathan found the Suypari village looming directly ahead.

The moment he saw it, Nathan's heart paused, as if to stop and question his sanity before taking another beat. His fingers grew numb. A cold sweat broke out on his furrowed brow. He had lived this moment countless times in his imagination. But now that he was here, he wanted to turn and rocket away at full throttle.

The last time, they killed my brother. Maybe this time they'll kill me.

Nathan did his best to still the dark thoughts.

This is a different time. The world has changed.

Still, at this distance, Nathan could see little change in the Suypari town. A few huts on one end lay crumbled to the ground. A large round house with a thatched roof reflected some evolution in architectural design.

The growl of the boats' motors brought the natives running to the edge of the plateau upon which the village stood. The people fanned out in a line. As they neared, Nathan could see the women now wore cloth dresses of the simplest design—a length of fabric folded back upon itself with a hole cut out for the head, either belted or sewn up at the sides, leaving holes for the arms. Gone were the grass skirts—a misnomer anyway since they were really made from *aguaje* palm fronds.

Most of the men wore shorts. The vast majority carried bows and arrows, with bone or bamboo tips. A few cradled shotguns in their arms. But Nathan knew they were mostly just for show. Shells were prohibitively expensive for people who lacked income. Most natives still relied on blowguns and archery to bring down their game.

Shotguns were reserved for war.

Dang. Civilization not only knocked on their door, it barged into their lives a long time ago.

Although the size of the settlement looked the same, the population appeared to be only a half to two-thirds their previous number. He didn't need to ask to understand why. It was the same story everywhere. Previously undiscovered tribes suffered terrible attrition from introduced diseases. The main culprits were influenza, measles and hepatitis B. As Nathan pondered the fate of the Suypari, his boat's prow slid with a grinding sound onto the lakeshore beside a row of dugout ca-

noes. Karintha jumped out and secured the bow-
line to a small tree. A moment later, their supply
boat slipped in beside them.

Once they were on dry land, Nathan was surprised to see the line of natives hold their position.
Nobody smiled or waved. None offered a sign of
recognition or an indication of welcome. When he
had known them, the Suypari had been a somber
people. Now, they appeared deeply suspicious
as well. He scanned their faces and, defying his
expectations, he saw a handful who might measure in the mid-fifties to early sixties. U'Yara was not
among them. In fact, none of the villagers regis-
tered recognition.

Nathan felt Tonto edge up to his side and join
him in scanning the line of natives for a friendly
face.

"What do you think? Do you recognize any of
the older ones?"

Tonto shook his head. "And they don't recognize us. Even some of the older ones were children
when we left."

"We'd better introduce ourselves."

"It doesn't look good, Nathan. Civilization has
hit this village hard. They look scared. And scared
people are dangerous."

"I'll wait here?"

Tonto nodded, never taking his eyes off of the
line of villagers. "Good idea."

Nathan watched as Tonto strode up the incline. A single man stepped forward from the

crowd. He wore cotton pants cut off at the knee, but his face was dotted with paint, his chest crossed with braided chest straps. In one hand he carried a shotgun, in the other a broad-bladed spear.

Nathan cast a glance over his shoulder. He found Karintha standing immediately behind him. The two boatmen squatted by the water's edge, conversing as if they couldn't care less what the outcome might be.

And they probably don't. If we get killed, they'll lay claim to our goods and return home happy men.

After many gesticulations and a longer discussion than Nathan had expected, Tonto called out and waved him up the incline.

"Karintha," Nathan said, "you stay here, keep an eye on our supplies. Whatever you do, don't let the boats leave without us."

67

Nathan followed Tonto and the chieftain to one of the community's longhouses. A low cooking fire burned at one end. Its smoke slanted away from a draft that snuck in through the open doorway, and spiraled up into the thatched ceiling. A colorful display of bundled cloth, fresh fruit, dried spices, cooking and field implements hung from the rafters all around them. Collapsed hammocks lay suspended along the walls and between some of the lodge poles, giving the interior the appearance of a giant spider's web that had to be cautiously navigated in order to get out alive.

They sat on logs in the middle of the floor. The community elders squatted or stood in a semicircle facing them. The chieftain appeared to be in his mid-thirties. Although strong and otherwise healthy in appearance, his face was drawn with lines of despair. Tonto explained that Chief Mutakkah had lived long enough to fear and hate outsiders. Had Nathan been white, the Suypari would have never allowed him off the boat—or would have killed him on impulse.

"Me, my daughter—we're welcome here," Tonto said. "You...he's not sure. I think you're the first black man he's seen."

"Tell him our story."

Tonto began. Chief Mutakkah listened intently with his chin in his fist.

As the story progressed, the chieftain leaned forward. He put his hands on his knees, one pinky finger twitching with excitement. Nathan could tell when the story approached its climax, because the chieftain's wide eyes danced between him and Tonto, as though he were watching the action play out on their faces.

When Tonto finished, the chieftain lowered his face to the ground. His shoulder muscles bunched rhythmically. His jaw clenched and unclenched as if he were chewing his thoughts.

Then Mutakkah mumbled a name. One of the oldest men there stepped forward. He planted the spear in his hand into the dirt at his feet. He leaned forward at the waist and stared at Nathan intently.

After a moment, he shook his wrinkled face with a grunt and stepped back.

"He doesn't recognize you," Tonto said.

Mutakkah muttered a different guttural-sounding name. Another elder—in his late-fifties to early sixties—stepped forward. As the man peered into his face, Nathan undid a few buttons on his safari shirt.

The man straightened with a grunt and shook his head.

"Ask him if he recognizes *this*," Nathan said. As Tonto translated, Nathan threw open his shirt, exposing the chunky bloodstone necklace and ceremonial shaman's knife that hung around his neck.

The elders bunched into a semicircle as they leaned forward to examine him. Nathan thought he saw fear contort a few faces.

Maybe it's just surprise, or confusion, he told himself as they straightened, and emitted a chorus of noncommittal grunts.

Tonto turned to Nathan and shrugged. "It was a long time ago, Nathan" he said. "The oldest men here were only boys back then. Could you remember a face you saw once or twice forty-five years ago?"

Nathan looked down at his feet and shook his head. If not for photographs, he might not remember what his *mother* looked like forty-five years ago. When he glanced up at the chieftain, Mutakkah's facial expressions wavered between fear and uncertainty. He waved a hand at them and spoke.

"He says we need to go wait at the boats. He needs to talk with elders and make a decision."

They stepped from the darkened longhouse into the crowd waiting outside. Nathan blinked from the sudden glare of light and shielded his eyes with his hand. Turning in the direction of the lake, the natives parted a path for them.

"They've changed," Nathan said, as he scanned their faces. He stopped in the peoples' midst and pointed to a number of children. "They look like they've intermarried with the Xuraquit.

They've taken something from their shorter stature, their deeper skin tone."

"That's your doing, Nathan," Tonto said. "Before we left, you made the Suypari chieftain marry the Xuraquit chief's daughter. Also, the Xuraquit gave the murderer's family to the Suypari," Tonto looked up at him. "Your punishment. Maybe that wasn't the only murder. Maybe there were other families transferred."

Suddenly, Tonto spun on him, eyes wide. Then he bolted ahead. Jolted from his thoughts, Nathan heard the voices rising straight ahead—then shouts. He lurched forward.

A shotgun blast exploded.

Nathan yelled at the villagers to get out of the way as he raced through the crowd. He leapt from the edge of the village plateau, windmilling his arms as he pedaled to keep balance in the air. He landed on the incline running. Then he skidded to a stop, vines from the groundcover snatching at his feet.

Karintha stood over one of the river guides. He lay unmoving at her feet, flat on his back in the mud.

The other guide backpedalled, hands thrust skyward. He pleaded as Karintha repeatedly jabbed his belly with the muzzle of her grandfather's survival rifle—all the while berating him with the voice of a banshee.

The guide tripped on an exposed root and fell in the muddy groundcover. Then he reached up protectively as she threatened to club him with the butt of the gun.

Tonto grabbed Karintha's raised arms from behind and muttered something to her. She faked a blow with the gun butt and the guide flinched. Then she allowed her grandfather to coax her away.

Turning from her victim, the ferocious thundercloud faded from Karintha's face. She actually winked at Nathan as she strolled past.

"Just another day in the jungle," she said in a singsong voice.

*What the...*Nathan cocked his head inquiringly.

"They were trying to untie their boats and leave with our supplies. I snap-clubbed him with the gun butt, fired a blast into the air to warn you, then reloaded and backed the other guy down. Like I said...just another day in the jungle."

68

After piling their supplies in the middle of one of the longhouses, Tonto sat Nathan and Karintha down in one corner. He'd been speaking with Suypari elders, and he had information to share.

"Most tribes have many shamans," he told them. "The Suypari only have one. Their chief is always the son of a chief. The shaman is the son of a shaman. If a bloodline dies out, the elders choose a new chief or shaman."

"I was shaman for a week." Nathan sat on a log and poked the dirt with a stick. "They must have had fun choosing my successor."

Tonto flexed his brow. "There's a problem," he said.

"What's that?" his granddaughter asked.

He glanced at Karintha. His aged face softened, and he patted the hand she rested on one knee. "The problem is this: Chief Mutakkah's not sure. He'll allow us to stay for now—but the shaman is stronger than the chief. When the shaman returns from hunting, he'll make the final decision."

"That sounds ominous," Nathan said. "*What* final decision?"

"Whether we can stay or have to leave," Tonto said. "I don't think we're in serious danger. At least not for the moment. If you were *white*, now, that would be a different story."

"So, worst case—they run us out of the village?" Karintha asked.

"There aren't any guarantees," Tonto said, "Anything can happen in the jungle. But that's pretty much how it looks."

"So…" Nathan wasn't sure how to ask. "Those old men…they were the oldest people in the village? Were you able to find out anything about… about…"

"U'Yara?" Tonto nodded. "Yes, Nathan. I found out that U'Yara remarried. She had many children. Sounds like she had a happy life. But, Nathan, I'm sorry to have to tell you this. She died of fever—seven years ago." Tonto paused to let the news sink in. Then he coughed into the back of his hand conspicuously. "There's more bad news, I'm afraid," he said. "The Xuraquit tribe…they're gone."

Nathan found himself on his feet, then felt himself sway. He grabbed a lodge pole with one hand to steady himself. "What happened?"

"A mining company came in, just upriver from them. Five years ago. They poisoned the river, Nathan. Animals died. People died. Then disease hit the Xuraquit—hard. Only a few survived. They'd been at peace with the Suypari ever since we left. There had even been some more intermarrying. The last few Xuraquit came here…and became Suypari. There are no more Xuraquit."

Nathan sank back down to sit. He shouldn't have been surprised by the story. As an anthropologist, it was an all-too-familiar tale. The mortality to native tribes from introduced diseases alone was so high that Brazil had adopted a no-contact policy. Previously undiscovered villages, when spotted by air, were charted—but declared off limits to outside contact. Nathan had only obtained permission from the authorities to visit the Suypari after providing certificates of health for all of their expedition members. As he mulled over what this news would mean, given the purpose of their visit, a native stepped through the doorway and jabbered off a few words.

"Shaman Yantamupu has returned," Karintha said, getting up to her feet. "We have to go to the main longhouse."

The native pointed at Karintha and spoke again. Tonto stood beside her. He took her hand, and the three exchanged a few words.

"He says only you can go," he said to Nathan. "The shaman—he speaks English. He learned from Christian missionaries."

"The plot thickens." Nathan stood up, and handed a pump-action shotgun to Karintha. Then he picked up his own shotgun and slung it over his shoulder.

Before leaving the hut, Nathan placed a quick call to Hawley by satellite phone. He provided their GPS coordinates and filled him in on their progress. Then he turned to Tonto and Karintha.

"Wish me luck," he said.

Nathan followed the crowd of villagers back to the main meetinghouse.

Chief Mutakkah kept them standing while he delivered a short speech. At the conclusion, Nathan turned to see the body of elders part as the shaman strode through their midst. When the last elder stepped aside to allow him through, Nathan reflexively sucked in his breath.

The man stopped, spear in hand, directly in front of them. Beneath the black tattoos and red lines of facial paint, and despite the snail-shell ear and nose adornments, Nathan instantly realized he was standing face-to-face with one of U'Yara's sons.

The man's fine bone structure, narrow nose and smooth skin spoke of her beauty as only direct kinship can. His dark skin, wavy black hair and mid-forties appearance shouted his lineage.

With a shock, Nathan realized the shaman wasn't just U'Yara's son.

He was his son as well.

For a moment, his mind churned in a flood of understanding. The two warrior-hunters who stood directly behind the shaman must be Nathan's grandsons. The taller, more swarthy children he had believed to be descended from the Xuraquit were his own great-grandchildren. He would never have considered the possibility in his own culture, even though his family had traditionally married and had children in their early twenties. In tribal society, natives married at puberty.

Nathan's immediate response was that he wanted to hug his newfound son. But when he gazed into the shaman's face, he saw a man primed to explode from hatred. Yantamupu practically snarled at Nathan as he reached out and ran his fingers over the bloodstone necklace he wore. Then he lifted the ceremonial knife that hung around Nathan's neck, dropping it with a snort of disgust.

"Our brothers sell these trinkets in the white man's cities. This means nothing."

Nathan opened his mouth to speak—but the shaman raised a menacing finger, crooked and pointed straight between his eyes.

"I heard your story," he said with a glance at Chief Mutakkah. "Devil's lies. What are you here for?"

The venomous way he spat out his words left Nathan feeling so deflated that for a moment he couldn't think to speak. Then the train of thought began to flow, and Nathan completed the explanation. He wanted the shaman to understand. He had loved U'Yara. The two of them—Yantamupu and Nathan—were bound by blood.

"Devil's lies!" Yantamupu spat.

"I don't lie."

"All outsiders say they don't lie. Then they make us sick. Kill us. Drive us off our land."

"Yantamupu," Nathan said, pronouncing the man's name slowly, with care, "I know your people have suffered. Maybe you even hate me for leaving when I did. But as much as I loved your mother, I couldn't live in her world any more than she—or you—could live in mine. I swear, I didn't know she was pregnant when I left. But now that I meet you, I see I am your father. Isn't this plain for everyone to see?"

Nathan ran his hand across his bloodstone necklace as he spoke. Then he pointed to the single bloodstone the shaman wore around his neck on a leather thong—the bloodstone he had given to U'Yara.

"Your mother must have told you...."

"Lies!" Yantamupu shouted. He raised his spear in a cocked arm, the tip pointed straight at Nathan's chest. Nathan backed up a step. With surprising speed for his age, he swung the shotgun from his shoulder and racked the pump action with the sound of slapping metal.

The shaman's eyes flitted to the barrel, still pointed at the ground. Slowly, he lowered his spear, his arm shaking with anger.

"You are a *man*," he spat, jabbing the spear in Nathan's direction. "My father was a *god*." Turning, he grabbed something from one of the sons who stood behind him. Then he shook it in Nathan's face—the Bible. Spittle frothed at one corner of Yantamupu's mouth as he ranted.

"My father entered our holy city on a donkey! He shook the heavens with the thunder of his anger! His thunder and lightning drove away the evil spirits of the night! He was raised up by a silver angel with a..." He flipped the Bible open and pointed to a halo in a reproduced painting of Jesus. "My father was all-powerful *God*! Xuraquit arrows could not penetrate his flesh. Our shaman could not cut him with his knife. You? You are an old man!"

Yantamupu thrust the Bible back into his son's hands. Before Nathan realized what he was doing, the shaman slashed with his spear.

Nathan raised a hand to a shallow cut on his cheek, and found blood on two fingers.

"An old *man*," Yantamupu hissed. "And you *bleed*."

The shaman raised his hands to the heavens. Nathan saw fear on every face, including Chief Mutakkah's. Yantamupu shouted a proclamation.

Nathan didn't raise his shotgun. He couldn't.

He felt the weapon snatched from his hands. Then the braided thong that held the ceremonial stone dagger was yanked over his head.

Armed villagers surrounded him from all sides with drawn knives and machetes, and pushed him roughly toward the open doorway.

69

Nathan looked around the empty hut as the villagers ushered him inside.

Warriors here, warriors at the door. Lake on one side, river on another. A village of warriors all around us, a hostile rainforest all around them. The shortest path to civilization is six days walking—and unless I'm off my mark, those outboard motors we heard a few minutes ago were the river guides running home scared.

His thoughts flitted to how his guns had saved his life before, usually by show, sometimes by bluff. *That won't work here,* he thought. *Their shotguns will trump my pistols any day. And anyway...*

After Wogan's expedition, Nathan feared ever having to shoot another human being. He only drew when his life was threatened, only shot when two natives in Micronesia tried to kill him for his possessions. He squeezed his eyes shut and once again saw the flame leap from the pistol in his hand, felt the explosion kick the barrel skyward, heard the blast buffet his ears. The native's paint and ash-streaked head snapped back, a pink mist airbrushing the forest leaves behind him. The dead man dropped the bloody knife in his hand and tumbled to the ground as Nathan spun into a crouch. A machete slashed through the space his head had just occupied, and all he saw was brown skin. He felt the gun bucking in his hand like a wild thing thrashing. The naked flesh in front of him jerked and twitched as an unseen hand punched holes through it. Then the smoking beast he strangled in his grip stood still, its black metal slide locked back, chamber gaping. Nathan blinked his eyes open and the light in his mental projector flickered, then switched off, and the vision faded from view. He self-consciously ran a hand over the left side of his ribcage, where a six-inch scar commemorated the battle.

"Shooting another human being," he muttered to himself with a shake of his head, "it's the worst feeling in the world. And that's not going to happen here."

Whatever else Yantamupu is, he's my son. I'll die before I kill my own flesh and blood.

Nathan spun at a knock on the door. Tonto and Karintha squeezed past the guards and stepped into the middle of the room.

"Thank God," Nathan said. "Tonto, call Hawley on the satellite phone and…." His voice drifted off when he saw his old friend shake his head sadly.

"They took everything," Tonto said.

"That doesn't sound right…that's not the Suypari I remember." Nathan recalled how he used to leave his possessions unguarded in his hut, and never found anything stolen.

"They asked me who the supplies belonged to. When I said you, they took everything of value.

Nathan—the shaman is planning to kill you. Not in three days, like before. No feast. No celebration. He's going to just kill you. Tonight."

Karintha patted Nathan on the shoulder reassuringly.

"Mr. Jones, we believe the shaman is your son," she said. "That's obvious to everyone but him. What did he say to you?"

Nathan sat on the ground, his back to the wall of upright wood poles. He leaned his head back and stared at the ceiling.

"Yantamupu obviously learned enough—badly enough—from Christian missionaries to know how to mangle the Bible to serve his purpose. None of the other villagers can read, so nobody can correct him. He heard I arrived with mules—and draws an analogy to Jesus riding a donkey. I scared the rescue plane away—a nighttime spirit in their minds—with my distress signal of three shots. That was my thunder and lightning. I dodged the Xuraquit arrows. I defeated the shaman and his warriors without a scratch, so presto, change-o, now I'm all-powerful. I was 'raised up' by a helicopter, a silver angel with spinning rotor blades that looked like a halo, so that made me God. He's playing the Bible off of the legends of my deeds, and leading the Suypari down a path of blasphemy to fuel his delusions. The mythical me was a God in his mind. That makes the real me—an aging, imperfect, ordinary human—an imposter. Or, worse yet, the devil."

"So how do we get you out of this?" Karintha glanced at her grandfather for an answer. Tonto clenched his lips and shook his bowed head miserably, his eyes on the ground.

"You don't." Nathan glanced out the doorway and saw the sky dimming with the approach of sunset. He leaned forward from where he sat, one arm balanced on an upraised knee. "Look, I want to live. But I'll never kill my own son. You two take off by foot. Or wait here if you think it's safe. When we don't check in by satellite phone tomorrow morning, Hawley will know something is up and send rescue boats. That was our deal. He knows our GPS coordinates."

"What about you?" Karintha asked, looking dazed.

"Me?" Nathan forced a smile. "What can I do? I'm going to face this stupid 'son of god' ignoramus son of *mine*—and either talk some sense into him or die trying."

70

Nathan knew his time drew near when he heard the drums beat their cadence an hour after sunset. The sound rolled through the village from the direction of the arena. He wondered what preparations the villagers had made for him.

Nathan tossed a half-eaten MRE into a corner. He glanced at the open doorway. He didn't know where Tonto and Karintha had gone. Only that they had been taken from this hut by warriors.

They hadn't gone easily. Karintha held on to Nathan tightly as the natives tried to drag her from the hut, pulling him to his feet. At the door, she broke away from them, and put her arms around Nathan, holding him in a strong embrace until the warriors pulled her away.

"Grandfather says you are a part of our family," she said. "We're not going to let you go easily."

That had been nearly an hour before. Now, Nathan watched as a knot of painted, half-naked warriors, backlit by the community's many fires, crossed the level plain and stopped outside the hut, in front of the guards. After exchanging guttural greetings, they filed into the small room, brandishing their spears and machetes.

Nathan stood as the shaman's two sons—his own *grandsons*—grabbed him by his arms and lifted him to his feet. He stared as the warrior in front of him raised his machete menacingly and pointed a finger at him to be still. He felt another man lash his wrists together behind his back with a leather thong.

Nathan tried to shrug them off and yelled, "Let me walk like a *man*," but the shaman's sons held him with a strength he recognized only from his youth.

Stumbling to keep pace with his captors, who hauled him forward by his shoulders, Nathan realized why the Suypari seemed afraid. Before, they had a certain style—a gentleness, even—in the way they treated their prisoners. Yantamupu, however, ruled like a tyrant. At any moment he could command a person's execution, as he had with Nathan. His own father. In a society where none were safe from the shaman's fickle whim, all were scared. Even Chief Mutakkah.

Nathan remembered the manic gleam in the shaman's eyes as he pronounced him a liar again and again. He had chalked it up to denial, coupled with public humiliation upon meeting the father who had abandoned him.

But it's more than that, Nathan now realized. *He's insane.*

They rounded the last longhouse. The waiting crowd fell silent as his captors dragged the condemned man into view. Nathan saw the circle of villagers ringing the arena. Chief Mutakkah sat in the place of honor on a dyed reed mat.

Yantamupu stood in the center of the arena. He was flanked by two village elders. He wore a grass skirt, elaborate waist and looped chestbands of beaded leather, and a headdress of exotic feathers.

Nathan's eyes froze on his own ceremonial stone dagger. It was the same one Yantamupu had dismissed as a tourist trinket. Now the shaman wore it with pride around his neck. Nathan's mind flooded with memories. He reflexively scanned the empty ground. There was the spot where the cowardly shaman had cut out his brother's heart. Over there, the place where the disgraced shaman's head had been impaled upon a pole.

This was the same arena where Mark was murdered. Where Nathan was reborn as the tribe's shaman. Where he forged lasting peace with the Xuraquit—and where Hawley rescued him and Tonto in the "silver angel" helicopter.

Most heart-rending, this was where he won U'Yara in the turtle wrestle—and then lost her forever in a clash of cultures that could not endure a lasting union.

Nathan's sadness was beyond words at the thought that the only legacy of their marriage was a deluded charlatan intent on killing him—just as a prior shaman had murdered his twin brother on this very spot.

As the warriors shoved him into the arena, Nathan scanned the crowd. He saw no ceremonial joy on the faces around him. There was no spark of enthusiasm in their eyes, no fever of righteous conviction. All he saw was apathy and fear...and what he suspected was shame.

As he completed his visual sweep, Nathan's spirits lifted to see Tonto and Karintha standing together to one side. Even though they could do nothing to help, it was somehow a comfort to have them nearby. Nathan knew he had to save himself—or die. If anybody else intervened, the shaman would kill them as well.

Nathan nodded to his old friend, who swayed on his feet as tears streamed down the deep creases age had sculpted in his chestnut brown cheeks. Tonto nodded back. Karintha reached over and clasped her grandfather's weathered hands in hers. She whispered what appeared to be words of comfort in the old man's ear, and Nathan thought the look of grief on his old friend's face softened slightly.

Nathan strode the last few steps.

How could he overcome the shaman? If he fought and won or humiliated Yantamupu, the disgraced shaman's own people would destroy him. No. Nathan's best chance was to convince his long-lost son to reverse his own decision, and thereby save face with his people.

"Yantamupu," Nathan said, as he neared. "How could I know the things I told you—things I could only know if I am who I say I am?"

The two elders who stood behind the shaman looked at one another. For one vain moment, Nathan thought he had struck a chord of reason with them. Then he realized the look they'd exchanged was one of confusion—not enlightenment. They couldn't understand a word he said.

"Because you are the devil," Yantamupu said. "You are here to mislead our people from true faith." He snapped his fingers, and his two sons spun Nathan around to face the crowd.

Straining to look back at him from over his shoulder, Nathan said, "If your father is God, as you claim..."

Yantamupu flicked a finger, and one of his sons buried a fist into Nathan's gut.

Gasping for breath, Nathan's vision turned grey from the pain that exploded, then radiated outward. He doubled over at the waist.

The shaman's sons shoved him to his knees.

As Nathan sucked great gasps of air, the shaman leaned over his shoulder and whispered, "I don't care what you are. I only care who my people believe *me* to be."

Who's the devil here? Nathan thought. He watched as the shaman straightened, drawing the ceremonial dagger from its beaded sheath.

Yantamupu thrust both hands skyward. The light of a dozen fires played across the rough stone blade in his right hand.

Without warning, Nathan felt the man's sons grab fistfuls of his hair and jerk his head back, exposing his neck. He wanted to say something—anything—but couldn't find air to speak. He saw the flickering light dance across the dark lines of dried blood on the knife, and heard the shaman pronounce what could only be a proclamation of death. He felt his vision blur, his mind detach.

All he could think was that in the next instant, his blood and Mark's would mix on the shaman's stone blade. He felt the leather thong cut into his wrists, still bound tightly behind his back. As he knelt, his hands brushed against the 22-caliber Beretta in his ankle holster.

For a split second Nathan considered snatching the gun and firing at whatever he could hit. But just as quickly as his mind conceived the idea, he dismissed it. In the crawl of time that accompanies death, he watched as a third hand rose up in the air. This one held a steel knife, as if the shaman had transformed into the multi-limbed Hindu god, Kali, the symbol of destruction. Nathan stared, waiting for one of the weapons to slash and end his life. Yet all his stunned mind could think was, "How very *peculiar!*"

The next moment, the shaman finished his proclamation. The steel knife slashed downward.

Nathan shut his eyes and felt a blessed wave of peace wash over him.

Somehow it seemed right that he die here, the place where his mature life had begun. The bitter, metallic scent of fresh blood flooded his nostrils. He waited for the tunnel, the light, and dreamed of finding U'Yara waiting for him on the other side...

Then the shaman's sons released their hold on his head. Nathan knew he should topple over and thrash in his death throes. For some reason he couldn't understand, he remained kneeling. He had seen enough death to know that this simply shouldn't be.

The whisper of this realization forced him to open his eyes.

He gazed upward to where the shaman stood. A black leather handle and an inch of steel blade protruded from the angle between the native's shoulder and neck. A river of blood tracked down his naked chest.

As Nathan watched through unblinking eyes, Yantamupu's hands fell to his sides, his right hand clenching the stone dagger in dead fingers. One knee buckled and he toppled to the side—revealing the elder who stood directly behind him. The man stood with his arms thrust into the air. His right hand was streaked with the shaman's blood, one rivulet twirling down his raised arm like the red ribbon on a barbershop's pole.

The elder shouted out some words that sounded like an announcement. Then he repeated them. The arena exploded with shouts of rage.

The shaman's two sons glanced at one another, their eyes wide. Then they snatched at the weapons that hung from their belts.

One swung his war club backward and stepped toward the elder, who threw his head back and puffed out his chest in proud defiance. The other turned and raised the machete in his hand, aimed directly at Nathan's head.

The air was split by the concussions of gunshots.

Nathan watched sparks shower off the machete as it flew from his would-be assailant's hand. With a scream of outrage, the shaman's son wheeled around to fetch his weapon—and a spray of bullets sent dust flying inches from his hands, stopping him short. The second son turned toward the gun blasts—and stopped dead in his tracks as more bullets exploded into fountains of dust at his feet.

The elder shouted hard words at the two men. Then he pointed a finger at Nathan, and spoke again. The villagers stamped their feet and shouted their approval.

Nathan raised his head to stare straight ahead—and saw Karintha ten yards away, cradling a 40-caliber semi-auto in a double-handed grip.

Fumbling at the small of his back with his bound hands, Nathan's fingers slid into an empty holster.

So that's what the hug was about. Thank goodness she considers me part of the family.

Chief Mutakkah stepped into his peripheral vision, swung up his shotgun and pointed it at the shaman's sons. He shouted a few commanding words.

The sons shuffled their feet uncertainly for a moment, then came toward Nathan.

Are they supposed to finish the job for their father?

The men took Nathan by the elbows and lifted him to standing. Then one of them released the cords that bound his hands behind his back. Mutakkah said a few words—and both men fell to the ground and kissed Nathan's feet.

Nathan remained standing at the same spot. His stunned mind struggled to keep up with the rush of unexpected events. Something inside seemed to slow his sensory input, switch off his emotions, perhaps to limit the shock to his mental system.

Nathan watched with an odd sense of detachment as the circle of villagers erupted with shouts and crazed foot stamping, celebrating the death of the tyrant—his own son—and the return of their long-lost shaman.

Tonto threw his arms around Nathan in a joyous hug. Karintha wedged the pistol into her waistband, and then joined the group embrace.

Chief Mutakkah and Enata, the elder who killed the shaman and saved Nathan's life, shuffled in front of them, as if embarrassed to interrupt a private reunion. Tonto and Karintha slipped to Nathan's sides, and they stood facing the natives together.

Enata's brown face cracked into a huge smile as he stepped forward. He draped the braided leather thong and ceremonial stone knife over Nathan's head, where it rested upon his necklace of bloodstones. Then he handed Nathan the shaman's single bloodstone—his gift to U'Yara—on its leather thong.

Nathan glanced down at the mementos. He knew he should crumble and cry. But he couldn't. Whatever mechanism had switched off his emotions was holding an iron hand on the controls.

Tonto listened intently to the elder's words, then turned to translate. "He said these things belong to you by right, Nathan."

Enata spoke again, and Tonto's face melted into understanding. Then the elder extended his arm. Draped over his open palm were the shaman's elaborate waist and chest-bands. Tonto nudged him with an elbow. "He says you were the shaman before—now you're the shaman again."

"He...remembers me?" Nathan spoke in a monotone, his words as dead and devoid of feeling as his heart felt empty of hope.

"He's your warrior."

Nathan blinked. He tried to will his mind to work, and failed. "My what?"

A sheepish smile played across Tonto's lips and eyes. "I'm going to take some credit for this one, Nathan. When the shaman killed Mark, so long ago, two very young warriors held you back. They later apologized. I told you to forgive them—make them your warriors. Remember?"

When Nathan nodded slightly, as if dazed, Tonto continued. "The other warrior has been dead for years. This one remembered you. But he was afraid of Yantamupu. Everyone was. That's why he didn't speak earlier. He was hoping you would go away—unharmed. But when Yantamupu tried to kill you, there was nothing else he could do. He had to defend you. He owed you his life. Now he has repaid. And he told Yantamupu's sons to honor you—their grandfather—the greatest shaman the Suypari have ever known. Obviously, the chieftain seconded the request. And it didn't hurt to have a little backup from Karintha."

Nathan shook his head first with wonder and then, more vigorously, with refusal.

He reached out with both hands and closed the elder's fingers upon the braided leather bands.

"Tell Enata that I must leave once again. This time I will not return. Tell him...tell everyone destiny brought me back to make him the shaman. When he dies, the honor will pass to his bloodline."

Tonto translated and Chief Mutakkah nodded.

The Chief turned, raised both arms, and shouted a proclamation. The villagers went wild with foot-stamping and shouts. Enata looked as though he might faint from surprise.

When the din died down, Mutakkah turned back to speak. Tonto translated. "The Chief says your grandchildren and great-grandchildren will become part of his family. Today you lost your son—but you gained a tribe."

A flood of emotions knocked Nathan to his knees. Burying his head into his hands, his tears rushed out in quiet sobs.

71

Laughter, giddy voices, and the cool rays of early morning sun sifted through the upright wood poles as Nathan sat on the ground in a corner of the longhouse.

He knew the Suypari were too polite to celebrate the end of the shaman's tyranny without giving him time to grieve. But nothing could suppress the joy he heard in their voices as they went about their morning chores. Nathan glanced at the satellite phone in his hand, then tossed it onto one of the bundles of supplies that lay piled against the wall—all returned to him on orders from Chief Mutakkah.

"He coming?" Tonto asked.

Nathan nodded. "Hawley wants to stay with us until the celebration ends. *I'm* not sure I want to stay until the celebration *begins.*"

"You should sleep, Nathan. You spent the night in tears."

Nathan nodded. He had spent the entire night grieving, and he was dead tired. He gazed at Karintha. She squatted in front of a cooking fire, tending a pot of oatmeal. She sprinkled salt, pinches of local spices, then stirred in a bowl of shredded curassow, a pheasant-like bird that, along with jacobins and guan, was greatly favored by the natives. Nathan knew it would turn the oatmeal into a meaty, tasty meal, although nothing like the sweetened porridge at home.

As appetizing as her cooking looked, Nathan had no interest in food. Karintha pulled the steaming coffee pot from the fire, using a folded T-shirt as a potholder.

"It must be a terrible thing for a man to see his bloodline turn bad—to realize his son caused so much grief to others," she said. She turned to face Nathan directly. "I'm so sorry things turned out this way."

"Yeah," Nathan said with a deep, shuddering sigh. "But at least now there's hope for my grandchildren and great-grandchildren. And it's been a comfort meeting you, Karintha. Your grandfather must be very proud."

"More than proud, Nathan," Tonto said. "Karie...she's my secret weapon."

Nathan looked down, deep in thought for a moment. Then he looked up at Karintha. "So, 'Karie,' is it? Well, Karie, I want you to have this."

He lifted Karintha's hand and placed something in her open palm. She stared down—at U'Yara's thong necklace with the single bloodstone. She clenched her fingers tightly around the gift, then she blushed and glanced at the floor.

"Thank you," Karintha said. "I know how much this means to you. I will always treasure it."

She tied the thong around her neck. Then she returned to kneeling by the fire, plucked a container of spices from the floor and dipped her hand into the bowl.

Nathan looked at Tonto and saw a single tear run down his old friend's face. Tonto gazed proudly at his granddaughter as she fed a stick into the fire—then shot Nathan a wink and a smile, his old spark and joy for life still very much alive.

Nathan suddenly felt hungry, after all. He willingly took the wooden plate that Karintha offered, along with a folded leaf to use as a spoon.

He smiled up at her. She nodded back, her entire face lit with a joyful serenity.

72

Nathan heard the helicopter's rotor late that afternoon. It began as a distant droning sound. Then it grew louder, setting the birds to flight and prompting protests from the howler monkeys. It broke out over the tree line, circled the village to draw the natives' attention, then hovered over the arena. The helicopter landed in the middle of the clearing and immediately cut its engine.

Hawley stepped from the cabin and strode over to the welcome committee as the rotors slowed, then stopped. Tonto introduced him to Chief Mutakkah and Enata, who stood resplendent in the previous shaman's braided leather waist and chest-bands. Then, once the helicopter was still, Hawley introduced them to the machine.

"Sorry I couldn't find a silver one," he said. "This was the best I could do."

Nathan had wanted him to bring a "silver angel." But bright yellow seemed to do the trick. The main thing was to show the natives it was a machine and not an angel. Mutakkah and Enata took a thrilling ride over the lake and back. After that everybody milled around and talked about the marvel until the pilot fired up the rotor and headed home.

"I told him to pick us up in six days," Hawley said. "But we can call him if we decide to leave earlier."

The next morning, Nathan stood beside Hawley and watched as Tonto and Karintha headed into the forest with a large group of hunters, armed only with blowguns, bows and arrows. They returned late that afternoon in smaller groups of three and four, but their collective catch added up to enough black and howler monkeys for a feast. The big prize, an adult tapir, was brought down by an archer in Karintha's group.

The feast kicked off that night with drums and flutes. Although Nathan still grieved, Hawley's presence lifted his spirits enough that he was able to leave his hut and attend. They sat in a line on reed mats beside Chief Mutakkah. The chieftain's extensive family, now including Nathan's own descendants, milled around behind them.

Mutakkah bade Nathan to stand. Two women in their mid-twenties stepped forward. In unison, they chanted the same apology three times.

"Wives of shaman's sons," Tonto translated to Nathan. "They apologize, they welcome you, and they thank you for sparing the lives of their husbands—your grandsons." Each woman presented Nathan with a folded bundle of hand-dyed cloth. "Their gift of hospitality, of thanks."

The women filed their children past, introducing Nathan's great-grandsons to him. The oldest was nine years old, the youngest a baby bundled into a body-sling.

After the children followed their mothers to the far side of the arena, Mutakkah waved a hand. Nathan's grandsons, who had held him when he was facing death, ran forward.

The warriors faced Karintha, then extended their arms. Laid across their open palms were spears, machetes, and bow and arrows.

Nathan jumped to his feet and stepped to Karintha's side.

"I think I can help you with this," he said. He cast a glance at Tonto, giving him a wink. His old friend broke into a grin.

"They surrendered to you in battle. Take their weapons, admire them—and then hand them back. In this way you will make these men your warriors. For *life*." He thumbed to the side, where Enata stood, and said, "If your grandfather hadn't made me do this with Enata forty-five years ago, I wouldn't still be here today."

Karintha did as she was told, marveling over the warriors' weapons before handing them back with a gracious smile. She nearly jumped in surprise when the warriors bent down to kiss her feet. The villagers burst into good-natured laughter, followed by their traditional foot stamping and shouts. The warriors ran back to their families to celebrate, the drums burst forth with an energetic beat, and the arena filled with dancers. As Nathan turned to reclaim his seat, he spotted Tonto staring at Karintha with unrestrained adoration, his face aglow.

Hawley nudged Nathan as he sat back down beside him, and head-nodded to the side. "Tonto's granddaughter is quite the little warrior. How old is she?"

"Just 17," Nathan said. "Even younger than me when we came here last. She's really something. I wonder what the future holds for her."

"Judging from what you've told me," Hawley said, a big, mischievous grin splitting his face, "I'd say her future is pretty bright. I mean, heck, she's already got two of your grandsons indebted to her for life. If she keeps going at this rate, in a few more years she could have enough warriors in her pocket to make an army."

Nathan stared at his old Southern friend, and shook his head. "Still worried about us darkies staging that revolt, are you?"

73

Nathan glanced at his right hand resting in his lap, and found himself cradling a cold cup of tea.

So...what did *you* learn from all this, Pops? What's the take-home message for our family?"

Nathan smiled at his oldest son and nodded. "The Suypari made me into a god. Amazon activists make native Indians out to have mystical unity with the rainforest. Both distort reality to promote a myth. We can do better than that. Especially regarding religion. Believing too little is lack of faith; believing too much creates false gods."

"So...is that the end of the story?"

"Not exactly. There is the hemosiderhonium," Nathan said, fingering the bloodstone necklace in his lap, "There's still a chance it can help the Suyparis. Hawley has a few old connections—pretty high up—in the mining business, and they're working on trying to give the tribe a better deal than what they'd normally get. Karintha is being trained to act on the tribe's behalf, as their agent. It's a potentially lucrative position for her. And with her warrior spirit, it's hard to imagine the Suypari having a better advocate.

"And anyway—as long as there are monkeys in the trees, fish in the rivers, and natives defending their tribal lands, the Amazon will keep writing new stories. The adventures won't end until the last tree is felled and the last Indian dies. Which hopefully won't be soon."

Martin clapped his hands together and straightened up. "And on that cheerful note, Pops—you must be starving." He glanced at a framed wedding picture propped on a nearby end-table, and sighed at his wife's youthful beauty. "Alisha's been slow-cooking a turkey, along with those peppermint candied yams you love so much. You know, the ones with that crispy, caramelized glaze?" He swept his hand over an imaginary dish, as if he were torching it himself. "It should be just about ready, and I think I heard the others arrive. So what do you say? Shall we go downstairs and join the reunion of your *North American* family? Or should I say 'tribe'?"

He reached for the camcorder on the tripod, just as Nathan's face broke into a wide grin.

Martin flicked a switch. Nathan's image disappeared from the screen in a snap of static lines.

The red record light dimmed, then blinked out.

Made in the USA
Charleston, SC
06 December 2011